Also available from **Adriana Herrera**
and Carina Press

Content Note

American Sweethearts deals with topics some readers may find difficult, including mentions of child sexual abuse and neglect.

AMERICAN SWEETHEARTS

ADRIANA HERRERA

carina
press

**carina
press®**

Recycling programs
for this product may
not exist in your area.

ISBN-13: 978-1-335-21598-7

American Sweethearts

Copyright © 2020 by Adriana Herrera

This edition published by arrangement with Harlequin Books S.A.

For questions and comments about the quality of this book,
please contact us at CustomerService@Harlequin.com.

Carina Press
22 Adelaide St. West, 40th Floor
Toronto, Ontario M5H 4E3, Canada
www.CarinaPress.com

Printed in U.S.A.

For everyone who has been able to see
even a small piece of themselves in these Dreamers.
These stories are for you.

AMERICAN SWEETHEARTS

"Each time you happen to me all over again."
—Edith Wharton, *The Age of Innocence*

Prologue

Thirteen Years Earlier
Priscilla

I let myself into the apartment, wired and excited to talk to J. I'd finally done it: put in all my paperwork to apply for the police academy. My big plan—no, *our* big plan— since we were like fifteen.

"Hey, where are you?" I called into the empty living area.

"I'm in the bedroom, still unpacking—shit!" he yelled, as what sounded like a bunch of rubber balls crashed to the floor. I hurried over, laughing, and found J on his knees picking up a ton of tennis balls and throwing them into a box.

"Hey." I leaned against the door frame watching him, his brown skin a little clammy from the summer heat. He had all the windows closed, but like always, refused to turn on the AC until it got so hot we ran the risk of melting. He could still get it though.

He looked up and grinned when he saw me glomming him up.

"You lost something down here." He grabbed his dick like the dirtbag he was and I almost wanted to forget about what I'd come here to tell him and jump into bed. It's not like we could get up to anything at my place with my three roommates. But J had this cozy one bedroom with the good mattress two blocks from the D train.

"I don't have time for your dick jokes, Juan Pablo."

"Oh I'm not playing with you." He licked his lips all suggestive and shit. I swear sometimes keeping my clothes on around this fucker felt like a full-time job.

"Stop it, asshole. I got something important to tell you." It was hard keeping a straight face when he was giving his "papi chulo" impersonation everything he had. He pushed up from the floor, those brown arms flexing every muscle, and pressed up against me.

"You smell." I did not sound like it was bothering me none, and that slick bastard knew exactly how to distract me from the enormous news I had to share. But maybe this was for the best. I'd sort of gone off script for our plan, by going on my own, and getting him off always put him in a more manageable mood. Not that it would be a hardship.

"What, you don't like my stank anymore?" He joked as he ran his sweaty chest all over my arms.

I could barely talk I was laughing so hard. "Ew."

"But you didn't complain last night after I came in from my run and ate—"

"Oh my God!" I took a step back because all of my body parts were tingling just from the mention of what we'd gotten up to last night on his couch. He'd been a sweaty mess then too and I had not cared.

"Time out, you ass." I backed into the hallway, my hands up. "I didn't come over to mess around with you."

He gave me a "yeah right" look, eyebrows raised high, but he stayed where he was.

"For real, J. I got something to tell you." He stiffened, and in an instant his face got serious. That was one of the things I loved about J, he listened to me. Like really listened. Being a girl in a Dominican family sometimes meant that you got told about yourself more often than you were given a chance to say what you actually wanted. Even when you had parents that were trying to at least not raise their kid like they were still living in the sixties.

Juan Pablo always listened to me, in bed and out of it, since always. I smiled, thinking how the two of us had been at this forever. We'd grown up across the street from each other. Him in his family's little house with a garden, and me in my parent's cramped two-bedroom apartment.

"Yo, what's going on in there?" He tapped my temple gently, as I tried to breathe through what was going on in my head. "You're starting to make me nervous, Pris. Are you breaking up with me?" He tried to sound like he was joking, but I wondered if he already suspected what I was going to say. We'd talked about joining the police academy for years. We'd said we'd do it right after graduation. Now we'd been done with school for a couple of months and he was still waffling, so I went and did it on my own.

I kept trying to get the words out and they just would not come. He'd feel blindsided. I knew I should've waited, but I wanted to get on with it. I wanted to be in the NYPD, for myself and to fulfill the dream my father was not able to get for himself.

I fisted my hands and pressed them to my thighs, my nails digging deep into my palms. The queasy want-to-kiss-J feeling replaced by a hole in my stomach.

"I signed up for the academy. I start in five weeks. Now it's your turn."

He took a step back and his expression went slack, like he had no idea how to react. He took a deep breath and ran his hands roughly over his head, not talking. There was a weird flutter in my chest, like there wasn't enough air in my lungs. I wanted to ask what he was thinking, but I didn't.

When he looked up, I knew the answer before he opened his mouth. "I'm not joining the academy, Priscilla. I applied for grad school."

I felt like throwing up, bile rising in my throat, because I couldn't shake the feeling that this would be what finally blew us apart. This would put our lives on different paths. He would do his thing and I would do mine and we'd lose this.

We'd lose *us*.

Chapter One

Juan Pablo

The flex is really fucking real.

I grinned as I tapped the caption onto the photo of me cheesing with my glass of XO on the rocks in the private motherfucking jet I was taking to the Dominican Republic. I ran my fingers over the corner of my mouth as I posted on Instagram with more hashtags and shit than necessary, but who could blame my ass for doing the most?

"Juan Pablo, get off that phone, sweetheart, and take it easy on that liquor. We haven't even taken off yet."

I rolled my eyes, pocketing my phone as I looked behind me to where my parents were sitting. "Okay, Ma, it's only my first drink," I protested as I pointed at the glasses of champagne she and my dad were sipping on. "And that's not water."

My father smiled at my whining. "It *is* an open bar, Irene. Let him live."

My mother shook her head, making her dark curls bop on her shoulders as she moved up to kiss my dad gently on the mouth—both of them looking like lovesick teens, even after almost forty years. "I can't take you two anywhere," she said, without even a hint of annoyance. She then turned to the other side of the aisle where the rest of our group was looking on with amusement. "Odette, you have to help me keep these boys in line."

Okay, so yes, both my parents were on the jet with me. As was my best friend Patrice, his partner, Easton, and Patrice's parents. We were on our way to our *other* best friend's wedding: Camilo. So I wasn't exactly ballin' on this trip. Camilo was, however.

He was marrying a zillionaire who seemed to live for showering him with every luxury he could get away with. Which meant we were travelling like fucking moguls. We would be, anyway, if we ever got in the air. We'd been held back because at the last minute a few other passengers were added to the flight.

I turned around to ask P if he'd heard who else was coming when I heard the flight attendant's radio come alive with a crackly voice giving her instructions.

She smiled in our direction and gestured toward the still open door of the plane. "Looks like our final passengers are here. We should be heading out very soon." With that she went to meet whoever had finally arrived. This shit of travelling in a private jet was pretty fucking swank. I mean, no security line and you basically just rolled up to the plane, which was waiting in a hangar at the Westchester County Airport. I could fucking get used to this. Also I needed the vacation. I'd been taking my time decompressing after coming off of what seemed like an interminable post-season. This trip to the DR was exactly what I needed.

I heard her before I saw her, talking to her mother and father—whose voices I'd also recognize anywhere—and felt that sickening dip of excitement mixed with barely contained want that always took over whenever Priscilla Gutierrez was near. Fuck, I wasn't ready for this.

I knew I was going to see her; her entire family was coming to the wedding. But I thought I'd have time to get there. Get my bearings. I never knew how my heart would conspire against my head when it came to Pris—just knowing she was boarding this plane made a tornado swirl inside my chest. My heart started pounding and my vision blurred a little as she chattered with her mother.

I had no clue how to act and for some reason panicked at the thought that she would be caught off guard by me being here. But before I had time to turn around and get some information from Patrice or Easton she was walking onto the plane.

It was November so even though we were headed to the Caribbean everyone was wearing fall attire. Pris was in what I always called her Bronx Girl Chic. Fancy leggings and sweater combo with pristine, matching Nikes. The whole thing was a mess of fall colors, olive green and terracotta and bright yellow. She'd taken her braids out and had her hair pulled back into a messy top bun. Glossy baby hair framing her face.

"Oh wow." She had that sickly sweet tone she used when she was too tired to even look aggravated, and as I stared straight ahead, it did not escape me that she was avoiding looking at me. Which in a tight space, like a private jet, required a hell of a lot of effort. I mean I was in the wedding party, so she knew I'd be in the DR, but I wondered if—like me—she'd been hoping for a little more breathing room. Or maybe she just didn't want to deal with my ass.

At thirty-five and after years of working a job that

had toughened her, she still looked so much like that sixteen-year-old girl that made my heart race every time I saw her. When she finally looked up from talking with her parents and saw me, she seemed hesitant. Like she didn't know if she was up for managing my presence. Like thinking about it made her tired.

Fuck, had it really been almost a year since I'd seen her? There had been a time when we couldn't go more than a few hours without touching or talking. Now months could go by without so much as a word. She of course recovered quickly, not about to give me stank face in front of our parents. Instead, she started greeting everyone and giving me an impressively wide berth given the size of the cabin. With each kiss hello she pressed on a cheek that wasn't mine—or every smile offered to someone just beyond where I sat in silence—the luxurious and intimate interior of the plane felt more oppressive.

"What's the good word, detective?" That was my dad. He always asked Pris about her job with more than a little bit of pride in his voice. He'd been her mentor since the day she joined the academy. Just one more way in which our lives were thoroughly tangled together.

I'd tried to tell myself for so long that was why we were better off as friends. Too many people with their noses in our business. But I'd weaned myself off my habit of not confronting my bullshit. Nosy relatives and friends was not the reason why Priscilla and I didn't work out. No, that was all on us, on me for being a careless fuckboy and on her for being stubborn and prideful.

"Rafa."

Pris's affectionate tone as she went in to hug my dad

wrenched me out of my seemingly ever-present regrets playlist.

The kisses, hugs and back slaps went on for what felt like hours until she finally got to me, and I knew I wasn't imagining everyone looking at us. Like she always did, Pris kept it surface and polite in front of the parents. We could go at it behind closed doors as much as we wanted, but our parents would never ever see any of it. Not if she had anything to say about it.

"Hey, J." She bent down to give me a quick peck on the cheek. But she popped back up so fast I could barely get a whiff of the expensive lemon verbena shower gel I'd gotten her addicted to and now couldn't use myself because it reminded me too much of her.

"Hey yourself, you looking fresh like always." I said, proud of myself for not sounding like a thirsty scrub. "You ready for this?" I asked, looking around the plane full of our raucous family and friends. Puerto Ricans, Haitians and Dominicans were notorious for their excitement whenever the time came to go back to their islands. Hell, we practically had our own terminal at JFK airport. We were rowdy by nature, but holy shit when we were on the way to the homeland we could reach rapture levels of celebration.

Pris smiled, looking around. "Let's hope Thomas got us a DR/PR/Haiti-proof plane, because this open bar is about to pop off."

My own parents were on their second glass of wine and we hadn't even taken off. I was about to make an awkward comment about her Nikes when the flight attendant came by asking us to finish up our drinks, since we'd be in the air soon.

That broke the tension and by the time she was done

giving us instructions, Priscilla was seated next to me. To be fair, it was the only seat left and she had Easton, her best friend, on the other side of her. I had no time to fret on things getting awkward or weirdness between us, because within seconds we were all in an easy conversation about the wedding, the obligations and tasks Camilo had given each of us. It was familiar and natural to be with Priscilla, but then again, that had never been our issue. Coming together had always been easy. It was staying that way that never seemed to work out for us.

Priscilla

Things *could not* be weirder. I was in a very confined space with my parents, who I'd also be rooming with. Because it wouldn't be a trip to the DR if we didn't regress right back to my pre-adolescence. It seemed like everyone I knew was on this plane. My best friend, my ex *and* his parents. Except it wasn't like that, because Juan Pablo was a lot more than my ex, he was family. Still, things felt awkward now, strained. I felt like my skin was too tight on my face and I didn't know where to look. We hadn't talked in months and sure, it was partly because we were both busy people, but we'd always been busy.

After that last time, I told Juan Pablo he needed to grow up and leave me alone. I'd been angry and frustrated, but before he walked out of my apartment he'd looked me straight in the eyes and said, *I will*. After that, it had been radio silence. No, "You up?" texts in the middle of the night, nothing. He'd stayed away like he said he would, like I'd asked him to.

As I mulled on that I felt something cold touch the tray that served as an armrest and looked up to see a stemless glass of wine, half full of rosé. The flight attendant smiled as she gestured to Juanpa, who was now taking a turn in the tiny, fancy plane lavatory.

"Mr. Campos said you wanted a glass of rosé." I dipped my head and took a sip. I had maybe mumbled it as I assessed the beverages that people were drinking, but hadn't said exactly what I wanted. It was a decent guess though. "Thank you."

She nodded, moving on to my parents and their drink order. "You're welcome."

I saw Irene, J's mom, gesturing for my mom to taste the wine she was drinking while my dad was pointing at Rafa's glass, indicating he wanted one of the same.

"It's like we got a reunion of the old block." I smiled at Patrice's deep voice. He was right, the old folks were getting on like they'd never stopped living up the block from each other.

I turned so I was facing Easton, who was using Patrice's gigantic chest as his airplane pillow. "Just wait until that plane lands, it'll be utter chaos. Are you sure you're ready for this, Mr. Archer?" I asked teasingly.

He winked at me and then turned so he could bring Patrice's face down for a kiss. It was short and tender, but the devotion flowed off those two in waves.

I'd never thought I'd see Patrice like this, his feelings like an open book. It was strange seeing all our friends paired off, settled, how love had changed them. It was bittersweet to think that for Juanpa and me, love had never been the issue. It had always been there, no question. It just couldn't fix all the other things that didn't work.

Easton turned again toward me, his expression content. "I know you'll take good care of me." He was talking to Patrice. But I nodded anyway as I saw Juan Pablo stepping out of the bathroom. He stopped to say something to his dad, who was engrossed in conversation with mine. My dad of course reached for him, a big smile on his face. My mother beamed at him too.

"Juan, mijo. How you been? You got any gossip for next season?" My father never missed a chance to ask J about his beloved Yankees.

They fucking loved him.

Like his parents loved me. After all these years of ups and downs with Juan Pablo it was hard to know how to feel with him around. Especially when he wasn't being his usual extra self and trying to act cute.

No, he was giving me space. Like *all* the space.

I knew that this was going to be weird and deep down I'd been on edge, knowing how hard it was going to be to stay off that fucker's dick when we were going to spend an entire week on the beach drinking. But him icing me out was much worse.

I needed air, from all of it. From my thoughts, from the friendly ease everyone seemed to have when I still felt like I didn't even know my place. I was looking around, just for something to do, when I noticed on the other side of the wood paneling separating our cabin from the front of the plane there were two empty large leather seats, and I needed a breather.

I got up but before I could take a step I had five pairs of eyes on me. "A donde vas m'ija?"

"Just to sit up front for a second, Mami. I have to send out a couple of emails for work and need some quiet. Since this thing has Wi-Fi I'm going to do them on my iPad." I gestured to the overhead where I'd stuffed my bag. "I'll be back in a sec." I tried my best to keep my tone peppy because there was nothing that put my mother on red alert faster than people needing "to be alone."

When I was a kid she'd threatened to take the doors *off the damn hinges* on more than one occasion.

I could feel my mother's eyes tracking my moves, probably worried that I was upset, but fuck, I was suffocating. Not because being around Juanpa was making me feel uncomfortable. No, it was because with him my heart and my head never seemed to want to retain the bad. Things would go up in flames and I'd tell myself to stay away…then after long enough had passed, I was right back in. Wanting him.

The seats were back facing, so I had a full view of the cabin. I wondered if they were meant to be for a security detail—far enough where you weren't too close but you had a pretty good view of the cabin. Juanpa was sitting between his mom and his dad. Legs spread and that slick grin that always, *always* did things to me.

My phone buzzed with a message blessedly distracting me from those powerful thighs.

You need some company? I'll ditch the hot teacher and come sit with you.

I laughed quietly and glanced up to find Easton looking at me with a knowing expression. We'd been friends long enough for him not to guess the reason for my behavior had a first and last name.

I'm good, just contemplating from afar all the things I can't indulge in this week.

I heard the scoff before I looked up and saw my best friend taking a break from his text exchange with me to whisper something to Patrice. It was hard to remember that only a year ago things for them seemed virtually impossible, their lives at odds in so many ways. And here they were, engaged as of a couple of months ago, and so solid it felt like they'd always been together. He tapped another message as Patrice engulfed him in another tight embrace.

I got your back.

I pocketed my phone after that and took another sip of my rosé as I quietly watched Juan Pablo. His shoulders were wider than they'd been a year ago, the last time we crashed and burned. Same tight fade, but now he wore a thick beard, which made his broad lips stand out. A shiver ran down my spine as I remembered how they felt grazing the back of my neck. How I could feel the imprint of them for days after.

Fuck, I needed to calm down. My parents were on this plane.

I made myself shift my focus away from his mouth and noticed he was wearing his usual travel ensemble. Fitted sweats, Yankees hoodie and Jordans. Nothing different there. Except he didn't seem like the old Juan Pablo. There was an ease to him that hadn't been there before. Like he didn't have anything to prove. He had his face turned to talk to my dad and I looked him up and down as he laughed at something.

I could tell you every mole, every scar on Juan Pablo's body better than I could my own. I knew exactly where to touch him to make him moan with pleasure, and he could do the same to me. Except beyond that nothing ever seemed to work for us since that first breakup. Since that awful night when we said too many ugly things to forgive. We broke things then, but instead of giving up we kept coming back to take more bites out of each other. Until there was nothing left.

Still, I wanted him as badly as I ever had, because no matter how much it hurt with Juan Pablo the pain always seemed *almost* worth it. I needed to watch myself and remember how that last breakup almost undid me. Juan Pablo couldn't deal with my job, and I swore to myself I would never change course because of anyone. So that was where we were. Stuck.

Chapter Two

Juan Pablo

Three hours into this flight, and it was sort of a scene. I mean, you got a plane packed with Dominicans, Puerto Ricans and Haitians, an open bar and free food…it's a fucking party. But something was missing. I spotted Pris sitting by herself on one of the seats furthest from the cabin. She copped that spot from the beginning of the flight and even though she'd come and chatted with the rest of us I could see she was keeping herself at a distance.

Of course I assumed it all had to do with me.

We didn't need to be like this. I wasn't going to push for more again. I swore to myself I'd keep my ass in check on this trip. No drunken begging Pris to take pity on me or greasy behavior. That wasn't what I wanted, I just missed her.

I looked around again and saw that people had finally settled down a little bit. Figured, just when we're about ready to land. I almost went over to P and tried to kill time talking with him and Easton. But they were sitting so contentedly. P's big ass arm like an oak branch draped on his man.

It was a fucking trip, really, to see my friend who

never let himself show too much looking like the very picture of contentment. I wasn't going to say he was glowing, but he looked really fucking happy. I must've been pulling a face, because P's eyes went right to Priscilla, who looked like she was trying and failing to fake sleep.

I didn't have the energy to have an eyeball conversation with P, so instead I did what I'd wanted to do since Priscilla stepped onto the plane. I didn't even know what I was going to say once I got there but I had to make sure she and I were cool. Just the thought of an entire week around all our friends and family while Priscilla and I tried our best to ignore each other made me feel a deep, bone-level exhaustion.

"Hey," I said, and she opened one brown eye.

"Hey yourself. You kill that $200 bottle of Henny yet? We only have like another forty minutes in the air."

My mouth twitched at that. Of course she was going to give me shit for freeloading on the booze. I smacked my lips and took another sip, knowing it would piss her off.

"I'm working on it. I see you haven't availed yourself of much of the free food and beverages. You sick or something?"

She snorted but didn't answer, finally training both of those chocolate brown eyes in my direction. "I'm trying to pace myself since we're about to go on a five day binge in the DR, but thanks for asking." This was us, always, giving each other shit from the moment we opened our mouths.

Fighting or fucking, that was me and Priscilla.

But that wasn't true either, we were—we'd *always* been—a lot more than that. I looked up at her again and my stomach flipped thinking it would be like this for us now. That we'd have to find fake shit to talk about, because we didn't know enough about each other's lives to know what to ask.

I saw her reach for her phone and raised an eyebrow. "Tying up work stuff?" I spoke before giving it too much thought. Her job and how much it interfered with her personal life was definitely in the red zone for us. I cringed when I saw her put her back up, her mouth twisting to the side. I braced for the tongue-lashing I knew was coming, but at the last second, she deflated.

"Nah. It's all under control. This new team requires a lot less from me." She lifted a shoulder and pushed out her lips, feigning an indifference I knew was not really there. Not for her job. Never for her job. "I'm not really sure how I feel about it, but at least for this week I'm off duty. Fully at the disposal of Camilo and his man."

That smile was real and I was sure a twin to the one on my lips. "He'll want us at his beck and call as soon as we get there."

"That's Camilo. Although Tom has gotten him to chill out a bit."

"Not enough that he won't be a fucking monster this week. You know how he gets."

She laughed at that and grabbed my glass. It was one of those things that we'd done with each other forever, but the stakes felt high. The moment she slipped the glass out of my hand and moved to take a sip she widened her eyes and thrust it back into my hand.

"Sorry."

I tried to give it back to her. "Come on, Pris, you can take a sip of my drink. Just because—"

I almost said "we didn't work out," but I couldn't make

the words come out of my mouth. One thing was to know that's how it was. Another was to say it.

"Take a sip, woman. That's XO and you don't want it to go to waste." That last part made her smile and she did take the glass from my hand for a small sip.

When she handed it back she smiled ruefully at me. "God forbid we leave any of the food and alcohol intact on this flight." I fake shuddered and she laughed, cracking something open inside that I didn't realize had been cutting off my breathing from the moment she'd walked onto this jet. Pris and I could still be us. Maybe that could be what I did this trip, remind her of that.

I was mulling on that when the flight attendant started moving around the cabin asking everyone to get ready for landing. The energy immediately shifted in the plane, everyone buzzing with anticipation. I leaned over so I could look out at the same deep turquoise water I'd seen on yearly childhood trips to Puerto Rico, and later when I'd come with Pris or Nesto and the guys for spring breaks in the DR. Like everything else with us, Pris's and my own roots were inexorably tangled. The islands our people came from only divided by a small stretch of sea.

We both sat back after a minute, our eyes still half focused on the view when Pris spoke. "How's the Uptown Center?"

The Uptown Center was my father's post-retirement labor of love, which, like everything he did, had taken a life of its own. I smiled, thinking about the bustling operation my dad now ran. A social services agency that served retired cops and other first responders from the Bronx. The idea had come from his own struggle finding services when he was recovering from the gunshot wound that shattered his leg. "It's good, he just got another full-time social worker, so they're doing some support groups now too. A friend of Camilo's from grad school. He's good, Papi likes him."

She nodded and smiled. Pris has a special bond with my retired cop father. He'd been her mentor and friend completely separate from anything she and I ever had. I loved that they were close like that.

"You still helping out in the off-season?"

I nodded, feeling the jet starting to lower itself in the air.

"Yeah, I'm there three afternoons a week, unless I have to go down to Miami to work with the players that go south."

She peeked over to where our family was having the best time ever and then turned to me. She looked…unsure, which was so unusual for Priscilla.

"What's up?" I asked, genuinely worried. It was so rare to see her hesitant. Hell, that had been part of our problem. We'd gotten together in high school, both obsessed with joining NYPD, with making a difference. Me to follow in my dad's footsteps, and Pris to in some ways fulfill her own dad's dream. He'd yearned to be a cop, but by the time he was able to get his papers, felt like he was too old to try.

But after my dad got shot senior year of high school I couldn't do it. Priscilla of course would not be deviated from her plan. Instead of being supportive of each other, we turned those choices into personal affronts and before too long, things got rocky. From then on we'd been on and off. I ended up dating a classmate from my master's program for a couple of years. She never got serious with anyone, but in the end we'd come back and try again. Until the last time, when we said we just needed to quit trying.

Pris's laugh brought me out of the swirl of regretful memories running in my head, and when I looked up, her smile was almost as maudlin as my thoughts.

"So you ask me to tell you what's up and then you go all into your head?" Her tone was a lot softer than her words and I wondered if she guessed what I'd been thinking about.

"Sorry." I tried for a wink and a smile, but gave up. "Tell me what's going on."

She ran a fingertip over the rim of the glass, her usual strident confidence still not there. "I've been thinking of putting together these workshops through Come as You Are."

"Oh?" I tried to keep my tone neutral, because Come as You Are was her online sex positive toy shop and I was still trying to figure out how that had anything to do with my dad's retired cop center.

This time Pris did laugh. "Oh my God, Juan Pablo, your face right now." She pointed at me, grinning. "Your eyebrows are almost flush with your lineup."

Well, I could at least still make her laugh at my expense.

"You're imagining me showing up at Uptown Center with mad strap-ons and dildos right now, aren't you?"

It was really hard keeping a straight face, but I managed. "No."

Another cackle. "Liar!" She waved her hands dismissively, telling me I had the wrong idea. "It will involve a few toys, eventually. I was just thinking that it might be fun to offer a class for spouses of cops. Something about sex positivity for people living with chronic pain or injuries. I've been taking all these online courses and certifications for sex-ed."

She looked so adorably unsure about this. I'd never seen Priscilla this earnest. Her side-hustle always brought a different, playful side of Pris. Being a cop suited her, no doubt she was a badass and she did her job well.

But the sex positive stuff just made her glow. The more I thought about it, the more I thought I'd pay good money to see her in a room full of cops and their spouses with all her prostate massagers and fancy lubes. "Do say more," I said encouragingly.

"It's this new thing I'm working on. I was going to tell Rafa I could volunteer to do it at El Espacio. I also have the M&M class."

I knew about that one. It was a meditation and masturbation class for women she'd been doing for a while.

I lifted a shoulder and looked at my dad. These days he was getting more and more irreverent. I was pretty sure he'd be up for it. "I think he'd go for it. He's all about mindfulness these days, and self-love. Taking care of all parts of life. Since you put him onto yoga he's pretty much obsessed."

She nodded and smiled, but it didn't exactly reach her eyes. "Good. I need to be better about my own yoga. I haven't been as consistent as I should be."

That was surprising.

"Oh, been working a lot?"

Another shrug and her tone was decidedly less friendly when she spoke. "Something like that."

"I'll tell Papi about it. You know he can't say no to you."

And neither can I.

Priscilla

The smiles and whoops of joy were already resounding through the plane and we hadn't even touched down yet. I looked at my mom and dad, who were sitting side by side, clutching hands, excited as they always were to come home. They'd left the DR only weeks after getting married at nineteen and twenty-one. No English, no promised jobs.

Nothing.

They made it work though, for us, for me, and I never forgot that. There wasn't enough that I could do to repay what my parents had lived through. Working multiple jobs, tireless, so they could hand me the American Dream they came here for. No, they weren't perfect, but I'd never seen anything in my house but work and love.

I felt a soft pat on my arm and turned to look at where Juanpa was pointing. "You'd think it would get old for them," he said with a smile, looking at his Puerto Rican father's beatific smile as he looked down at the turquoise waters of the Caribbean Sea.

I laughed softly and shook my head. "Nunca." Seeing their land would never ever get old for them. For us either, if we were honest.

Suddenly I felt a strong, rough hand gripping mine and time stopped, as the plane finally touched the tarmac. I should've pulled it back, but as I sat there and cheered as we always did when we landed home, I let J's touch be part of the moment.

"Landing in style. Que cache." That was my dad trying to make us all laugh. "Rafa, who could've told us we'd be flying in a private jet, mano?"

"If anyone was going to figure out how to get himself a billionaire from DR it would be Camilo." That was Patrice, and we all lost it then.

This was going to be a good week. There was too much good to celebrate for anything to mess it up. As long as I kept my shit together and didn't land on Juan Pablo's dick. And because that motherfucker could read my mind, I felt his breath right by my ear as the captain told us that we should be arriving at the private gate soon.

"You feeling more relaxed? Ready for nonstop family time?"

I wasn't sure why his perfectly reasonable questions sounded like a lascivious offer, but I could feel a bead of sweat forming at the base of my back. I almost shook my head, marveling at the fact that Juan Pablo Campos still had that effect on me. Thankfully our parents were all half drunk and raring to get out of the plane, so no one noticed our little private moment.

I looked around and Juan Pablo's eyes on me were… blistering. But we were having none of that.

"No bullshit, Juan Pablo."

That grin was the one I knew meant he saw right through my protests.

"No BS, Morena." He crossed his thumb over his index finger and brought them up to his lips. "Promise."

Him using the nickname that only my family ever used should've annoyed me, but it just made me ever more flustered. Fuck, why was it always like this?

I could fool myself and act like none of it felt good or familiar. Tell myself that being here with everyone I loved was not just a little better because Juan was here, but I'd be a fool. And a liar. I'd be doing what I always did: pretending that he was not getting under my skin with every word.

"No BS. I will keep you to it, Juan Pablo Campos. Nobody needs our mess this week. We're here for Milo and Tom. No games, please."

Something about the way it came out made his expression change. Suddenly all playfulness was gone, and I hated myself a little for causing that.

"I've never played games with you. But I promised you something the last time and I don't plan to go back on my word."

There it was, the words I'd wanted. He was giving me what I'd asked for. But as I stepped onto the hangar, feeling the sea breeze running through the rafters, and as Juanpa hung back with the others, I wished I'd kept my mouth shut.

Chapter Three

Juan Pablo

"Ma, hurry you're gonna make us late." It was way too early for anything that required this level of energy. We were rushing to get on some sort of limo-bus thing getting ready to head out to a morning tour to some famous caves about an hour from the hotel. Since arriving last night, we'd been on some sort of Instagram dreamscape: Camilo's fiancé had rented out an entire boutique hotel for the week. The whole wedding party and our families were staying there and the place was pretty swank. We'd had an insane seafood dinner waiting for us when we arrived and everyone had turned in early, so we'd be ready for the tour.

Things with Priscilla and I had cooled off significantly after we'd landed, but I hadn't been in my head too much about it. This wasn't the Juan Pablo and Priscilla show after all, we were here for Camilo.

"Are those mimosas?"

I rolled my eyes as my mother gaped at the clear plastic cups that Patrice and Nesto's mom were drinking from. "No, Ma, it's just OJ. You don't want to get to those caves all dehydrated, do you? We'll have plenty of cold bubbly waiting for us when we get back." My mother nodded, not looking a hundred percent convinced that there wasn't a bottomless mimosa situation on the bus.

Nesto grinned and leaned down to give my mother a peck on the cheek. "Don't worry, Irene, you'll get your drink on soon enough. It's been like this since we got here. Milo's really getting the hang of spending Tom's money, because the flex is real." I laughed at the awe in Nesto's voice. He'd been at the hotel for a few days already, working out the details for the food at the reception and the rehearsal dinner. Nesto ran his own successful Afro-Caribbean restaurant in Upstate New York and Camilo and Tom had asked him to help them come up with the perfect Afro-Caribbean fusion menu for the wedding.

It was still sort of unreal that my three best friends were coupled off, getting married, engaged. It all felt so fucking grown-up. Seeing Patrice in love and not afraid to show it, Camilo actually getting his fairy-tale love and Nesto living his dream with Jude up in Ithaca…it was the greatest gift. But also a reminder of what I didn't have.

I looked over at Priscilla, who was busy chatting with Jude and Easton and I wondered if, like me, she was thinking that the two of us should've figured it out already. I felt like I'd spent half my life certain I was meant to be with her and the other half trying to figure out why we never seemed to work.

I was still mulling it over when I was flanked on either side by Nes and Patrice, who probably saw me sulking by myself in the back row, and came to do a welfare check.

"You looking like a Drake video back here, my guy." That was Nesto. Asshole.

I pursed my lips while they grinned at me. "Fuck off, I'm just chilling and wondering how it is that Camilo's still running my life. Why are we up so damn early? We're supposed to be on vacation."

"See, that's where you're wrong. We're here to be at Milo's beck and call and y'all know he's going to ride our asses all fucking week." Patrice grunted in agreement as he spanned his freakishly long and beefy arms over the entire back row.

When he finally spoke, he could barely keep the grin off his lips. "You think with the way Tom looks at him that the guy would be fucking some of that edginess out of him, but that fucker just can't stop bossing people around."

Nesto just shook his head and laughed at Patrice and, even as moody as I was, I had to crack a smile.

"Speaking of dick related issues." Nesto paused, his eyes trained right where my mom was chatting it up with Pris and her dad. "You gotta stop with the glaring, pa. I thought you said you were keeping things chill with Priscilla." There was just a hint of an edge there and I knew that was Nesto's protective side. Looking out for his cousin.

I let out a long breath and rubbed my hands over my face, hard. "I'm trying, Nes, but I don't know what's gotten into me on this trip. Since I saw her getting on the plane yesterday, it's like I can't get my head straight. I swear I'm not looking to start up something with Pris."

I winced even as I said it. "I mean, at least not anything that she's not up for. I promised myself I wouldn't mess with Pris unless she made the first move." I glanced at Nesto, whose face for once was devoid of emotion. I knew I always put him between a rock and hard place whenever shit with me and Pris started up over the years. "I fucked up with her last time and I don't plan to miss my shot if she gives another one, but I'm not starting anything. And even if I was, I would *not* do it here where I have the entire peanut gallery ready to take a bite out of me."

That at least got me a laugh.

"I'm not going to begrudge for biding your time, I know I would've waited an eternity for a chance to make things right with Jude." Nesto gripped my shoulder hard and settled in the seat next to mine as he looked up at where his partner was in deep conversation with Nurys, Nesto's mom. "I'm glad I didn't have to, but I know what it's like to know in your gut that everything you ever wanted slipped through your fingers because of your own stupidity."

I closed my eyes, feeling the weight of that hard truth, not wanting to get into any of this. Pris and I had a moment on the plane, but that didn't mean I had free rein to step up to her and ask for things. Like Nesto said, she was worth me waiting for her to be ready, and I would have to learn how to live with the possibility that she may never feel ready again.

"Are you coming?" I must've dozed off despite all the chattering in the limo-bus because the next thing I knew, I was opening my eyes to the vision of Priscilla Yudelka Gutierrez leaning over me in a halter top. She was offering me a view I was not equipped to deal with at that exact moment.

I quickly leaned back and made a show or rubbing my fists over my eyes. "I'm coming. Did those two clowns really leave me back here?"

Pris gave me a funny look and angled her head toward the front of the bus. "Patrice and Nesto told me to come get you. They jumped out to go to the bathroom before we go down to the caves."

Yeah, right. Knowing those two they were probably up to something.

"The bus driver is getting our tickets and the guide that's showing us around, so there's no rush." She pointed out of the window where most of our group was standing around by the bus chatting and passing around snacks and water bottles.

I looked around, trying to get my shit together. I grabbed the small backpack I'd brought with me and my Yankees fitted and stood up, just in time to watch her walk out of the bus. I got a full view of her strong, dark brown back and shoulders. Her shorts hugged her ass so tightly I didn't have to try very hard to remember how it felt to hold on to those curves as I pushed into her.

I literally had to shake myself under control as I followed her out. After all these years, Priscilla's body and the way she moved turned me on like nothing else could. I knew exactly where a soft touch made her purr and where my teeth could make her scream. She could do the same for me. But like I'd told Nesto and Patrice, I was going to keep my hands and thirst to myself this week.

The cave turned out to be pretty cool. It was a huge system of underwater tunnels with hundreds of Taino paintings and hieroglyphs. It was sort of unreal to see signs that there actually had been people here before colonization razed through everything. I was walking around looking at some of the lit drawings, taking a breather from the group, when I felt her come up behind me. I didn't have to turn around to know it was Priscilla, I could recognize even the sound of her fucking feet.

"You're worrying the mothers, Juan Pablo. They sent

me to find you." I could hear the grin in her voice. No matter how old we got, all our moms regressed to when we were in elementary school whenever we travelled together.

"I'll be right there, just needed a minute."

"The hovering and micro-managing every move is already getting to me. You should've seen Mami telling me how to open a water bottle just now. Because apparently Dominican water bottles twist different." The exasperation in her voice did nothing to hide the humor.

"Did Papi try to read the signs in English for you?" I asked, and could tell she was laughing from the way she was huffing. "They hammer Spanish into us our entire lives and as soon as we get here they start acting like they need to translate every word." I turned around and found her sporting a grin that perfectly matched mine.

She shook her head, shoulders still shaking from laughter. "They can't help themselves, they get too excited."

"I know, which is why I took a moment to myself before impaling myself on one of those rock spikes."

"They're stalagmites." I rolled my eyes while she grinned.

But after a moment she went back to observing me with a very serious look on her face. She even raised an eyebrow, like she was figuring something out. She came closer, looking at me with an intensity that I hadn't gotten from her in a long time. Detached and indifferent had been the vibe with her and me, at least for the last few years.

That shit was dangerous, because with me, Priscilla did not have to look very hard to see everything. When she finally spoke we were so close that I felt the hem of her linen shorts brushing against my legs.

"So instead of mouthing off, you walked over here to cool off." The incredulity in her voice almost pissed me off, but I took a deep breath and nodded. She was right—this was not my typical approach. I could let my stress or exhaustion turn me into an asshole sometimes, but I'd been working on not letting that shit get out of hand.

"I've learned to dial it back. People *can* change, Priscilla." As soon as I said it, I wondered if I'd made a mistake, but the sneer or dismissal I'd expected never came. Her eyes so focused on me I almost felt them burning my skin.

"People *can* change, you're right about that, Juan Pablo. The trick is wanting to."

I could tell myself I got closer on instinct, without thinking, but I didn't. I moved because I wanted to kiss her, and the way she pushed into me, I knew she felt the same way.

I could just let go, lean down to close the few inches between our lips and kiss her, remind her of how good it always was with us.

My hands trembled with the anticipation of touching her, and when I looked at her I knew she was barely containing her own need to reach out. But I'd promised myself that if I ever got the chance, I'd do this differently. That I would not fall into the same patterns with Priscilla again. I'd promised myself, my friends, and her, even if she didn't know.

So, I took a deep breath and stepped back. My shoulders tight with the tension of not going in for a kiss. "We should go back to the group—you know the parents must be about to send a search and rescue for us."

She didn't move, taking her time to assess me, like she was seeing me for the first time. "What's up with you?" Her tone wasn't so much hostile, just baffled. Like she really could not figure out what was going on with me.

"We're good." I tipped my chin in the direction of the group. "Let's get going."

I'd leave the question open, because I wasn't sure either of us could answer it right now.

Chapter Four

Priscilla

"I thought my folks were a little over the top, but Tom has them beat. Are those entire lobsters on that lunch buffet?"

I rolled my eyes at Easton's delighted tone. You'd think a guy who was, for all intents and purposes, heir to a world-famous vineyard would not be fazed by free seafood. But this was just one of the reasons why Easton was forever invited to the cookout.

I laughed as I pointed at the dozen grilled prawns on his plate. "Damn, East, you really have been hanging out with my family too long. You won't be able to eat all that."

"For your information," he said, haughtily pointing at the end of the pier that was part of the beachfront hotel restaurant. "I got some for my man too. He went to grab us one of those lanais. These views are really spectacular." We both turned to look at the white sandy beach and turquoise water. The lanais in question were lined along the pier. They looked like big four-poster beds covered on all sides with gauzy fabric that fluttered in the ocean breeze. I took a moment to appreciate the beauty of my parents' homeland and wondered once again what it would've been like to grow up in a place like this. Where everything just beckoned you to slow down and play. To not be so focused on the next thing. Easton's voice pulled me out of my thoughts and when I looked up the smile on his face got me out of my fretting. "Come on, babe. Patrice is over there shirtless and horizontal."

I had to laugh. "You'd think after a year your thirsty ass would've calmed down about Patrice's dick, but I guess that's not happening anytime soon," I teased, as we made our way down the wooden boardwalk.

He just shook his head, eyes trained on the man in question. "If anything, it's worse." He laughed and I marveled at the lightness in his voice. No reservation, no doubts.

"God, this place is pretty." I grunted in agreement as Easton admired the view.

I'd been coming to the DR my whole life and had stayed in pretty gorgeous beaches and hotels, but this shit was next level. Dominican beaches were world-class, there was no question about that, and Juan Dolio was a stunner. You could walk until the water was up to your neck and still see your feet; that was how white the sand was and how clear the water. Except my dumb ass was not paying attention to any of it. My head was still stuck on Juan Pablo's vibe at the cave.

I'd pushed and gotten close, half-expecting him to jump on it. Do something to give me an excuse to take things further, but he hadn't. He'd kept his hands to himself. I needed to do the same. Was I little taken aback by the fact that Juan Pablo didn't even try to leer or say something ridiculous when it was just the two of us in that cave?

Of course.

But I wasn't going to be the one to play games either. The last time we'd tried, things had gone up in flames and I swore I would not be the one to break. So far I wasn't doing super great at it, but I wasn't cracking either.

When we got to the lanai we passed around plates of food and drinks. There were four huge chaises that could probably fit four people each, but of course the couples had already commandeered three of them. Jude and Nesto were literally feeding each other ceviche in one, Easton dropped his ass on the one Patrice was clearly saving for him and no one else, and Camilo and Tom were on another one. That left the fourth one, where one Juan Pablo Campos was chilling, a cold Presidente in his hand.

For fuck's sake, how was I supposed to get through this fucking week with that man looking like an entire fucking meal? He was wearing his usual tight swim trunks and Ray Ban aviators...with a Yankees fitted on his head. He'd been picking on a plate of tostones and fried fish, and his lips were just a tiny bit greasy. The way my stomach dipped just from the thought of leaning in and licking it off should've been the first sign that I was in real fucking trouble.

"Here." I legit squealed and jumped about a foot in the air when he lifted a hand gesturing for my plate. "I'll hold it for you, so you can get comfortable." I passed him the glass of wine and plate then went around the to the other side of the chaise, trying hard not to look directly at the tattoo which just made the muscles on his smooth chest look that much more delicious. The man waxed and groomed more than any other person I'd ever met, and you'd think all the high maintenance bullshit would put me off his dick... Well, you'd be wrong. Because I was actively refraining from running a hand over all that brown skin.

As soon as I sat on the chaise he placed my wine and food on the built-in wooden tray between us. As I worked on getting my top back in place, I kept my peripheral vision on him long enough to see him noiselessly suck on his teeth. My heart tripped inside my chest at the gesture—which was usually the precursor to him saying something filthy and extremely hot—and I fought the urge to push up to him. The electricity in the air that was ever present whenever Juanpa and I were within touching distance practically burning my skin.

And he was right there with me, close enough I could smell his citrusy aftershave and the shea butter and jojoba coconut oil he religiously rubbed on his skin each morning.

Fuck, drinking and this much contact with Juan Pablo was not going to end well.

"There's really some hashtag 'living my best life' shit happening right now." His voice startled me again, this time at least I managed not to scream. "I'm too overwhelmed to even post to my Instagram account," he said, making me laugh. I nodded in silent agreement, as I took a long sip from the delicious Chilean sauvignon blanc they literally had on tap.

"Leave it to Camilo to find a man that hot and *that* fucking loaded and then make him so crazy he has to beg him to spend money on him," Juan Pablo joked, referring to Camilo's refusal to take money from his fiancé at the beginning of their relationship. Thankfully our prickly friend was now embracing the flex, which meant we were getting treated to a pretty fancy vacay.

"I'm not going to say I'm mad at Camilo seeing the light," I muttered around a mouthful of grilled octopus.

"Ey, nobody's complaining, least of all me—"

Juan Pablo suddenly stopped talking then cleared his throat and stared somewhere around my mouth.

"What?" I asked, running a hand over my cheek.

"You got a little bit of the sauce on your chin, here," he said, leaning in to rub his thumb over the spot.

Fuck, he smelled so damn good.

I squeezed my eyes shut, trying mad hard not to do something crazy like lick him, but it was a very close call. He kept his thumb on my face for just a moment longer than necessary and we both held our breath, caught up in touching again. Everything felt like this with J, like I was always on the edge of a precipice. Constantly on the verge of falling. I had to make sure I never forgot it was a bad idea to take the plunge.

But like back at the cave, just when I was about to let myself take what I knew we both wanted, Juan Pablo pulled back. With his eyes hidden under mirrored glasses I couldn't exactly see what was happening, but the flush on his chest and neck told me that he was just as heated as me.

He stood up, pointing at my half-full wineglass, his empty bottle in one hand. "I'm gonna go to the bar for another. You need anything?"

I shook my head as I attempted to compose myself, "Nah, I'm good."

He angled his head in the direction of the beach bar where some of our family was still eating as I tried to discreetly watch him walk away. That wide back tapering down to a narrow waist and God, that ass, which had always been my weakness.

"Nice to see that even though we're living the *MTV Cribs* life these days, some things never change. Pris, your thirst is showing, Mama."

I glanced up to see Camilo and Easton both grinning at me but before I could tell either of them to fuck off I got flanked on both sides and got matching looks, which all but guaranteed I was about to get a session of twenty questions. "Don't you two have men you need to be paying attention to?"

Camilo flicked his hand in the direction of his silver fox who seemed to be in a very engrossing conversation with Patrice. "They're talking about the elections. They'll be at it for a while, and I'll have plenty of time to get all the QT I need with my man soon." He gloated, as he raised his left hand to admire his very understated engagement ring. Tom had managed to get a rock on that ring, but I'm sure he restrained himself for Camilo's sake. "From here, we're going to some bougie place in Greece for two weeks of what I hope will be nothing but fucking, eating and day drinking, not necessarily in that order."

I smiled at how happy he was. It seemed that while I wasn't looking all my friends had become...fulfilled. The Priscilla who had been through more than a few breakups with them and knew how fucking amazing they were was happy, no, elated for them, because they deserved it. The other Pris, the one who was starting to feel like every part of the life she'd worked so fucking hard to build was suffocating her—she felt just a little bit jealous. Not because I wanted exactly what they had, but because I felt unsatisfied and I had no clue how to fix it.

Actually that was a lie. I knew what could fix it, I was just too scared to try. But instead of going down that anxiety-inducing rabbit hole, I focused on my reason for being here and pulled on Milo's hand so I could kiss his cheek. "You're a smug little bastard, but I'm happy for you."

He made a "move over" gesture with his free hand, and I obliged as he directed his knowing gray eyes in my direction. "Thanks, but don't change the subject. What's up with you and J? I've been catching some serious powder-keg vibes from the two of you."

Easton nodded in agreement as we all looked at the man in question making his way back to us. He stopped about halfway when his dad called after him. Turning around only gave me another look at that ass.

Easton made an appreciative sound, which I knew was more to make me laugh than anything else. "I got more than I can handle with the professor burning the sheets off my bed on a regular basis, but, friend, I gotta tell you, at another time, I'd have happily taken a bite out of that."

Camilo cackled as he stole a sip of wine from my glass.

I laughed too, keeping an eye on J. "He probably would've let you too. And please stop, I don't need this kind of dangerous enabling when I'm in an all I can drink type of situation, Easton Archer."

Camilo cut his eyes at me and spoke in a low voice. "Like you've ever needed substances to fall on that dick or vice versa. The two of you have always been that thirsty for each other and it looks like time has not taken off the edge."

There was no use denying what we all knew was true. "We work better as friends."

"If you say so" came across loud and clear on Camilo's face, but thankfully J's return put a stop to the conversation.

Before he even had a chance to say something, Jude came over waving a finger in the direction of Juan Pablo and Camilo, then turned to do the same at Nesto and Patrice who were sitting just a few feet away still talking to Tom. He smiled widely as he looked at the foursome. "Wow, I don't think I've ever seen the full set."

I didn't even have to ask—he was referring to seeing the matching tattoos the four of them had gotten while we were all in college. Each of the guys had a beating heart tattooed over where their real ones would be. Each one covered in flags. Juanpa's had the Puerto Rican and the American flag; he'd had the last name of his Italian mother done in a heavy cursive font on the other side of his chest. I'd gone with him to get both pieces. Back then we were inseparable and still talking about the future.

I shut down that line of thinking immediately, nothing good was going to come from me reminiscing on shit that was done with a million years ago. Instead I looked up at the guys who were now lined up showing off their tats. Juanpa's chest was like chiseled marble. Since he'd started the job with the Yankees he'd been taking better care of himself. His body, which had always been lean, was now hard and strong.

Checking myself again, I held up my camera, desperately trying to get out of my very unhelpful thoughts. "We should document this occasion. Before the very first one of the GA crew gets officially hitched."

That got a laugh from the group and they started posing right there in the lanai, but Camilo, who always had to have a say, shook his head and pointed toward the water. "Let's do it with our backs to the water, so we get the view."

The other three all shook their heads and griped about

Camilo's bossiness, but made their way to the exact spot their friend had indicated.

We all shuffled out of the shaded refuge and stepped out into the afternoon sun. Out of nowhere, an image of me lying on a chaise with J's head between my legs almost made me drop my camera.

"Shit." I sounded as flustered as I felt, while trying to adjust the lens for the picture.

"Prima, you all right? This sun is killing us." That was Nesto.

"Sorry, here we go on the count of three." I got a few weird stares for spacing out, but I kept it moving. I felt a twinge of resentment at their surprised looks. Once again, I felt burdened by the expectation that I was made of steel or something. That everyone around me could falter or fall apart, but somehow I could never have a misstep, a moment of doubt. I looked down for a second, trying and failing to shake off whatever this was, and when I glanced up Juan Pablo was looking right at me. The intensity in his eyes telling me he sensed something was wrong.

I flexed my shoulders and made a show of adjusting the camera. "Here we go." I took a moment to look at them, the boys I'd grown up with, now men. Handsome, successful…happy men. It was almost overwhelming to see them all standing there, so much history. I took a couple of shots as their partners and lovers looked on, the mixture of adoration and possessive pride all over their faces.

Right as I brought the camera down Juanpa caught my gaze and held it. There was too much there for me to process. I knew we were thinking the same thing: this was the end of an era. Our friends were all stepping into their future. Juan Pablo and I were getting left behind.

I wondered if I'd ever find someone that got me like Juan did. I knew it would be impossible for anyone else to understand what my family and my people meant to me, because at the end of the day…my people were his.

That I could never get with anyone else, the short-hand of so many years knowing each other as we did. I'd thought more than once that the history we had was part of what made it so hard for us to work. I'd always felt a little caged in by the family in my business, the meddling. But as I stood there, feeling the love that surrounded us and would always lift us up, I wondered if embracing all this was a better approach than trying to contain it.

Chapter Five

Priscilla

I wouldn't ever have to imagine what a fairy-tale wedding looked like. I was in one.

It was a small wedding; less than a hundred people. I sat in the second row of comfortable chairs lined across the white sandy beach. The sun was lower in the sky and the breeze coming from the ocean made for a pretty perfect moment.

"This is quite spectacular," Easton whispered from the seat next to mine. On my other side were my mom and dad, and right in front of us were Nesto's parents and Patrice's mom.

"It is," I agreed, as I took in the scene. The event planner, a high school friend of Tom's, had outdone herself. She'd built a small canopy, under which Tom and Camilo would say their vows. It was covered in what must have been thousands of white and green orchids. And to the side was a music quartet playing instrumental versions of old merengue. After a moment, they began playing a more solemn piece and Tom's mom and dad came down the aisle, looking like royalty and beaming at all the onlookers.

"It's perfect." I didn't mean to sigh, but it was hard to resist getting a little maudlin. I'd never wanted any of this for myself. I still didn't; my idea of a happily-ever-after had never involved a wedding dress or a white picket fence. But bearing witness to one of my dearest friend getting his own version of a happily-ever-after was beyond special.

"God she's so cute." I smiled distractedly at my mother's comment then looked over to see Tom's six-year-old daughter, Libertad, walking toward the front, a little red cushion holding the weddings bands.

That was something else I didn't want: children. I'd never envisioned domesticity for myself, which had not been exactly an easy sell for my Dominican parents. I was their only child and I knew they'd always dreamed of getting to do this. Of seeing me walk down the aisle and stand up with the person I loved.

Juan Pablo and I would laugh, wondering how we'd break it to our parents that there would most likely be no wedding or grandkids, at least not from us. The rustling of people moving in their seats and Easton's gasp got my attention back on the proceedings, and my eyes landed on the guys who were walking in that easy rhythm of people who were used to making space for each other.

They were wearing pastel blue linen Cuban guayaberas with gray slacks and leather sandals, with Ayako, Camilo's work wife, heading up the line in matching blue linen romper. They all looked sun kissed and handsome; fades fresh, breads trimmed. They could've been a destination wedding fashion shoot.

Tom's side came up after, with Priya, one of his best friends, wearing the same romper as Ayako but in a golden yellow, her arm linked with her husband Sanjay's.

Behind them, Tom's other best friend and his brother walked along, smiling in their yellow chacabanas—the Dominican equivalent of the guayabera, minus the intricate embroidery on the sides. Tom followed them and, after a minute, Camilo came up with his mother.

There was a collective gasp on our side when we saw the two of them beaming as they made their way to the canopy. Seeing Camilo and Dinorah glowing had us all in tears. I looked up and saw that Juanpa and the guys were doing their best to hold it together while Ayako was trying, and failing, to blot her mascara as tears ran down her face. Tom's face was the definition of adoration as he stood on the tip of his toes, clearly holding back from running down the aisle. The rest of us could disappear and he would not even notice, all of his attention on his beloved.

After Camilo got to the front and hugged Dinorah, all of us were ready to lose our shit. But when Milo walked up to Tom and the older man enveloped him in a tight embrace and mouthed "I love you," with such intensity he could barely get the words out, there was not a single dry eye in the place.

There would be no judge, gay marriage not being legal in the DR. Tom and Milo had already made it official in New York City. This was the celebration of their love they wanted to share with all of us. Tom's dad stood up to say a few words in English and Spanish about Tom and Milo and we all settled in to hear the vows.

Tom told Camilo about the ways his love had changed him for the better. How for the first time in his life he felt like he could step into all the parts of who he was without fear. And Camilo reciprocated by telling his man that because of Tom's love he was finally able to trust that he deserved the fairy tale he'd always yearned for, but never thought he would get.

As Camilo and Tom made promises to each other about forever, I glanced at Juan Pablo and found him looking at me. Each time the intensity in his gaze almost made me jump in my seat.

What was he looking for, looking at me like that?

I wondered if this new Juan Pablo I'd been seeing glimpses of all week wanted something different. If he wanted something more "normal" than the low-key shared apartment we'd dreamed about as teens. I couldn't tell. He looked at me with a mixture of longing and hope, I couldn't quite decipher. As Milo and Tom finished their vows and then ended the ceremony with a swoon-worthy kiss, we all whooped and cheered. With that, the first notes of Celia Cruz's "La Vida es un Carnaval" sounded across the beach and we all headed up to where the reception to end all receptions was waiting for us.

I let our family and friends hurry up the sandy path to the cocktail hour area and lingered behind, giving myself just a minute to breathe through the wave of emotions that had hijacked me during the ceremony. It was so strange to feel so alone when I was literally surrounded by every person I loved. I could see them all right now, and still I didn't know what to do with myself.

I sighed, sick on my own bullshit, and decided I'd take a stroll on the beach before rejoining the rest of the group. Just as I was about to turn I felt a light touch under my elbow. It was almost like my body could recognize him before my mind did.

"You bracing for what our nearest and dearest are about to do to that open bar?"

Just like that, the tension balloon that had taken over my chest popped.

I tried my best not to laugh, but then stopped fighting it and busted up. When I looked up he was grinning from ear to ear. "You think you're funny," I said through fits of laughter. "Although my dad's been availing himself of the Blue Label like it's his job."

He scoffed as we took a few steps toward the darkened beach. "I can't talk, my parents took so many crab legs from dinner to their room last night they could barely walk."

I shook my head and grinned, certain he was only exaggerating a little bit, then bumped his shoulder. "You guys looked great up there."

"Shiiit. Is that a compliment?" I could barely make out the grin on his face, now that it was fully evening and we were getting further from the lights of the reception area. But it was there.

"Don't let it go to your head, this day has us all in our feelings."

"I know. Milo's so damn happy that for a whole ten minutes there he forgot to boss us around." That made me laugh for real. I lifted my face to the sky and felt the briny sea breeze as we walked.

For a second I felt him hesitate, but then he lifted his arm over my shoulder. He didn't drop it though, just let it hover over there for a second, waiting for me to pull it down. I didn't question my impulse as I brought a hand up to settle his arm around my shoulder.

Juan Pablo

There were many sides to Priscilla, and over the years I had seen most of them, but her vulnerable, quiet side was not one I'd seen a lot.

I wasn't sure what to think when we reached the edge of the hotel property and she had her hand gently resting on the arm I'd draped around her shoulder. It was too dark now to see her clearly, but at the ceremony I could hardly keep my eyes off her.

She was wearing a long gray and turquoise maxi dress. The top hugged her breasts and showed off her strong brown arms. She'd braided her hair in an intricate design, which made her look like a Taino princess. I was never any good at coming up with clever or romantic words, but for Priscilla corny shit always seemed to be right at the tip of my tongue.

"Do you need to get back to the reception? Photos, speeches?"

I startled when her voice pierced the quiet, and turned to look at her. "We took all the pics beforehand, because it would be too dark after the ceremony." She dipped her head once at that. "But I do have to be there in—" I lifted my arm to look at my watch "—about fifteen minutes. We let Priya and Ayako convince us to act out a poem for our joint speech, and I have to go look like a jackass in front of a hundred people."

She busted up at that. "Of course they did. I can't wait to hear what those two came up with. It's so great that Milo and Tom's friends get along so well." She said it in that same glad-but-a-little-sad tone she'd been using all week. As we walked back up to the hotel, I wondered if all this was also getting to her.

I almost asked her what was wrong, or if this weekend had just a tinge of bittersweet to it for her too, but getting to Priscilla's soft underbelly was almost never a pleasant experience and I didn't want to ruin the moment. "We all do get along well. Ayako and Priya are thick as thieves. They've been working on that program together. Sanjay and Priya are giving a ton of money to start a South and East Asian LGBT+ Youth center in Queens and Ayako's been really involved with that."

Pris nodded and when she spoke I could hear the smile in her voice. "Leave it to Milo to find the one set of millionaires in New York who are not only all gorgeous and nice, but seem to be hell-bent on spending all their money on helping people."

I cracked a smile at that. "And that little monster still finds shit to complain about."

"That's why we all love him. You never need to know where you stand with Camilo. He will let you know."

I grunted some kind of affirmative response, feeling that a little more intensely than she probably meant me to. As we got closer to the lit reception area, we could smell the jerk chicken on the grill, but Priscilla spoke before I could. "Damn that smell's making me hungry.

I didn't think I'd be able to eat after that gigantic lunch, but I could use a cocktail and some wings right now."

I laughed at her ravenous expression. "Same. The food this week has been amazing." Because Camilo was Cuban *and* Jamaican, we would have a Jamaican-themed cocktail hour, and dinner would be Dominican/Cuban fusion.

"Nesto really outdid himself on this one." Pris's voice was full of that pride she always had for her cousin. Nesto had asked two of his friends from culinary school—one Cuban and the other Jamaican—to come help out. Last night we'd had an amazing Afro-Caribbean fusion meal at the rehearsal dinner, and from the scents hitting us right now, we were in for another treat.

As we started walking up the stone path to the large covered terrace where guests were milling around various food stations I slid my arm from her shoulders. I almost didn't say anything, but no matter how much things had changed I still had to be me. "I'm gonna take this arm off you right now, but know that it's ready and able to be deployed whenever you need it."

She just gave me some side-eye…and a smile. "Duly noted. Not that we want to give any of these people the wrong idea. Team JuanScilla is going strong in the Gutierrez family." I grinned when she mentioned the nickname the guys had given us during a particularly hot and heavy time for us.

"Fuck no!" Throwing my hands up as if to shield myself. "Don't even mention it in front of Camilo."

I was about to make another joke about all the grief we put up with over the years when I noticed Patrice hurrying toward us. "Oh good! Here you are. We're going to go practice this poem fiasco one more time before the speeches start."

I just rolled my eyes as I stepped up to where he was with Pris next to me. "It's a little difficult to buy how annoyed you are about this when you're grinning so hard I can see your molars."

Pris rolled her eyes at him too, pointing at Easton who was walking toward us with two champagne flutes in hand. "He probably thinks this is going to earn him points with Easton." She clicked her tongue at Patrice, who was now waggling his eyebrows and mouthing, "You know I am."

"Oh how the mighty fall. Patrice Denis, trying to get ass by acting a fool at a wedding. I never thought I'd live to see the day."

We all cracked up at that and by the time Easton made it to where we were, we had tears in your eyes. He handed Pris one of his glasses after giving Patrice a kiss. "Stop teasing my man, Priscilla."

She balked at that. "How do you know I was teasing him?"

If any of us didn't know her as well as we did, we'd think she was dead serious.

"I can tell. Now drink your delicious signature champagne cocktail so we can go get food from that unbelievable cocktail hour spread while these men go practice."

She saluted us with one hand as she took a sip and moaned. "Damn. This is good. Champagne and what?"

Easton nodded in appreciation. "Tamarind and passion fruit."

"Thank you baby Jesus for making Camilo skanky." She pressed a hand to the champagne flute as if in prayer. "Because we are all reaping the fruits of his efforts."

Man, I hadn't seen that glint in Priscilla's eyes since we'd gotten here. I didn't want to get a big head and say our walk turned her mood around, *but I could think it*. I didn't want to leave, just so I could get a little bit more time with her.

But before I could mess more with her, P clapped me on the shoulder. "Let's go J."

Pris and Easton lifted their glasses to us as we turned to join the others.

"Are you two patching things up?" That was another big change in Patrice, since he'd joined the ranks of the coupled off and blissfully happy. He now *volunteered* to know about people's feelings.

"I wouldn't say patch things up, but yeah it's all good." As we headed to join the rest of the wedding party to figure out how many ways we could make asses of ourselves in honor of our friend's marriage, I thought about how good it had felt to have my arm around her, to see her at ease and joking, the way her laugh still did more for my soul than anything else in the world, how it probably would forever.

I knew it then. It was time to take my chance.

Chapter Six

Priscilla

No matter how I was handling my own feelings about my love life or my future, tonight had me feeling grateful. Tom and Camilo's wedding had been not just beautiful but it had been a freaking love fest. It was impossible to be sad in the presence of two people that much in love with each other. It was also so good to be with family and friends to lift Milo up. No one deserved a happily-ever-after more than him.

The guys and Ayako had brought down the house with their adorable and hilarious speech. Even Milo's prickly ass hadn't been able to keep from cackling as they relayed hilarious stories about Camilo's reputation as the group's ring leader and all the ways in which they loved him. For their first dance, Tom actually flew in Juan Luis Guerra, whose music meant so much to both of them, and they danced to "Cuando Te Beso," as we all basically melted from how monumental it all felt.

It was past midnight and the party was still going strong. And another one of the merengue bands Tom hired for the wedding had all the Latinx people still going hard on the dance floor. I'd danced about three songs in a row with my dad and was about to call it quits when I felt someone tap my shoulder.

Before I could turn around I saw my father's face light up. "Juan Pablo, you cutting in?"

He moved so he was standing next to my dad, a shy smile on his face, and my traitorous stomach dipped. He'd been dancing all night too. With his salsa skills he was always in high demand at weddings. At some point he'd unbuttoned his shirt, so I could see just a peek of that chiseled chest I'd been getting eyefuls of all week.

My dad released my hand and looked between the two of us. "Que dices, Pris?" What *could* I say? No?

I mean, I could but… I may not have wanted to admit it to myself but I'd kept an eye on him as he'd danced with other partners tonight. No matter who it was he was always the one leading, he was a beautiful dancer. I wanted to dance with Juan Pablo. He knew it too. I winked at my dad, trying to keep the mood light and not make this a thing like I seemed to do with everything lately and extended my hand to him.

He took it immediately, as my father clapped a hand on his shoulder and pointed to my mother, who was sitting at our table watching the dance floor with a tired smile. Her gauzy yellow dress hiked up to her knees. "I'm gonna get Maritza and head to the room. You got your key, right?"

I nodded and my dad walked off, leaving me in Juan Pablo's arms. Just as I was about to make a snarky comment about his dance card finally having an opening, the first notes of "Entre tu Cuerpo y el Mio" started and he and I both stiffened at once.

Of fucking course our old song would start playing the moment we began dancing.

"That's a throwback." Juan Pablo wasn't even trying to sound casual as we started moving. I couldn't even remember the last time we'd danced together. It'd been years, but as soon as he pressed his hand to the small of my back we were in sync again. Our feet stepping in unison, hips swaying to the same exact beat. I closed my eyes, confident in J's lead as I listened to the singer belt out the lyrics to what had been our anthem. I felt his grip tighten when she sang about lovers that gave each other their very souls, bodies that fit so perfectly there was no space at all between them when they came together. He pressed closer and I let him as I mouthed the words from the song, my head thrown back.

I felt his beard brush against my face, as I pressed closer. We were almost the same height but with my heels on I was just a little bit taller. I smiled at that, because for all his posturing and vanity, Juan Pablo had never cared about that. On the contrary, he loved seeing me in heels.

"How did you enjoy the rest of the night?"

Oh shit. He was going to talk to me then. Because I wasn't having enough of a problem not swooning over what his hips were doing or the man sweat and Tom Ford aftershave combo he was rocking right now. I slowly opened my eyes and he was looking at me expectantly, but again with that sort of Zen thing that he had going on these days. Like he could wait for my answer for as long as I needed.

"It was good." I shook my head to clear it, because there was a lot going on in there and I'd had quite a few of those signature cocktails. "You have to stop looking at me like that. I let Easton convince me to have a few Henny shots, because he thinks he's Drake now."

That only got me another laugh from J and that wide

grin that made his dimples pop…fuck. I was weak, and that motherfucker knew right when my defenses were at their lowest, because he put both hands right at my back and pushed in tight. "How am I looking at you?"

I closed my eyes again, breathed in deep and thanked the universe for my room, which was fully equipped with a set of parents. "You're looking at me like you want to start something."

When I opened my eyes, I expected him to be looking at me all seductive and shit, but he wasn't. He just looked…happy. Before he spoke he smiled again and my chest tightened. I missed Juan Pablo still, no matter what happened. I missed him, and not just as a lover, but as a friend.

"I mean, I'm not going to lie. I'd love to start something with you, but I'm not going to push. I told you the last time, Pris. I don't want to wreck things."

That was another thing that the new Juan Pablo did, he talked. Shared his feelings openly. The song ended and the new one was an old bolero. One of those old ones that Luis Miguel had brought back in the '90s and my mom had played 24/7 for months.

"Damn that's old *old* school." Juan Pablo grunted but didn't make an attempt to bring me any closer. Boleros were a slow, tight against each other dance. If there was too much space between you and your partner, you were definitely not doing it right. But it seemed he was taking some sort of stance. I had to be the one to put us in the proper position. When I saw that eyebrow hiked up high on his forehead and that lopsided smile I gave in.

"Okay, fine." I had my arms around his neck and was swaying with him after a moment, and I had to admit, it felt nice.

"This has been a good week. I won't lie, there's been some sexual frustration and confusion on my end." He laughed as I eyed him suspiciously. "You've been giving off some really unusual vibes, Juan Pablo Campos."

"Nah, I'm just not being my greasy shameless self." He came to a dead stop on the dance floor, as if whatever he needed to say demanded his complete attention, and mine too. "These days I'm trying to be more cautious of how I approach things, being a little more careful with the people I love."

It's not like I hadn't noticed it. He was different—contemplative, almost. Paying attention. Juan Pablo was the youngest and the only boy in his family. All his cousins were girls so he basically grew up as a prince, and he acted like it. He could be selfish sometimes. More than once his assumption that the world just had to accommodate to what he wanted had been a source of contention for us. But the hubris that usually accompanied that seemed to be done now. The way he carried himself was different. The line of his shoulders was stronger, and softer at once. That set to his chin that challenged the world not to give him what he wanted was softer now. The more I thought about it, the more I felt like this was a Juan Pablo I could almost take another chance on.

"Sorry," I said with an embarrassed laugh. "I zoned out."

Without asking me to give more of an explanation he started moving again. Once we were back in a groove, moving together in unison, he spoke.

"It's not that deep. I'm just trying." He didn't say what for, but he didn't have to. I knew what he meant.

"We all are." I sounded tired and just a bit more jaded than I used to, and for the first time I felt bothered by it. I wanted to shake that weariness off my voice. Sound like I used to, purposeful, satisfied. "I guess the mid-thirties life crisis hits everyone differently, for you it's been a positive change."

As I looked for words for wherever I was going with this conversation the song stopped and some Latinx pop song came on. I wasn't in the mood and suddenly the urge to spill my guts to Juan Pablo was almost overpowering.

I took his hand and angled my head to the beach. "I think I may call it a night." J's brow dipped in disappointment, but I shook my head and tugged on him. "Do you want to get out of here?"

At any other time this would have been his cue to say something suggestive, to rake his eyes over me, knowing just how to get my blood boiling. Tonight he just pulled me along with him and said, "Let's go."

Juan Pablo

I knew I had Priscilla on pins and needles with my new vibe, and I wasn't going to lie, it felt good to know she could see it. That she noticed there was a change in me. Because I'd wondering if it was only obvious to me. That all this shit I'd been working on hadn't made a difference.

Before heading out we walked to one of the tables where Patrice and Easton were also getting ready to call it a night. Camilo and Tom had left hours ago, since they were flying out first thing to start on their honeymoon in Greece.

On a whim I grabbed a water bottle and couple of the tiny champagnes from one of the huge ice buckets that were placed all around the reception area. Once Priscilla had her gauzy shoulder wrap and small bag in hand, we headed to the beach.

"So what is this mid-thirties crisis thing about?" I asked as we walked out onto the sandy beach, the grains soft and still warm under our feet. Remnants from the sunny day.

Priscilla sighed and wrapped the sheer fabric around her shoulders. That thing didn't look like it would do anything to keep her warm and I wished I had a jacket or something to give her. The breeze from the ocean had picked up with a vengeance now that it was more early morning than late at night. "It's just work-related bullshit."

"The Inwood precinct isn't working out? I thought you liked it there."

She gave me a curious look and I realized she hadn't said this to me. I'd heard it through my mother, who heard it from the Dominican News Network, as Nesto always called it.

"My mom said you'd come by to talk to Papi after you took the job. She mentioned you seemed happy."

She pursed her lips but her dark brown eyes had a glint of humor in them. "Our parents are serious busy-bodies, damn."

I laughed at her stank face. "True."

When we passed one of the covered cabanas on the beach she stopped and jerked her head in its direction. "You want to go in there? I'm freezing."

I didn't answer, just followed her into one. The cabanas in this place were seriously pimped out. There was a huge double chaise with a small stack of towels on a shelf to the side. It was dark as fuck inside, but we both had our phones with us and with the help of the flashlight app got situated. Pris draped a couple of the towels over herself like blankets and one over her shoulders.

Once she was settled in she put her head back and let out a long sigh. "This wedding was bomb, but fuck, I'm tired."

I grunted in agreement as I arranged the three small bottles between us. "You up for some bubbly or you want water?" She looked down at our beverage bounty and smiled. The smile she always had when she was pleased by something or someone. It was just a turning up of her lips, but her eyes went liquid with warmth. I'd missed that smile most of all.

I'd placed my phone in between us with the flashlight on and could see her face half cast in shadow. I spent a moment looking at the lines of her face. Her long neck and the way her skin seemed to be glowing in this light. Her makeup was not perfect at this time of the night. The humidity making her a little shiny, and her deep red lipstick having worn off after hours of food and drink.

She looked like she'd had a long night of fun and she was still, as always, perfectly kissable. I swallowed hard and lifted the beverage offerings to her.

She grabbed them both, first taking a few gulps of the water and then cracking open the little champagne bottle. I did the same and we clinked them together, saying "to Camilo and Thomas" almost at the same time.

She took a long sip and sighed again, and I debated on what to do. There was so much to say. There was so much *to do*. But a lot of those things were about me, and what I wanted. I'd promised myself that if I ever got the chance to do so again, I'd give her my full attention.

"So what's up with the job?"

She laughed, shaking her head at me. "Damn, Juan Pablo, you really are a changed man. You're actually volunteering to hear people whine about their job?"

Okay that stung a little, because even though I could be a little impatient about people's drama, I wasn't a total asshole. I could go into my feelings about this, turn her comment into a thing, or I could just keep the focus on her.

"I always want to hear about you, and that will never

change." She looked a little reluctant, like she didn't know what to do with this new version of me, but it was true. It felt good to look her in the eye when I said that.

"Okay." She sounded only slightly suspicious, which I guess was an improvement. "It's not even that it's bad. This new captain is pretty good and I like working with her. The rest of the team, even though it's mostly guys, is decent enough." She slumped and I could feel the weariness radiating from her. "I'm just tired of the politics and educating people that should know better."

I didn't know what to say. My job was pretty straightforward. I mean yes, I dealt with some bullshit for sure. There was a whole lot of toxic masculinity and entitlement in that clubhouse. Sure, a lot of the players were Latinx or black but the guys sitting in the executive suites were...not. It made for weird moments. However, I rarely dealt with that. I had a job to do and I did it. And for the most part I got along with everyone.

"I can't say that I'd have a lot of patience for politics, and you've been fighting your way up the ranks for ten years now. I can only imagine that shit's gotten old for you. Do you like the work at least?"

She lifted a shoulder, obviously trying not to be super down on things but barely succeeding. "I did."

The dimness in her smile told me the love she'd had for the job in those first few years was no longer there, or it was nowhere near as strong. I hated the idea of Priscilla's fire being snuffed out by politics and bullshit. Most of the time with Pris I could sense where she hurt and where I could make things better. Tonight I had to remind myself I no longer had a right to any of those places. I'd talked and fought my way out of being the person she came to for comfort.

"I don't think I can handle *I told you so's* right now." I could hear she was wary of what I would say. She thought I would go back to old arguments and disagreements to hurt her, and in the past I probably would have.

"I have fucked up in so many ways when it comes to us, but I really hate myself for saying things that would make you think I care more about being right than seeing you happy."

She took in a breath and let it out slowly, eyes still locked on mine. "You're different, J."

I shrugged, not wanting to make any of this about me, but something in my chest loosened from her words. Unbidden and completely unfiltered, the words came out of my mouth before I could do anything to stop them.

"You looked beautiful today." I did something halfway between a cringe and shrug. "You always do, but with the sun in your hair and little bit of a flush you get when you feel like crying but you really don't want to…" She bit her lip, trying not to laugh and my head swam from how much I wanted her.

I let it hang for a moment and in the way her chest moved, fast and a little erratic, I saw that the moment had turned for her too. In this dark little corner of the Caribbean with white sand under our feet and the ocean breeze serenading us, I wished we were still Pris and J from high school, from college, from even two years ago.

Again, my mouth was faster than my head. "I miss kissing you."

Pris's breath caught and fuck I wanted to, but I wouldn't make a move. I would not encroach on the space she asked for. I would not be the one to break the promise. I was practically vibrating as I waited for her to say something, to ask for what she wanted.

"J." The way she said that made me feel like I was on fire. I'd missed how just the first letter of my name could sound so fucking hot slipping from her lips.

We both reached out at the same time, mouths crashing together, chests heaving and hands hot on each other.

"Fuck." I wasn't sure if it was regret or it was rapture, but tasting Priscilla felt like my entire life was realigning. Like all the things that had gone old and stale shone again.

I kissed her hard and, as always, she gave it all back to me. Hot, hungry. Lips nipping, mouth open and I couldn't hold it in. I could almost smell her.

"Are we blaming this on post-wedding haze?"

I was so caught up in all the places I wanted to get to on her body that I almost missed the question. When I pulled back, again I could see the vulnerability in her eyes. It hit me hard to know that she thought wherever this was going could hurt her.

I lifted my hands off her and tried to get myself under control. I didn't ever want to be one of the things that Priscilla regretted. Not again.

I didn't want to say it, but I made myself do it. "Why don't I walk you to your room? I don't want to make you uncomfortable." I was more stating a fact than asking a question, and no matter how much my dick was going to hate me later I was glad I said it.

She looked at me for a long moment without answering, her gaze scrutinizing me, as if she was looking for the answer to my question somewhere on my face. Like I'd just turned into a puzzle she was set on solving. I always forgot the way Priscilla could make my skin feel like I was on fire. Like my lust was a tornado swirling inside, powerful enough to lift me clear off my feet.

"I missed kissing you too, J, and I was lying."

My heart thumped in my chest, because we never did this. Heartfelt and earnest was not us. We were usually too busy slaking whatever thirst we'd built for each other to think about feelings or consequences.

"I don't need a wedding haze excuse to want you."

Chapter Seven

Priscilla

No matter what lies I told myself all week, I knew this is where we'd end up. In a quiet corner tangled up in each other. I wracked my brain for a reason not to do this. But the way Juan Pablo was looking at me. How he was letting me take this where I wanted, it was burning me up inside. It was always like this with him—I could take charge or let go as I needed to without ever having to explain. That's why I always came back; because with J I never had to explain and always got what I wanted, what I needed.

Without breaking eye contact I placed the little bottle of bubbly on the table by the chaise and then pushed forward until his lips were right against mine.

I could feel his arms stiffening, as if he wanted to touch me or pull me closer, but was waiting for me to make the next move. Letting me set the tone. But his tongue still darted out slowly, and I ran it over the seam of my lips, making me gasp. "Tell me what you need."

I slid a hand over his arm, my pointy nails digging into the skin. "I miss your mouth and your hands." I didn't even need to say where, it didn't really matter.

When he kissed me again and I pushed against him, he finally let himself touch. His hands ran over my thighs, then my calves, agonizingly slow, until finally he slipped them under my dress.

"Touch me, J." I usually chased my orgasms with single-minded determination, but with J I let his touch set the tone and he almost always wanted to explore. He was thorough, and not by going hard and fast. He always took his time, slowly undoing every knot, unfurling every nerve ending until I was a panting, sweaty mess.

He could always wreck me.

He laughed in that filthy way he did when he was getting me so revved up I lost the ability to talk. I wanted to move. Spread my thighs for him, raise my knees, so that he'd touch me like I he knew he could. But he would not be rushed. It felt illicit to be doing this out here, the breeze of the ocean lifting the flaps of the cabana as J made his way over every inch of my skin.

I felt liquid and wild under Juan Pablo's hands. He could always do that. With his eyes locked with mine he moved so he was kneeling between my legs and ran his hands—rough from years of gripping baseball bats—on the inside of my thighs.

He crawled up on his knees as my thighs widened, adjusting for him. As if he could not hold himself back any longer he pushed my dress up. I threw my own arms over my head, feeling languid and wanting to enjoy the familiar buzzing under my skin.

"You're soaking through this, Nena." He leaned in to kiss me as he palmed my sex over the wet lacy fabric.

I gasped as he gripped my thigh hard and circled his thumb over my clit.

"Juan Pablo." I wasn't sure if I was laughing or

screaming, but he was touching me so I'd beg. I felt myself tighten and my hips started moving without my bidding, needing more.

"You know I go a little crazy when you get like this, Priscilla. Imma have to put my mouth on you." He sucked his teeth, neck muscles tight from holding back until I told him he could.

"Tú no eres fácil, Juan Pablo." It was more of a gasp than a statement, as our gazes were locked tight and I exhaled with a laugh.

"You only say that when you're taunting me to turn you out," he said, as he flashed me a filthy grin, and with the same thumb he'd been driving me out of my mind with he slipped my underwear off.

He balled the lacy bit of fabric in his hand and pressed it to his nose, closing his eyes in apparent ecstasy. He spoke, eyes still shut tightly, as I laid there vibrating.

"You know what I miss?" he asked, but it wasn't a question. Before I had a chance to say anything he lowered himself to kiss me, his hands roaming over my belly. Fingers tracing the edge of my dress until he got my nipple out. My skin buzzed, anticipating what it would feel like to have his mouth on me.

"I miss this." He traced a finger over the dark brown areola, and without a word brought his head down to lick at it. His tongue tracing the edges and lapping at the tip.

I hissed at the sensation and pressed the back of my head to the chaise, the ache between my legs getting more and more intense. He took mouthfuls of me, tongue sliding over my nipple as two fingers took turns moving over my clit and dipping into me, looking for the place he always seemed to find so effortlessly.

I had both my hands on his head, keeping his attention on my breasts as I breathed choppily, just on the cusp of coming apart.

"Don't fucking stop, J," I begged through gritted teeth, already feeling the waves coming. He grunted, redoubling his assault on my senses and soon I was lost, body pulsing in an orgasm that left me weak.

When I opened my eyes, the way Juan Pablo was looking at me made my belly molten again. The want there, gut deep and all-encompassing like my own. When he was like this, it was so easy to forget all the ways things seemed to fall apart for us.

He ran the back of his hand over his mouth, eyes still roaming over me. I probably looked a mess, but from how he was breathing I knew we were both on the exact same page. No stopping. We'd just keep going at this, kissing, touching until we'd had enough. We'd always been good at pushing off catastrophe as long as we focused on what we could make each other feel.

I ran a hand over his hardness, focusing on him. "Can I have this now?" I sounded a lot more in control than I was, my mouth practically watering for him.

He jerked his head, already making his way down my body. "Not yet."

I could feel the tingling before his mouth was on me, and when he closed his lips around my clit and pulled, all I could do was fall into the soft deep cushions of the chaise and feel. My hands fisted at my sides, trying to relax into the sensation.

He took turns between sucking hard and circling the hard tip of this tongue to that little nub. The crackle of electricity worked itself up my limbs and gut, until I was vibrating, so close to coming again. Juan Pablo could always get me off in record time. Fleetingly I thought that nothing ever felt this comforting and hot at once.

Soon the tingling in my limbs increased to waves of pleasure and I was coming with a long lazy moan. "Fuuuuuuck that's so good."

I lay there panting as J softly ran his hands over my thighs, which he knew was one of the only spots where I didn't feel hypersensitive after an orgasm. Finally, he pushed up again and searched for my mouth. While we kissed I reached for his cock, but it was soft.

I grinned and pulled back. "Did you jerk it while you were down there?"

I could feel the smile on his lips as he kissed his way down my neck. "I'm good at multi-tasking and need to get these pants dry-cleaned anyway."

"Gross." I did not sound disgusted. I wasn't. I felt satisfied and understood in this little cocoon by the ocean J and I had made.

After we'd each had some more sips on less than optimally cold but still quite delicious bubbly we laid there next to each other, in comfortable silence, and before he opened his mouth I could feel J getting ready to trample right into my post-coital bliss.

"If things don't get better, would you consider leaving the force?"

My initial reaction was to bristle. Over the years J and I had had more than one blowout over my job and his constant worry that I'd get hurt. So this line of questioning made me defensive, even when I'd been asking myself the same thing. A lot.

I didn't turn around to look at him, but I made myself come out with it.

"I've thought about it." He didn't say anything and

I knew he wouldn't until I'd said whatever was on my mind. "But I'm not sure I can, not yet. The multi-disciplinary team is pretty good and I want to keep working in it."

J would not let me hide the truth from myself. A lot of times that didn't work out well, but I could always rely on him to hear what was on my mind and tell me what I needed to hear.

"Is that the same kind of group you were in in Ithaca, with the CPS people and the prosecutors?"

I smiled and turned to look at him, not really surprised, but still touched that he recalled the details of a job I'd left years ago. "Yeah, pretty much the same. Of course the team is a little bigger, and we work with the FBI too, but the same idea. I can't believe you remember that. I was a baby cop when I was on that Ithaca team."

He gave me a pointed look. "When have I ever forgotten about something that made you happy, Priscilla?"

Never. But that road was not one I was going down right now.

"You have a good memory." That elicited a scoff, but whatever it came with, he kept to himself.

Again I veered us off the lane that would put us on the path to talking about our feelings. "Anyway the work is goodish, and some of the guys are assholes, and problematic, but I can mostly deal with it. I also love the forensic social worker from the child advocacy center that sits in on the meetings. Bri."

There was a shift and I could feel he was refraining from asking more about Bri.

"He's in a very committed relationship to a man, so you can unclench your jaw. Not that your ass needs to be pressed about men I like."

"Says you." *That* was a verbal pout if I'd ever heard one.

I would not find his whining cute. "We were talking about my dissatisfaction with my job, Juan Pablo."

He gave me a serious look, almost as if to gauge if I really wanted to hear his full opinion on things. "So are you feeling like things are as good as they'll get?"

It's what I'd been *avoiding* feeling.

Before I could censor myself or change the real answer, I said it out loud. "I just wonder if this is what I want to do forever."

Another grunt. "You don't have to. I mean, look at Papi. I think he's happier running that center than he ever was being a cop, and that man bled blue. You can reinvent yourself, Pris."

I felt a flash of resentfulness, because that was easy for Juan Pablo to say, he had the dream job with the Yankees making six figures. Meanwhile, *my* dream job involved coaching people on how to masturbate better and peddling vibrators. Which didn't exactly come with benefits and I was still not sure I could ever even tell my parents about it.

No. I was going nowhere.

I sighed, the easy feeling from before dulled by the conversation. "I think I'll sit tight in the NYPD. I love my side hustle and that's good enough for now."

It was dark, so I couldn't see his face, but I could tell he was trying to figure out what I wasn't saying, but when he finally opened his mouth, I almost fell over. "Your blog is good and so is your podcast. I honestly think people would pay for what you have to say."

"You listen to my podcast?" I asked, floored, because I wasn't exactly advertising among friends and family.

"Milo turned me on to it, since somebody didn't let

me know about it." He sounded a little hurt and my dumb "never going to learn its lesson" heart skipped a beat. "It's good. You're talking some next level woke shit on there. Sex, blackness, queer issues, feminism. It's dope."

Before I knew what I was doing, my hand—probably by instinct—searched out his. I squeezed and pressed a kiss to his lips. "Thanks for the vote of confidence."

"You know I think you're the smartest woman on the planet," he griped. "No matter what mess is going on between us, I will always cape for you."

This was true; even when we could barely stand to be in the same room, if anyone dared say anything to me about Juan Pablo, they were getting their ass handed to them and I knew for sure it was the same for him.

"What do you think?"

I realized that in my musings about all the ways we were inexorably tangled for better or worse, I'd missed something he'd said. "Sure," I said, and he laughed.

"You have no idea what I just asked, do you?"

I snorted and sat up. It was getting mad late and the sex and bubbly had me a little woozy. "Tell me again."

"I asked if you've given any more thought to doing one of your workshops at the center. Papi is happy to lend you the space."

I was glad for the darkness because I knew my face had to be slack from surprise. "You asked your dad already?"

He scoffed again and found my hand. "Your stuff is needed. My dad's been trying to find more ways to work with LGBT+ adults Uptown."

I tried to dissect the last few minutes for any kind of hidden agenda or if this was just J's way of keeping the lines of communications open now that we'd hooked up.

But I was either too moved by the offer, or too addled by the sex to catch it. "I do have this workshop I do with Bri about pleasure for trans and black bodies. We've been trying to find a spot to do it. I also have the one about pleasure after sixty."

"Papi will be down for both of those, and I'm there a lot during the off-season. We can make it work. So can I hit you up when we're back in the city?"

I was tempted, so tempted to say yes, to just let the things I was feeling make my mind up for me and accept the olive branch J was extending. The offer to be back in each other's lives. Still, I wasn't sure I could open that door just yet. What had happened just now felt too good, safe. And I wasn't sure I could handle losing it again.

So I leaned in and kissed him long and hard, like we usually did. Then I got up, and grabbed my sandals from the sand.

"I'll let you know. Take care, J."

Chapter Eight

New York City, Two Weeks Later
Juan Pablo

"Did you call her?" I didn't have to ask who because my mother had been asking me the same question every hour on the hour for the last two days. She was throwing a surprise party for my dad's sixty-fifth birthday in a few days and she'd decided the party couldn't happen without Priscilla. Meanwhile I was still smarting for the way she'd ghosted me after that night at the beach. Not because she hadn't been jumping at the chance to pick up where we'd left off—or maybe just a little bit. But because I'd hoped that, like me, she'd felt like we were worth another try.

I looked up from my overthinking to find my mother glaring at me, obviously over my bullshit. "Ma. She's busy. I don't know if she's going to have time to come. Besides she's not in the Bronx anymore."

The reality was that even as I told myself that I was willing to be patient, deep down I'd hoped she would be as eager as I was. But as soon as I tried to push for a little more contact, for the possibility of seeing each other once we were Stateside, she'd literally walked out

on me. The morning after our sex on the beach, when
I'd asked Easton where she was, he'd said she'd left for
Santo Domingo. Without saying goodbye to me. I hadn't
heard from her since.

It seemed like she'd finally gotten over whatever it
was that we'd been doing all these years after all. But my
mother was obviously on a whole other timeline.

"Juan Pablo, I will tell Camilo to call her."

Oh hell, no. That little prick was such a terror my parents still used him to scare me into doing shit.

"Damn, Ma. Chill. Let me just get something to eat
and I'll call her."

That got me an eye roll and a big shake of her head.
"No, Caro. Call her now. I've been on you for days. You
know how much Rafa loves her and she might not be
in the Bronx but she's still close." She stretched out the
last part too. Yeah, Pris was in Yonkers now and so was
I. Except she wanted nothing to do with my ass, so it
didn't really matter.

My mother put down the iPad she was using to in-
ventory some coats and boots we'd gotten for the kids
in the neighborhood, and walked around to where I was.
"I loved seeing all of you back together for Milo's wedding. Like the old days."

She sighed with a forlorn look in her eyes. Probably
remembering the years when we'd all be at our house
after school. My mom, being a teacher, would come home
with us and most days, Milo, Patrice and Nesto would
end up at our place until their moms got them after work.
Pris too.

I knew it wasn't my mother trying to meddle, at least
not intentionally, but it nettled. I didn't like people in my
business. After years of dating my best friend's cousin

and the daughter of my own father's best friend, we both got tired of having everyone we knew all up in our business.

"Juan, son."

I sighed and turned to her with my phone in my hand. "I'll call her, Ma, but aren't Tonin and Maritza coming down. Why can't they ask her?" I knew pointing out that Priscilla's parents could let her know about the party was not going to dissuade my mother in the slightest. No, because she had an agenda. She'd been walking by every ten minutes while I worked with one of my PT clients at my dad's center.

"We're the hosts and we should confirm." There was no dissuading her when she got like this.

I didn't know why we were suddenly going by the Ina Garten party etiquette rules, but this was not an argument I was winning. So I sighed and walked back to the PT room to call Priscilla.

There were a few people there working with the weights and other equipment under the supervision of the other physical therapist and two of the interns we had working for us this semester. Too crowded. I wasn't talking to Priscilla with this many people around.

I didn't know what the hell was wrong with me. I was practically coming out of my skin at the prospect of calling her and getting ignored. I knew that it wouldn't be easy for us to become friends again and the cabana sex was probably not the best idea, but I really didn't think I'd get shut out like that.

I knew I hadn't been the only one that night at the beach who'd been blown away by how easy, how all-consuming it was when we were together. I'd always been up for sex and had been with enough people to know that when it came to feeling good, I did not discriminate. Pleasure was pleasure and chemistry was chemistry. But I didn't believe in soulmates. Not really. There were a lot of people out there I could be with that could make me happy. That *I* could make happy, but there wasn't another person on this planet who knew me like Priscilla Gutierrez did.

We'd talked like we hadn't in years. Hell, that whole week we'd been tight. Almost like the old days—well, not quite. In the old days I wouldn't have had to ask her how work was. I would've known that. I would've been the first to know. But then again, maybe not. Her job had always been a contentious issue for us. So maybe even if we had been together, she would've kept her uncertainty about staying in the force to herself.

I wasn't one to give up easily, but at times like these it did seem like it might be too late for us. Like I should let go of the idea that Priscilla could be in my life again. But it wasn't like she seemed happy. No, she'd sounded disillusioned and tired. And I hadn't been able to get out of my head that she seemed lonely too. Like she didn't trust that anyone could understand why she was tired, why she didn't just move on or do something different.

I'd always wondered if eventually Priscilla would outgrow her job. Or if like my dad, it would take her being forced out of it to realize there was more out there that could fulfill her. Other jobs that could make her feel like she was doing something with purpose. Because I knew ultimately that is what she'd always wanted—to feel useful, to help. And from the way she spoke that night I was sure her job wasn't fulfilling that need like it used to.

That I also knew to be true. And I knew *her*—even when she didn't want me to see too much, I knew her.

But Priscilla did not take kindly to people getting all up in her business. She hated feeling talked down to, especially when she was feeling unsure. Just like me, when she needed an opinion she asked for it. And unless you asked her for it, she did not put her nose into anyone's business. Not even when she saw you trifling.

Growing up as the only child of two very overprotective Dominican immigrants, Pris craved her space more than she craved anything else. The way she set boundaries for herself was by not ever giving her parents any reason to believe she didn't know what she was doing. Pris's boundaries were non-negotiable. So my blowing up her phone with a shady ass excuse, when she'd let me know in no uncertain terms that I didn't need to be calling her, was probably going to get me an ass chewing.

But nobody else needed to know that I'd been looking for an excuse to call her again and my mother had finally given me one.

I leaned against the brick wall next to the door of the center and called, with my head pounding more than it should have over a call to a woman who I'd known my entire life. And yet here I was with drops of sweat beading at the small of my back. It rang three times, then four, and finally it went to her voicemail.

I considered not leaving a message and just calling back. Then thought better of it and decided it would look even thirstier for me to call and not say anything like I was some creepy asshole. I got my shit together just as the beep for the message blasted in my ear.

"Hey. So hope you're good. My mom told me to hit you up and remind you that my dad's sixty-fifth is this weekend. It's a surprise party on Saturday at 6:00 p.m. here at the center."

I took a breath and sweated some more, knowing I was acting a fool on this damn call. "Anyways, we hope to see you there. We miss you. *I* miss you."

I tapped on the screen and exhaled, thinking that last part was probably going to send her running in the other direction. I knew that Priscilla had left that night because the power of our connection, the way we fell into each other again like barely a day had passed was scary as fuck. Because even though neither of us could deny the highs that being together brought, the lows always wiped us both out.

Priscilla

"Well, today was particularly shittastic. We'll never have to wait too long for a fucked-up take as long as that guy from probation keeps coming to these meetings."

I sighed and kept walking out of our weekly multi-disciplinary team meeting, and turned to my friend Bri.

"I appreciate you and your patience, Bri."

He gave me a rueful look and rolled his eyes in the direction of the conference room we'd just exited. "Well, it's all for the children." He delivered that deadpan, because that's the BS that the problematic people in our team usually lead with whenever they were about to say something dumb.

The meetings *were* useful and I appreciated being in the loop about the cases we worked on, which all involved children who had been abused, so a team approach was great. But my tolerance for bullshit seemed to be at an all-time low. Only the fact that Bri and the two ADAs we worked with were there to hold it down, kept me from snatching one or two of the usual assholes in that meeting. Thankfully they usually intervened, so I didn't have to be the one to constantly point out shit like

"I'm not sure what they do in Peru about child abuse, Ted, because I was born here and my parents are Dominican." Or "Latinx people don't all live in the same country, Karen."

Bri looked at his watch and angled his head in the direction of the Child Advocacy Center's exit. "Reyes's mom sent me lunch. You want to walk over with me? I know there's enough for five people."

I smiled at that and nodded, as I patted my jacket looking for where I'd put my phone. "Sure. I can use some Dominican arroz con habichuelas. Leave it to you to score the one Dominican dude in the Tri-State area willing to bring you his mom's cooking to work."

Bri's angelic face reddened. He had two small black gauges in his ears which really stood out in contrast to his slender and pale neck. He was small, about three inches shorter than me, but he was very strong. His forearms corded with muscle. He always wore slacks and sweaters with leather vans. He was pretty, and he took meticulous care of himself. He said it was a ritual that felt almost sacred for him after his transition. To be able to dress and groom himself. To look on the outside how he always knew himself to be on the inside.

"You look good, Bri. Are those the ones Reyes did for Vans?" I pointed at the burgundy leather slip-ons with soles that had the Pride colors on top. The left shoe had the words *We Are* and the right had *Orgullo* the word for *Pride* in Spanish.

Bri's man, Reyes, was a renowned Dominican pop-culture graphic artist and lately was working on some pretty big projects.

Bri blushed again and nodded. "Yeah, they're not supposed to come out until April, for Pride next year, but I got some early ones."

I winked at how happy he looked. "You got the connect. He better get me a pair."

He laughed. "Of course, I told him already."

I threw an arm around him, a smile on my own lips. Seeing Bri's glow whenever he talked about his boyfriend was infectious. "That's why you're my favorite, and why that man of yours is a keeper."

Bri's blue eyes sparkled at the mention of his partner. Like they always did. Bri was from the Midwest, Wisconsin. But he'd come to New York for college and stayed. Once he decided to transition things with his family became strained, but they'd eventually come around. He was amazing and doing so much for trans youth Uptown, together with his man, who was the most woke Dominican cis dude I had ever met, and my bar was high. When Bri and I met through work when I'd started here a year ago we made fast friends.

He'd also gotten an earful when I got back from the DR and had to tell someone about what had gone down between J and me.

As we walked out of the center and headed the few blocks to his boyfriend's studio I remembered to check the messages on my phone. As soon as I saw the missed call and voicemail from Juan Pablo my heart pounded against my chest.

How the hell could he still do that after all this time? Just seeing his name on my screen sent my heart into a gallop in my chest. I'd been thinking nonstop about him reading my blog and listening to my podcasts. About the way he got the essence of what I was doing, because he knew, he got me. And I was avoiding what all that meant at all costs.

Other than Bri, Easton and Camilo, I hadn't really told anyone about this new venture. How happy it made me to write and share my thoughts on sexuality, desire and my own journey in all that. A journey that, in large part, Juan Pablo had been along for the ride.

"You're pensive today."

Bri's curious voice brought me out of the swirl in my head. He was looking at my phone which I was now clutching tightly. "Bad news?"

I shook my head once and then sighed. "It's Juan Pablo."

"Oh?" Bri knew me enough to know that with J nothing was ever simple for me. Not because he was making it complicated these days, but more because my feelings for him never seemed to get less confusing, or consuming.

"I don't know what he's calling about. I haven't talked to him since I got back."

Bri raised an eyebrow in question; he was well aware the lines of communication had been severed on my end. Thankfully we were almost to Reyes's studio and that bought me some time to digest why I was making such a big deal out of a voicemail. When we arrived I held my phone up and waved Bri off. "Let me listen to the message, I'll catch up with you in a minute."

As soon as Bri was in the store I tapped on my phone and pressed it to my ear. J's voice as always made my guts go liquid, and as I listened I felt a mix of feelings I wasn't sure how to untangle.

I knew his mother had probably asked him to call me. I knew Irene's agenda and it involved me shacked up with her son after a white wedding.

There was no nefariousness to his message. I could be polite. This was family business, and J and I had never let our mess interfere with that. So I texted him back.

Priscilla: So your mom's got you calling people for an RSVP?

After a few seconds the three dots appeared and a response came shortly after.

Juan Pablo: Nah. You're my only assignment.

Why did my belly have to flip over like that?

Priscilla: She gave you the toughest case then.

Juan Pablo: Always, but she knows I like a challenge.

I didn't have to wonder, I knew what this was.

We were flirting, and for the first time in days I felt something loosen in me. Felt the tightness around my mouth and in my shoulders ease just a little bit. It had taken eight words from Juan Pablo. I could come up with a thousand reasons not to do this. To steer very clear of playing a game with J that would end up with my heart torn out of my chest. But right now, I didn't want to let go of this easy, light feeling I had.

Priscilla: I know you do, but yeah, I'll be there.

I saw the three dots pop up and disappear a few times, until a bubble with a message finally appeared.

Juan Pablo: See you then, Pris. Take care of yourself all right?

I was unreasonably annoyed at the disappointment I felt when that was all he had to say. I should've left it alone. I should have walked into the store and had Dominican lunch with Bri and Reyes. Juan Pablo was abiding by the boundaries I'd set and I should do the same. Instead I'd stepped right onto the Road to Perdition and sprinted.

Priscilla: Okay. Looking forward to seeing you, J.

I closed the message app before the three dots on the screen could turn into a message from Juan Pablo and pushed the door open to the store, where I found Bri doing what could only be called canoodling with Reyes.

"Dimelo," I said, as I walked up to Reyes for an air kiss hello.

I looked around the store, the prints on the wall and the racks with t-shirts and sweatshirts all original designs. Reyes as always was wearing some of his merch. He was a big guy, but kind of precious. The very definition of a bear. He was fucking gone for Bri, and I really loved him for it.

"What's good, Pris? Are you two staying out of trouble?" He said that as he tightened his arms around Bri, who was leaning against him.

"We try." I pointed at Bri's shoes. "That hustle is really bearing fruit, huh."

Reyes, gave a lopsided smile as he looked down at Bri, a besotted expression on his face. "I can't complain. The sweatshirts and hats with the design you wanted are in."

He pointed in the direction of a rack of black sweaters. I'd asked Reyes for them after seeing him post about them on Instagram right after I'd gotten back from the wedding. My heart sped up remembering who I'd wanted the sweatshirt for.

Juan Pablo. It was a simple design but it had El Bronx emblazoned in a heavy gothic-looking white font in the center. I picked one off the rack smiling. Repping the Bronx was basically J's brand. It occurred to me that he and Reyes would have a lot to talk about if they ever met. I found myself thinking I'd like to see that. I waited for the self-recrimination that usually came with ideas about Juan Pablo, but in the end I didn't have the energy for any of it. I wanted to give him the sweater. See his gorgeous smile as he read what it said.

Just to make it less reckless I grabbed a fitted hat that said Uptown for J's dad. A solid birthday present. I placed them both on the counter as Reyes and Bri observed me.

"Your mood has shifted. Shall I take a guess?" That was Bri.

I lifted a shoulder and tried not to give too much away, because honestly I wasn't too sure what I was doing anyway.

"Same old. Same old."

I left it at that and averted my gaze from Bri's knowing eyes. Because that piece was a lie. Nothing about this felt like the same old thing. Juan Pablo felt new in ways which made me feel like there was something worth exploring there, even if just until I figured myself out.

Chapter Nine

Juan Pablo

You know when in a book someone says something mad extra like, "I could feel when she walked into the room"? I'm here to tell you, it's not all bullshit. Because I swear I could sense Priscilla coming into the crowded room where we were hosting my dad's party. Before I even heard her the hair on my arms stood up and the back of my neck prickled, like my entire body was picking up her vibrations.

She hadn't arrived in time for the actual surprise, but both her parents were there and had assured me she'd just gone home to change after work and was not far behind. It didn't even faze me that they acted like she and I were still a thing since my parents were the same exact way.

"Look who's here!" That was my dad. When I turned I saw her walking in wearing a short parka and jeans so tight I had to swallow hard to keep my tongue in my mouth.

It was like my field of vision honed in on her and nothing else. She smiled wide at my dad as she unzipped her jacked to reveal a tight bloodred sweater. She had her big gold hoops in her ears and tall brown boots on. Her hair was pulled back tight in a fluffy long ponytail that bopped along as she walked.

She looked just like the girl I'd fallen hard for at sixteen and who had been my first everything. I wondered if we'd ever be able to be around each other without me feeling like she was the only person in the room. Even when I could barely stand to be around her, I could never keep my attention off Priscilla for long.

She stopped to give a hug to her parents who I knew were staying with her and then started looking around for someone, I assumed my father.

"Rafa! Happy Birthday!" My father engulfed her in a hug as he winked at me over her shoulder. When he pulled back he was grinning. "Querida, so glad you could make it.

"You arrived just in time," my father said approvingly, with an arm around her shoulder, and a finger pointed in my direction. "This one's arguing with me again about the Yankees bullpen."

She laughed and shook her head at me. "You starting arguments with the man on his birthday, Juan Pablo?" She turned to where I was standing next to one of my sisters and winked. It was sad that I felt my face heat just from her saying my name. But by this point we were all under her spell. She looked down and pointed at my father's shoes with a big smile on her face. "Are those Gucci loafers? Are you letting J take you shopping?"

That got a laugh from Patrice and Easton, who had come to New York for the weekend so they could be at the party.

My dad beamed as he gave her another hug. "You know I would never let that boy convince me to spend so much money on shoes. This was my birthday present."

Pris grinned at me as my dad rolled his eyes, then pulled something out of the shopping bag she had in one of her hands. "This is for you."

It was a black fitted, with Uptown embroidered in white. When my dad saw it he literally beamed and immediately put it on.

"Damn, Papi, that's tight," I said, a little jealous.

"I love it. Thanks, mija." Something straight up squeezed my insides whenever I heard my dad call Pris *mija.* She of course, waved him off, like getting him a perfect gift was no big deal. Soon my dad was launching on the one thing he never ever forgot to ask her.

"How's it going, detective. Have the good people of the 34th precinct wised up and made you lieutenant yet?"

Her smile fell for a second at the mention of her job, but she regrouped fast. "Not yet. But I'm giving them plenty of reasons to." There was a hollowness there that I would've noticed even if she hadn't clued me in about how things were going. My father didn't miss it either, his face getting serious at her answer.

She pulled back from him without a word and came over to kiss me on the cheek. I refrained from putting my hands on her, unsure that I'd be able to pull apart if I did.

"Pris. How's you?" She kissed my cheek and then ran a thumb over the spot where I presumed some lipstick had rubbed off, while I tried my best not to shiver or, worse, growl like a caveman.

"I'm good. Sorry I didn't make it for the surprise," she said, looking regretful. "Things ran late." Her face looked somber at whatever she was remembering.

I waved a hand as she moved to kiss my sister Sylvia on the cheek. "I know how it is. You're looking fresh. I like that sweater." I tried hard not to smack my lips as I ran my eyes over her without pausing on the deep plunge of her neckline for too long. I did run my tongue over my bottom lip, because I wasn't made of stone.

My sister snorted from somewhere on my left as I tried to focus on anything that wasn't Priscilla's cleavage, or her neck, or mouth. I found a spot where her baby hairs were curling up and tried to remember what the hell I'd been saying. But before I could, she lifted the same bag she'd pulled the hat from and handed it to me.

I took it, a bit surprised, and before I had a chance to ask who it was for, she said in a surprisingly shy voice. "My friend Bri's man is an artist and does all these dope designs on hats and sweatshirts." She lifted a shoulder and gave me a helpless smile. "I thought you'd like this one."

"Oh?" She rolled her eyes at my response and moved around to hang her jacket on one of the pegs on the wall behind me.

I opened the bag and peeked in like she'd told me it had a rattlesnake in it. I wasn't sure what to think, because this gesture was very far removed from the ghosting and icing out that I'd been getting from her. This was sweet, and that was *not* what we'd been doing. Not for a long time.

Sylvia shoved my shoulder softly as I stood there like a statue. "I want to see it."

"Fine, chill, Syl." The sweater I pulled out was black like my dad's hat, but the words at the center were El Bronx.

"That's certainly on brand for you." My sister sounded impressed, which wasn't exactly new. She, like the rest of my family, caped for Priscilla 24/7.

Priscilla was still squirming, but I bent down to kiss her on the cheek. "I love it."

Her neck was red and she looked pleased with herself. But I also knew pushing her on why she bought me a present would get me nowhere. Not in front of all these people. "I thought you'd like it." There was a whole lot happening between the shy looks she was giving me and the roiling in my gut that told me something was shifting between us. But in the end, I took her lead and gave her a nod, another thank you and let it go for a time when we didn't have all of our family and friends watching.

So I moved to the easier and familiar. "You want to go get some food and drink? Ma made the lasagna and there's mofongo too."

She grinned at that. "I love the Italian slash Boricua flavors of your family's parties. Is your mom still using sofrito for the lasagna meat?"

I barked out a laugh and looked at my grandpa, who was shoveling in some tostones. "Much to Nonno's horror."

I didn't want to scare her off by making a thing out of her bringing me a gift, but I was feeling too warm inside to not at least say a proper thank you. Or at least a proper thank you for us. I bumped her shoulder as she scooped a piece of lasagna from one of the pans on the buffet table. "I really do love my sweater."

She focused a little harder than necessary on getting some salad and maduros on her plate before lifting up her eyes at me. Our gazes locked and held for a moment, before she said anything in response. I expected her to say something flippant, like "don't let it go to your head." From the way her chest puffed up and then slowly deflated I guessed I wasn't too far off. But as she considered our surroundings and then made her way to two empty chairs in a hidden corner I let her come up with a way to respond.

Once we were seated she stabbed a piece of the yellow and brown sweet plantains on her plate and took a bite. She closed her eyes as she chewed and when she swallowed she finally looked at me. "I saw it and thought you'd like it, so I got it."

Period.

I knew enough to not push for more or try to get any ulterior motives out of her.

"I'm glad you made it tonight."

She took a couple more bites of food before answering. "No matter where things are with us, Rafa's family."

I wanted to tell her to enlighten me as to where exactly things were with us. Because I had no idea. We'd gone from barely speaking to a hot as fuck night at the beach to me getting ghosted, and now she was here…with gifts.

My head was spinning a little bit, but I was going to put a positive spin on this thing and keep the lines of communication open. If we were talking, then at least there was a chance for something—what, I didn't know anymore. But I could not deny sitting here with her eating a plate of food my mom and I cooked surrounded by the people we'd known our whole lives, felt pretty perfect.

What she said next had me almost pumping my fist in the air. "Were you serious about my podcast? Do you really think the workshop could work?"

I schooled my expression when I noticed this was far from a casual question. Priscilla was putting her heart out right now. "When have I ever lied to you, Priscilla Gutierrez?"

She nodded, and picked at her food. My hands itched

to lift her chin up. Kiss that sadness away. "Is the offer for a space to do my workshop still open, then?"

"It's yours whenever you need it." I bumped her shoulder again, then stabbed a piece of maduro from her plate and popped it into my mouth before she could protest, which of course she did anyway. "Hey, get your own plate." I laughed, as she turned so that the plate was out of my reach.

She pinched my arm softly and looked down at her plate, letting me only catch a glimpse of her smile. "I think I may take you up on it, then."

I wanted to ask what had brought this on. If she'd been planning to call. If she'd been thinking about what happened between us after the wedding constantly, like I had. I realized then that I wasn't sure I knew what Priscilla needed like I used to.

I didn't know what to do with that. I wasn't even sure if there was anything I *could* do. We'd changed, both of us and more than anything I wanted to tell her that every version of myself, the worst and the best one, still thought she was the most amazing person in my life. That with the wealth of people who loved me, she was still the one I yearned for.

I didn't tell her though. I was too scared of what she'd say to that confession.

"Is work going all right?"

The lightness in her eyes dimmed a little bit and I wanted to kick myself, but after a moment—like she always did—she regrouped.

"It's going. We have some tough cases right now." She frowned at whatever she was remembering, but after a moment she shook herself and looked up at me with a smile. "I've been meaning to call you, but work has been hectic since I got home from the wedding." She was almost whispering and I kept having to come closer until our heads were almost touching. The plate of food on her lap forgotten.

"Oh." It was the best I could come up with as my head buzzed, wondering what it was she wanted to tell me. I'd been swimming in what-ifs ever since she'd walked out on me that night. Wondering if I should've told her how I felt. Wondering if like me she hadn't stopped thinking about how good we were together, in every way.

My heart pounded at the possibilities. "I just wanted to say—"

And because every single one of our dearest and nearest was a gigantic pain in the ass, at that very moment, Patrice and Easton decided to come and chat.

"Hey, babe, we haven't had a chance to talk yet." Easton sat down next to Pris and gave me an apologetic look. I wanted to get up and pull her by the hand to a quiet place. Instead, I got up to give P dap.

"What's up, man?" I said, trying very hard not to growl at him.

He looked down at his man and Pris, who were already engaged in deep conversation, and raised an eyebrow in question. I guess the fact that we'd been sitting together in seemingly friendly conversation was noteworthy.

I shook my head and tried to convey as much as I could that I didn't want to get into it. Not that Patrice would push. Since he'd gotten more serious with Easton my closed-off and too-quiet friend had changed a lot, but he hadn't changed so much he would willingly walk into a conversation about feelings.

I rolled my shoulders and shook my head, this conversation was over, but she'd opened a door with the work-shops and I was making sure she knew it would never be closed to her.

Priscilla

I'd been about to spill my guts to Juan Pablo. I'd actually been about to suggest that we start hanging out again. But it seems like the universe wasn't up to seeing me start down the road to self-destruction again, so Patrice and Easton interrupted us just at the right moment.

That had been a couple of hours earlier, and now the party was winding down. Easton and Patrice had excused themselves and headed out, claiming they had an early start back to Ithaca. They had to get back because they were leading a community conversation around the school to prison pipeline in Central New York. I smiled thinking how far those two had come and how the things that seemed destined to tear them apart were now a joint passion. They'd found common ground and figured out how to build a life together on it.

That line of thinking got me right back to Juan Pablo. Almost involuntarily my eyes moved around the room, searching for him. While I'd been talking to Easton, he'd gone off with Patrice and since then we'd only caught glimpses of each other. He was wearing his black diamond studs tonight, with a black turtleneck and fitted jeans. Black Gucci loafers to match his dad's brown ones. Juan Pablo was always out to stunt. I smiled, surprised at the warmth in my chest even that thought brought.

He *was* a little vain, but he worked hard for that body. Even if his fuckboy tendencies had made me want to kill him on more than one occasion over the years, I had to admit J was damn fine.

"You're staring, mija." I almost jumped at my mother's amused voice right behind me.

"Ay, Mami. Stop, that's not very nice."

She clucked her tongue then moved so she could put her hand in through the crook of my elbow. "Just teasing you a little. He's been looking at you the same way all night. I wish you kids would just get over yourselves and make up."

I sighed, feeling defensive and wanting to shove down my own thoughts about finding a way to fix things with Juan Pablo. I wanted to be a brat and tell my mother that there was no chance anything between J and me could work ever again. Because this was part of my issue, sometimes it felt like our relationship was a communal affair. That everything we did was under a microscope that got passed around to everyone we knew. It was exhausting, and I didn't know if it would ever get less so.

"Ma, I don't have time to get involved with anyone right now. Work is hectic as always and I have my other projects."

As soon as I said *other projects*, my mom's sunny expression changed. My parents weren't exactly in the loop when it came to my side hustle, because no matter how much I wanted to front like I was a grown ass woman and I did whatever I wanted, there was one thing that I was not sure I'd ever be able to do—make a living doing something my parents couldn't be proud of. And maybe that was *me* being vain. But they'd come from the DR because they wanted a future for their kids. And in the end it had just been me. After almost a decade of miscarriages and false alarms my mother finally had me, and I was *it*. The vessel for all their hopes and dreams. The reason why they'd left everything behind and come to this country. The least I could do was hold down a job that could make them feel like I'd been worth all that sacrifice. No matter how much I told myself what I wanted mattered, I knew I couldn't bear seeing disappointment in my parents' eyes.

"Ay, mija, you put too much on your plate. I wish you could relax for a minute, not pile on so much. More than you need to." She shook her head and ran the back of her hand over my cheek. "But you came by it honestly. All you saw in our house was a revolving door of your father and me coming and going to work. I wish we could've had more time to sit still. Spend it with you."

I put an arm around my mother, as we stood in one corner of Rafa's community center, and thought about that. I had no resentment toward my parents. None. They worked hard, so I could have everything I needed. Everything they never got themselves and I knew from a young age that came at a cost.

"Mamí, I grew up in a home where all I saw where two hardworking people who loved on each other and on me as much as they could. There is literally nothing to be sorry for. As for my side hustles, they're fun for me and I like staying busy. I don't have a relationship or kids that require my time when I'm not working. So, I do things that help me relax."

My mother's back went up at my slipping in the no-kids thing, but she kept quiet. That was a fight that we'd put to rest years ago, and finally it seemed she'd accepted that there would be no grandchildren in her future. One more disappointment.

"Are you going to come up for Christmas?"

I shook my head at my mother's question, as if she had to ask. "Claro Mami, where else would I be at Christmas?" I looked around trying to spot J, as I talked to my mom. For some reason it seemed important to know where he was right now. "Patrice and Easton invited a few of us to go up to Easton's family's cabin in the mountains for a couple of days after Christmas so I may do that too."

She looked a little disappointed she wouldn't have me to herself for the whole week, but I'm sure the prospect of me being holed up in a mountain with J mollified her enough to not push. Just as I was about to ask when they wanted to go home, Irene, J's mom, made an appearance.

"Priscilla, sweetheart. Do you mind giving that boy of mine a ride home? He took an Uber over here, but he's taking the dogs to his place for a few days, since Rafa and I are going up to the Hudson Valley." I wasn't one hundred percent convinced this wasn't another ploy of the parents to get J and I together, but the request seemed reasonable enough. I knew we lived only like ten minutes away from each other, even though I'd never been to his new place.

"Sure. Are the pups ready to go?"

Irene nodded as my mother beamed at this new development. "Yes." At that same moment Juan Pablo made an appearance carrying a tote bag with mesh sides which I assumed carried his parents' two Yorkies. They were yappy little shits, but they were mostly harmless.

My mother spoke before I could. "Juanpa mijo, we're giving you a ride home today. Pris drove in her truck." Then like the faker she was, she yawned like was about to fall asleep on her feet. "Pris is just going to take us home first. We're driving back first thing tomorrow."

Wow my mother had legit no shame, but we all seemed to be playing this game tonight.

"Sure. I'll bring the truck around and get us going." I turned to J's mom, who was doing some kind of elaborate eyeball exchange with her son. "Irene, do you need help with clean up?"

Irene waved me off as if I'd said the craziest thing she's heard all day. "Oh no, hon. We got a few kids from the block all primed to go. Juan Pablo offered them twenty-five bucks a piece and they're all waiting to get started." With that she turned to give her baby boy the beatific smile I'd been seeing my whole life. "He loves to keep those kids motivated. He's got half of them on staff helping out one way or another in the afternoons." That was followed by a kiss and pinch on the cheek.

This was why I'd kept my distance when I'd come back downstate. Getting sucked back into the block and J's family was like a slippery slope. I had way too many things I needed to figure out and this was all too comfortable. Comfort was not my friend right now. Not when there was so much about the life I'd built that seemed ill-fitting and restrictive. Being back here with J and his family would mean having to perform. Act like everything was great. Chat up his dad about the precinct and the job, and I was so burnt out on all of it.

"You okay, sweetheart?" I practically jumped at my mother's question.

"Yeah, of course." Had to keep it moving, because my

mother would be able to tell I was in fact, not okay, very easily. "I'll bring the truck around. See you up front." I didn't look at J, because he'd see right through me too.

Once the cold early-December air hit me I was able to get it together and soon we were driving out of the Bronx and up to Yonkers. And I should've known my mother would still be on her bullshit, because we were barely getting on the expressway when she spoke up from the backseat.

"Mamita, can you take us first? Your daddy is so tired and we have to be on the road in the morning."

I turned for a second to look at my father's face and could see he was trying very hard not to bust up. When I looked in the rearview mirror I saw that Juan Pablo was not faring any better sitting next to my mother. But I also knew there was no winning this, so I smiled and nodded.

"Sure, Ma. Is that okay for you?" I looked at J in the mirror and he just shook his head, grinning.

"Sure. I'm good with that."

I made a noise that would have to suffice as an acknowledgement and distracted myself by talking with my dad about their plans for the week and what route they were taking up to Ithaca. The drop-off involved long goodbyes and requests for J to come up and visit soon. As if this development of me and J driving off with his parents' dogs to his place was nothing noteworthy.

Chapter Ten

Priscilla

We didn't talk much. Once I'd let my parents into my building and Juan Pablo was comfortably in the front seat with Tita and Pepe yapping their little fool heads off in the back, we headed to his place in almost complete silence. All the way there I had a feeling I couldn't quite put my finger on. Not exactly comfortable, but not unpleasant either. It was a new kind of being together.

I wanted him. I always did, but I didn't feel helpless to it, and that made a difference.

When I took the turn that lead to his fancy ass condo, he finally spoke. "You want to come up for a drink?"

It was casual, no innuendo. No suggestive tone. A friend asking another to come up to his place for a nightcap after an evening of a lot of family time. I'd pulled into one of the spots of the guest parking lot and looked up at the tall tower where J lived now. There was a lot of glass and metal and the view of the Hudson had to be amazing.

I took my time to answer. "How far up are you?"

His top lip twitched and I couldn't tell if he was annoyed or just laughing at my lame ass attempt to avoid giving him an answer. "I'm on the twelfth floor. I bought early so I got one of the units with a view of the river. It's pretty baller. I have some prosecco in the fridge."

I laughed at his cajoling tone. He knew all my weaknesses. I didn't get more time to think about it because Tita and Pepe started bitching again and made the decision for me.

"Just for a minute. It is kind of ridiculous that I haven't seen your place yet."

He'd been in it almost two years. At another time it would've seemed impossible for Juan Pablo to be living anywhere where I wasn't present. A home of his that wasn't at least partly my own.

I got out the car and helped J get the dogs out of the carrier and on their leashes, so we could let them do their business before going up to his apartment. They were old hats at apartment life, so within a few minutes we were on the elevator with freshly relieved fluff balls.

"Sorry about Mami," I said. "She doesn't take a day off, ever."

He laughed and gave me a long look that I couldn't figure out. That was another thing that had happened in these last two years and with this new version of Juan Pablo. He was mysterious and so very calm. Nothing riled him up.

"It's fine. You know I have mad love for Maritza, besides Irene isn't any better."

This was true, between my mother and his it was hard to tell who was thirstier for us to get together.

"I was happy she suggested it. I've been meaning to invite you over to see my place." Just as he said that the elevator doors opened and we walked into a well-lit hallway lined with white doors.

It was nice. *Really* nice.

I knew his grandfather had promised all his grandkids he'd help them buy their own place when they were ready, and that old man never let his family down.

"This is really bougie, J. You fancy." My tone was light, but his cheeks flushed.

We got to the last apartment at the end of the hall with Tita and Pepe getting more and more excited the closer we got. He laughed when they started circling around by the door.

"They stay over sometimes, so they've got a ton of toys and shit in here. They think this place is their vacation spot."

"Wow so this is what you get up to on the weekends these days. How the mighty fall, Juan Pablo Campos."

"Damn, Pris, you're savage." He laughed as he ran a hand over his fade, a flush of red staining his cheeks. "I do the parents a solid when they want to have some alone time. These little fuckers keep putting scratches on my hardwood floors too." I laughed as the toy-sized dogs ran into the apartment with us close behind.

I stepped in and had to take a deep breath.

"J." I moved to put down my bag and, with my jacket still on turned around the room, words failing me. What I was seeing was nothing that anyone else would find remotely remarkable, but I was having a hard time controlling my emotions. I looked at the wall-to-wall bookshelves on one side of the room. The blown-up photographs I'd taken on our many trips back to DR and PR and others from trips we'd taken together to Kenya and Ecuador, all hanging from a bright yellow wall. He even had the leather armchairs with a little table in between.

Just like we'd always talked about.

Like we'd said we'd set up our forever place. A big

room with books, art and a comfortable spot to read together.

He let me look around in silence as he leaned against the mantel of his gas fireplace. It wasn't a huge room, but there were floor-to-ceiling windows facing the Hudson. I could imagine how great it would be to drink my morning coffee from one of those chairs with J next to me.

I didn't know why this was getting to me as much as it was. I wondered if he'd known what it would do to me to see this room. On second thought, I didn't need to wonder. He knew *exactly* what I was thinking. Without any fucking warning my mouth started moving.

"You know what's funny?" I asked, giving my back to him as I studied the shelf where he'd put all the travel books we'd pored over before our many trips together. So many years of shared moments with J and here I was, walking into the place he'd been living for almost two years. The person who knew me the most in the whole world was in so many ways a stranger now.

That thought filled me with sadness, and soon it was all coming out of me. "I always thought I was the one who wanted all this," I said, as I lifted a hand to the framed photographs on the wall. "That part of the reason things seemed to always go awry was because I wanted something you didn't."

I sat on the arm of the couch, listening to the soft snores of Tita and Pepe who were snuggled up on their little dog beds in one corner of the room. J, who was never one to rush into an answer, especially one that might lead to an argument, took me in. His stance closed off. Cautious.

His arms crossed over his chest and his eyes focused on something far away. I looked at him and thought once again, how much I missed having him in my life. How I wished things could be different, that *I* could be different, and able to let go more. When he finally spoke it was like thunder crackling through the room.

"When have you ever known me to do something I didn't want to do?" He pushed off the mantel and walked over to stand in front of me. And because when it came to Juan Pablo Campos my body was a traitorous bitch, I had to dig my fingernails into my palms to keep from touching him. "The issues we've had were never about us not wanting the same things. They were about us being too stubborn to make the changes we needed to make for that to happen."

I could feel my hackles going up, my mouth pursing, ready to curse him out. Tell him that it was easy for him to call me stubborn when he'd never had to wonder if his choices would trap him. But like he'd been doing since we got on that plane to the DR, Juan Pablo surprised me.

"And you know, that's not fair for me to say. I never had to wonder what I'd lose when I decided not to go to the academy. I knew I had a backup plan and Nonno would help me with grad school if I wanted that. I knew my parents didn't need my help or wouldn't in the future. Your choices were always harder, and you've never shied away from them."

He smiled bitterly then, and looked up to the ceiling. "My choices were never that hard, and when it came down to a difficult one, I bailed on the idea of being a cop without a second thought. Even when it meant breaking my promise to you."

I'd been waiting for him to say that for over ten years, to admit that he'd broken my trust, and it left me cold to realize that hearing the guilt and sadness as he spoke brought me no relief.

I shifted where I was sitting again, trying to keep myself from reaching out to him. "We were kids, J, and becoming a cop isn't exactly something you want to do just to keep your girlfriend happy." I let myself slide onto the chair, since it was clear this conversation was long from over. "I was unreasonable, and I wonder now…"

Shit, this was something I'd avoided telling even myself, and because this new Juan Pablo always seemed to know the right thing to do, he sat down on the couch next to me and waited me out. "I wonder if the reason why I could never get past you backing out of the academy was because I was scared I'd made a mistake by joining."

At that his eyes widened, as if he couldn't really believe he'd heard me right.

"It's hard to remember sometimes that the hard ass thing is not who you are." He shook his head and closed his eyes as if the words he needed were somewhere deep inside, in a place where he didn't think he'd need to go looking ever again. "I never pushed or asked if things weren't going well because I thought if I did it would just start a fight. Like you'd forget I'd bailed on you and bringing it up would remind you."

He was still regarding me with that knowing gaze he'd been sending my way lately, and I decided to say the last of this, and be done. "It's not that I did this against my will. I like being a cop. I feel useful and it gives me purpose. But it hasn't been easy and I think in those moments when I want to quit—when I wonder if I can keep tolerating the toxic shit that always seems to be sitting right under the surface—that if I vent to you I'll get a big

'I told you so.' If I mention it to my parents that they'll be disappointed."

The relief of being able to say that felt like an anvil had been lifted off my shoulders. It shouldn't have come as a surprise that in the end it was to J I'd been able to say what I'd been holding in for what felt like eons.

He looked down at the little marble top roundtable between us. I could tell he was trying hard to figure out how to say whatever he was thinking. "I'm going to say this now, too late probably for it to make a real difference." His voice was earnest, like he needed me to hear how important this was. "I'm sorry I ever made you feel like you couldn't tell me how you were feeling."

I swallowed hard and took a few deep breaths. This was so much more than I'd been ready to deal with today. It felt good to hear him say that though, and I knew it was the truth because despite all the ups and downs, he was right, Juan Pablo had never lied to me. When I finally opened my mouth to speak, I found that I felt light. Freer somehow.

"Thank you, and don't whine when I'm over here all the time complaining about everything. You asked for it, Juan Pablo." I winked at him and he blushed again. I leaned in closer, just because the more I sat here with him, the less sense it made to have any distance between us. That old ache of constant want that ravaged me when he was close wreaking havoc on all my boundaries.

My breath caught when his tongue slid over his upper lip, a gesture that was usually a prelude to him doing some inflammatory shit that ended with us in bed. "I feel like this is some sort of truce and I don't want to ruin it by letting my dick call the shots."

I actually clapped a hand to my mouth to keep the

bark of laughter from coming out, but the way his face broke out into a huge smile told me my eyes were communicating my current state loud and clear.

"What?" He was barely able to choke that out and his cheeks were practically by his eyes. "You know we keep it real, Pris. I'm glad we could talk, because I'm not gonna lie to you, I've been really fucked up about how things have been with us." He shook his head and the regret there had to be a mirror image of mine. "I hate it."

I wanted to glom all this up. To take it all in, tell him we were good to go and that we could start where we'd left off. But I was scared. The last time everything had blown up between us had changed something in me. It had hurt so much and for so long I could still remember the pain. The way that I couldn't take a deep breath for weeks. How for months after it would hit me out of nowhere that I couldn't call him when I needed him and I'd just burst into tears. Even know, just recalling it made me flinch. The pain of losing the only person who I could really be myself with. And that wasn't even true either. I had friends and family who loved me just like I was, who I could be myself with, but they weren't Juan Pablo. No one could ever be what he was to me.

And because that truth was so massive that it felt like it was the load-bearing beam of my life, I stood up from my chair, went over to stand in front of him and pulled him up for a kiss.

Juan Pablo

If anyone ever asked me about the place where every-thing made sense, I would unequivocally say it was with Priscilla Gutierrez's arms wrapped around my neck.

She didn't give me a chance to think or to even ask if she was sure before she'd pressed herself against me, her lips scoring my skin. Leaving a trail of heat and firing up all the places that I'd thought would never be stoked alive again.

"Pris," I said reluctantly, but I'd never been too strong when it came to her. I licked into her mouth, my hands already roaming to touch and grip those places that had been mine for so long. The ones that I'd owned with my mouth and my hands hundreds of times. The ones I'd given up on having again.

Her teeth and tongue on my neck had me panting, and I grabbed her tight, trying to ground myself for a second, because I had to ask. "Are you sure about this?"

The hand tightening around my dick was more than enough answer and also the cue for my legs to give out. I dropped onto the leather armchair with Pris on my lap, and it was on.

My head felt fuzzy with want. I wanted to tear both our clothes off, bite, lick. Her lips on my neck were like embers. I was burning up, like there was livewire right under my skin.

"Tell me something." Priscilla's mouth was right by my ear, and she had that fucked-out voice that meant I was minutes, maybe seconds from having my brain shorted out. With that steady right stroke, I could barely string two thoughts together.

"What?" It was more a shudder than an answer, but my dick was fully in the driver's seat now. Making words was getting really fucking hard.

Before she answered she nipped on my ear and I was sure I'd black out or come before she got my dick out. "How bad do you want my mouth on you? My tongue on your balls?"

"Puñeta." Cursing was all my mouth was good for, and that was exactly the right answer, because it got the button on my fly open and her hand on my dick.

"You still like it a little rough? Just a little bit of teeth." She inhaled, like she was looking for a scent in the air. "I'm feeling really fucking reckless right now, Juan Pablo."

Groans and moans were my mother tongue now. I wanted her to take me all the way out of my head like I knew she could. Like she always did. "Pris, fuck." I was begging, and I would keep doing it too.

My knees were shaking and I wasn't sure what would happen once her mouth was actually on me. "Tell me how you want it, pa." That last part was said as she slid down my body and ended up on her knees eye to eye with my cock. For a second I had a crazy thought and imagined her making fire, we were that hot together.

"I want you to put your mouth on me, Priscilla." She didn't answer, just pressed a fingernail right to the slit and I bucked like she'd tasered my ass. I couldn't fucking think with Priscilla like this. My head felt loose on my neck, like it could snap off from how revved I was. I closed my eyes and felt her as she pressed up, coming in closer, hot breath on me. She pulled down my briefs, scraping my skin with her fingernails just enough to make me gasp, and when she had me just like she wanted, she let out a satisfied groan.

I opened my eyes slowly, trying to see through the spots in my vision and looked down just in time to watch her take me all the way in. My guts, my legs, my ass all of it went molten, hot and liquid. My hips thrusting of their own accord as she moved up and down my length. Owning me. When Priscilla had me like this, I felt like I could fly apart from pure pleasure. She knew just how to touch me, that when she tugged on my balls right as she sucked hard on the head, she could reduce me to a babbling mess.

"Oh shit. That's so good, Pris." I bit off another curse as she slid her thumb to my ass, while she stroked my dick and sucked on the head. I gripped the arms of the chair so tightly I was sure I'd tear them off with my bare hands, just to keep from gripping her head and shoving myself as deep as I could into her mouth. "Fuck, that mouth of yours." That was more of a long moan than actual words, and when she got a tight down stroke just right and then took me in to the hilt, it was a wrap.

The white haze on the edges of my consciousness took over and all I could do was twitch, my mouth open in a silent scream. Priscilla took it all and by the time I was breathing normal again she'd climbed on to my lap, kissing me with ravenous intensity. My taste on her tongue almost made me want to try CPR on my dick, just so I could fuck her like this, with our bodies locked together so tight each movement felt like we were melding into each other.

"That was good," I said, as I made my way down her neck, trying to get my tongue on her tits.

When I looked up at her she was smiling, no trace of regret in her eyes, no skittish weirdness. The relief loosened my chest, and if I was a praying man I would've plead for more time like this. Just enough, so I could show her that when it came to her, I would never get enough. Just as I was thinking of how to get us horizontal, she said the thing that made me want to pound my chest and howl at the moon.

"We're always that good."

Yes, we fucking were, and I was not nearly done with her. I paused from my attempt to lick right through her sweater so I could get my tongue on her nipple and with a growl pushed us up and off the chair. I was winded, but my dick had ambitious plans. Before she could protest, I put my mouth right next her ear and tried my best to get actual words out. "Can we take this to the bedroom?" I asked as I palmed her ass and walked to the hallway.

She was holding on tight, both hands gripping my head. "You know I hate when you do this caveman shit, Juan Pablo. I'm not a wilting flower."

Because she was doing her best to get her tongue in my mouth, it took me a second to respond. "Is that a yes to the bed? Because my entire mission in life right now is to get you out of these jeans and riding my face within the next sixty seconds. I can't even fucking see where

I'm going right now and if I die *I die*, but I need to get my mouth on you."

Her answer was sucking on my neck and grinding on my dick. That was the last push I needed to get us to the room. As soon as I walked in I placed her on the bed and kicked the door shut. Ready to get reacquainted with every inch of that dark brown skin.

I literally bit my fist to hold back from mauling her, but as expected, Priscilla grabbed the bull by the horns and skinned out of her jeans, sweater and thong in one go. I smiled when I saw her tattoo. It was a string of rubies around her waist. A few of the bloodred stones etched on her skin dipped in a curved line to the top of her mons. Priscilla's not at all subtle way of letting anyone who ever got there know they were getting a fucking gem.

I'd always called it her Bronx girl tat, and was always more than happy to let it guide me all the way down to where I wanted to be. "Are you looking at my rubies, Juan Pablo?"

Once this woman made up her mind there was no stopping her. If she wanted to fuck, she would get what she wanted. Pris had no shame about her desires and she let me know, unequivocally, how and where she wanted me. We'd tried it all after so many years together, but she always burned through my sheets. Always.

When she licked her lips and dipped two fingers into her pussy, I listed as a growl rumbled in my chest. I was about to take off my own clothes, but I couldn't stop staring as she pleasured herself. Lusty sounds escaping her lips. "That's mine tonight, Priscilla."

She laughed and licked her lips again, working her clit as I watched, and when one long reedy moan left her lips…that's when I pounced.

Chapter Eleven

Priscilla

This had not been my plan for the evening, but I couldn't care less. We'd figure out the details later. Right now I was going in hard and not coming up for breath until we were both wrecked. I'd left my bra on, but was naked and so horny I could barely think as J got on the bed still fully clothed. In the back of my mind I wondered if he remembered how hot that made me, to know he couldn't even wait long enough to take off his clothes.

I would probably regret this later, hell the thoughts were trying to creep in right now, but *I deserved this*. To have this man like this tonight. To get the satisfaction I knew he could give me. The only place in my world where I could shut out everything was when I was like this with J. Playing that game where we anticipated what the other needed, where to kiss and touch to make all thought and reason fly right out of our heads.

Without saying anything he knelt on the bed and tugged on my ankle. "Come here." His voice was strained like he could barely contain himself. Like he couldn't decide what to do first.

I shifted on the bed and moved closer to the headboard, until I was kneeling with my back to him.

"You must really want me to smack that ass."

Oh it was on. No more tentativeness, no more questions. J was in it to win it, and I was already shaking with the anticipation of having his mouth and hands on me.

"Don't take your clothes off." I didn't need to explain why. Within seconds he was on his back, head propped on two pillows between my thighs. I had my forearms resting on his headboard, looking down at him. Breath coming fast as my clit pulsed, my walls clenching with need. I wanted to scream I was so fucking hot for him.

"Come on, pa. Lick it," I urged him, and brought my hand down, showing him my engorged clit.

He smacked my hand away, hitting me with his palm right where I was aching and my vision blurred. "I told you that's mine. Put your hands on the headboard." He knew the one time in my life where I was fully compliant was with his mouth inches from my pussy. I obediently leaned on my forearms and threw my head back as he pulled me closer and sucked hard on my clit. My hips started moving, circling in a tight grind as he flicked the hard tip of his tongue against every nerve.

The pleasure made my whole body throb. I hummed and moaned as he slapped my ass hard, sucked and licked me.

"Shit, J. I'm gonna come. Ungh, your mouth." I bit off another curse and focused on the knot of sensation at my core.

He breathed through his nose as he doubled down on his efforts, lapping up every drop from me. I was panting like I'd been running a marathon as he worked me hard. That tongue circling, then licking. Lips locking in on my clit and sucking hard. Juan Pablo loved eating me out, he went into this kind of meditative state while he was doing it, he could go for hours, until I was a boneless heap in his hands.

"Ooooh, don't stop, J, fuck." I bucked hard as he did something particularly filthy with his tongue and fingers. We stayed locked together, him not letting go, and sucking and fingering me until my vision washed white as I twitched through a literal mind-melting orgasm.

"That's good. I'm good." I moaned, feeling hypersensitive. He finally loosened his grip and I slid down his body until my ass bumped into his raging hard-on. With my eyes still closed I gripped his head and kissed him.

He smelled like me. His lips swollen from sucking on me. I glided my tongue with his, feeling hollowed out by my orgasm. Like my insides had been blown out from all the pleasure, and still I wanted more. It was like now that I'd decided I'd let myself have him, I wanted it all.

I ground my ass on his erection, making him hiss, and when I pulled back from the kiss and looked at him, his eyes were squeezed shut, mouth twisted in a painful grimace. He was holding back. Giving me what I needed and not asking for more than what I'd freely give.

"Pris, shit. You're gonna make me blow. You know my dick can't handle your ass when you're grinding on me like this." That last part was more a long shudder than words, since I was now propped on my hands and really trying to make him sweat.

"Get a condom, Juan Pablo." His arm shot out to the side, blindly pulling open a drawer as I tried not to laugh.

Fuck, this boy could always ruin me.

I pushed up and started pulling off his sweats and briefs.

"Gimme," I said, extending a hand while I stroked him with the other.

He shook his head and sat up fast, and without comment went to undo my bra. "I want to see them." He loosened the hook with the ease and efficiency that only came with years of practice, and flung my bra somewhere in the room. He leaned back on one arm, eyebrows high on his forehead and a smile appeared on his lips that meant he was deciding where to put his mouth first.

"I could write sonnets to your tits. You still have the piercings, I kept wanting to say something in the DR, but I was afraid you'd ream me out." I chuckled, as he stared at the two gold hoops I'd had since college. I'd taken them out for a few years but put them back in on a whim.

"They feel nice. I like to tug on them." This was said purely to get a reaction from him and I got one. No words though, just more grunting. He leaned in and put the tip of his tongue through the small hoop and then pulled on it with his teeth.

I sucked mine at the sensation and cupped the breast he was playing with. Wetness pooling at my core. "Umm that's nice. Suck on it."

He did. I hummed in pleasure, letting my head loll back on my neck. Resting my hands on his shoulders as he pinched and sucked on me. Teeth and tongue doing what he knew would make me wild for him.

He kissed up my neck as he worried my nipple between his fingers, making my skin tighten with every brush of his lips. "Put the condom on me. I want to see your tits bouncing when you're riding this dick."

His breath was so hot on my skin, and I was sure I could come just from the tip of his cock rubbing on my clit. I made quick work of the lubed condom, as he leaned back on the headboard. I pulled off his sweat-shirt, so I could see his chest. I leaned in and nipped at him as I rode him.

He moved back and forth, pushing in and pulling back until I had him all the way inside. We both exhaled as if something tight and suffocating had been loosened in our chests. I closed my eyes, hands gripping his shoulders, hard. Getting my balance. Feeling him, deep, so deep. And fuck, I could've wept.

This was what I needed.

"J," I pleaded as he gripped my waist and started to thrust into me.

"Move with me, Pris." He sounded…lost, like his whole life was hanging on the balance of this moment. Of how our bodies would work together. I didn't want to open my eyes. I was afraid of what I'd see there. Of what it would feel like.

"Abre los ojos, mi amor. Dejame verte." I didn't know if I could let him see. I didn't know if my eyes wouldn't betray me. But I'd never been a coward, and J and I could always say more with our bodies than we ever could with words.

I opened my eyes slowly, as I started to move. My hips undulating in sync with his movements. Those brown eyes, the ones that had seen me naked in every way. That could see in my heart and my soul like no one else, focused on me.

"You still with me, ma?" That was said while he licked his thumb before circling it on my clit.

"Asi, Juan." The way he was moving, with his hands on me was like lightning crackling through my body. Soon we were moving against each other hard and fast.

The sounds of our bodies coming together and our ragged breaths the only sounds in the room.

"I'm close," he said through gritted teeth, as he pushed into me.

He kept rubbing my clit and I tightened around him as he bucked into me. "Fuuuuck." I felt the first spasm of his orgasm, right as my own was crashing into me.

He pressed me tight to him, our skin clammy with perspiration. The exertions of the last hour had wrung us out. And when I was finally coming down falling into the bed in Juan Pablo's arms, still too blissed out to say a word I thought to myself again, *This is what I needed.*

I kept my eyes closed and rested my head on J's chest as he kicked his sweats all the way off. Once he was settled in, his arms tight around me, I could feel the tension of the question he was afraid to ask. But J had never been a coward either.

"How are you doing?" That wasn't any kind of simple question, but the answer came easier than I thought.

"I don't want to think about the long game with this." I dug my nails into his chest, surprised with everything I was feeling. "Or how it's going to end badly or how we can make this last. This is good for now."

He tightened his arms around me, a deep sigh rumbling on his chest. "If you're good. I'm good. We can figure out the rest later." The gentle kiss he planted on my forehead made the last of my reservation seep out of my body and I settled in.

"Okay. Later."

Chapter Twelve

Juan Pablo

"You know what's wild?" Priscilla asked, as she cut off a piece of the omelet I'd made for her. Spinach and feta, her favorite.

"I'm sure you'll tell me," I teased as I wiped down my granite countertops trying to keep my cheesy grin under control. I was feeling pretty fucking good.

We'd laid in bed, messing around and talking until her stomach growled, making us both laugh. She was always starving after sex, and that usually meant I cooked while she kept me company. I was sort of blown away by how not freaked out she was. I almost didn't want to tempt fate by getting too deep. But this felt good. To have her here like this. Not just making love, although that had been great. But us opening up to each other after so much hurt. I wanted to keep this going forever.

"I don't even believe in soulmates." She lifted a shoulder and shook her head, still clearly baffled by this fact. "I'm one hundred percent sure there are hundreds of people out there I could be happy with. That I could have hot as fuck sex with and feel satisfied by in real ways."

Okay that's not where I thought she was going, but

I tried hard not to scowl. She knew me too well not to know what was going through my head.

She held a hand up with a grin on her face, as I stood there confused. "It's just…they're not *you*, and that's why I've stayed away." That was said with her looking at the plate. And fiddling with the sleeve of one of my hoodies which she was now wearing.

I nodded again, a sharp brisk movement, and really tried to figure out why she'd told me that. Why now? Did she want me to know that what happened tonight was a one-off? Did she feel compelled to stress the point that this hadn't mattered to her as much as it had for me?

I'd been working hard at not making assumptions, so I would take what she was saying like I thought she meant it. That things with us were never simple. That we had hurt each other a lot over the years, so it was best not to tempt fate.

She was right about all of it, and I had to tell her I knew that.

"I'm not going to say I never meant to hurt you, because that's not true. I've done it too many times to not take responsibility for it." I ran a hand over my mouth and pulled on my beard, hard. Looking for words that could work right now. Words that could allow me to tell her I'd discovered that losing her was the one thing in my life there was no safety net for.

That the Priscilla-sized void stayed empty and aching no matter how hard I worked on filling it back up.

"I talked to my therapist about this." My mouth always did me dirty at the most critical moments.

Her eyes went comically huge. "Your therapist?"

"I have a therapist." I wasn't going to make a big deal

out of it, but a little sense of pride puffed up in my chest at how surprised she seemed.

She leaned back, her arms crossed over her chest, and grinned. Okay so that fun fact landed better than I thought it would.

Her smile was devilish and I had to remind my dick that this was not the time. That motherfucker never learned.

"So after all those years of you shutting me down, you finally started going to a therapist. I'm gagged that you finally got your stubborn ass to find one."

I did laugh then, because I should've known. "Okay, so basically all you needed to hear was that you were right all along to get all relaxed and shit."

She laughed again and leaned closer, her hands gripping the edge of my breakfast counter, but whatever she was going to say wiped the smile off her face. By the time she opened her mouth her eyes were as serious as I'd ever seen them. And just under that seriousness I saw a flicker of the small flame of hope that was burning in my gut. "What are we going to do, J? Did we just ruin our chance at being friends?"

She looked scared and it carved out a hole in my chest.

"Can we start by *trying* to be friends again, Pris?" I swallowed, having trouble believing I was actually saying it. "I mean you know my dick and pretty much every part of my body is always up for whatever with you, and after what we just did, I'm gonna need a dick cage or something when I'm around you." That at least made her laugh, but I wanted to say this next part. "I'm not going to lie. I'd love to keep exploring this," I explained, as I came closer so that I was standing in front of her. "But

I don't want anything that stresses you out. I want to be a good part of your life again."

She closed her eyes and I had to squeeze my fists hard to keep from reaching out for her. But we needed to talk this out. "This doesn't have to happen again. We can go back to just friends, no benefits." My heart was galloping in my chest, my vision blurry from the fear that Pris would walk out of here today and that would be the end.

But when she opened her eyes they weren't sad anymore. "I don't know if I can do a relationship right now, J. Or maybe ever again."

Okay that hurt, that really fucking hurt, but I wasn't going to fight her on that, so I just nodded, resigned.

"But." She tapped a finger on my chest, and gave me a sad smile. "Tonight was good, so thank you."

"I'm not gonna ask if I can get some of that good good again," I said, as I sucked my teeth, flexed my biceps and generally acted up. "But you know I always, always want it. And now that you know where I live, you know where *you* can get it."

"You're a fucking clown." There was no malice in her words, just the familiar helplessly amused tone Pris sometimes got when we were together and I goofed around on her.

"This is true, but I am a clown that's been in therapy for a while now and I don't want to fuck this up. I want you back in my life, Priscilla. I miss you."

She nodded once and then leaned all the way over the table to kiss me once, gently, on the cheek. She looked content, if still a bit reserved. And something that had been cold and dead in my chest for years, pulsed with warmth.

"I can't promise anything beyond knowing I don't

want to close this door. That's the best I can do right now. And I'm not gonna lie, this place is pretty swank, I wouldn't mind dropping by every once in a while."

I pounced on that in a hot second. Even though neither of us would say it right now, we both knew her taste and the things she'd always said she liked were present in a hundred different ways all over the apartment. "Tu sabes que mi casa es tu casa. Siempre."

"Okay, Imma eat my food and get back into that bomb bed of yours for a nap before I head home. I can't show up at dawn with my parents there, but you wore me out." A shy smile, a nod, and it seemed like we'd sealed the deal, and started a new page.

I looked at her for a second and held my tongue because I wanted to say all kinds of reckless shit. But I wouldn't fuck this up. No, I'd slowly show her that I could be the person she leaned on, who got her. Who could hold it down when she needed it.

That I wanted to be all of that for her. Not because I was her soulmate, like her I knew that there were probably other people I could be happy with. But still, Pris was the only one I wanted. And if tonight had proved anything it was that we still worked a hell of a lot better together than we did apart.

Chapter Thirteen

Priscilla

I got to the Uptown Center about thirty minutes before my first ever workshop there was about to start, feeling a hot mess. I saw through the glass doors that the place was still busy almost at 7:00 p.m. and despite my foul mood a small frisson of excitement ran through me. It was scary to blend my two worlds like this, but being able to do one of my workshops in my old hood felt special. Things with J had been…interesting since that night we hooked up. I'd expected salacious texts at midnight or other suggestive behavior pushing for more. But nothing came. He'd been more than clear about what he wanted, but the ball was in my court when it came to taking it further.

So far I'd resisted the temptation of showing up at his house. Not just the sex, and I would be a liar if I didn't admit I wanted it, all the time. I wanted what we'd had that night, the ease, the comfort. But it almost felt like a mirage. Like that night had been a fluke to trick me into believing in something that wasn't really there. But I wasn't here to agonize about J on the sidewalk. I was here to work.

I leaned against the cold brick wall of the building

and took a couple of breaths, trying to let the tension of the day seep out. Just as my breathing was getting back to normal my work phone buzzed. The dread swirling in my stomach over a simple call from work should've been indicator enough that I needed to rethink my career. But that was yet another topic that would need to stay in the "Avoidance" shelf for a bit longer. I sighed, hoping it wasn't more bad news and pulled it out of my jacket pocket. As soon as I read the first few words of the message from Bri, I knew it wouldn't be good.

Hey, babe, I hope you don't get this until after your class AND I don't want you to worry, but looks like April didn't come home last night or to school today. Sanchez is on it. But since you asked me to let you know if anything happened with that case I'm giving you a heads-up. Good luck. Call me later.

Fuck. This was one of the cases that was keeping me up at night. A twelve-year-old who in the past year had gotten pregnant and miscarried and, not surprisingly, had been acting out since. She lived with her mom and step-dad and the story was that she'd been hooking up with some thirteen-year-old who'd only been in town for the summer, and had gone back to Georgia. No one could give any details on this kid, who he was staying with, even a last name. None of it added up.

But that was the story, and she was still sticking to it. Something about the stepdad gave me the creeps. But since he seemed to have his shit together, no matter how much I pushed about it, the rest of the team—other than Bri—didn't think anything was happening there. I'd been keeping tabs on her, certain things weren't good at home, but I couldn't do much if she didn't give us much to go on. Except now she was starting to stay out all night.

Dammit, Bri. Something is seriously wrong in that house.

I gripped my phone, trying hard not to get all worked up. This was technically not even my domain yet. Not until she gave us more information. And that was not happening just yet. I was looking intently at the dots indicating that Bri was working on a response when I felt someone tap my shoulder.

Before I could even think about what I was doing I turned around, my fist in the air.

"Jesus, Priscilla, chill." J looked startled and a little pale as his chest heaved up and down, but I was too on edge to think him sneaking up on me on the street like that was cute.

"No, you know better than to run up on a cop like that. I'm PMSing too, you're lucky you still have all your teeth. What the fuck, Juan Pablo?" I was yelling at him, full-on screaming, and something about my face must've been really scary because he didn't say a word. I was expecting to see the vein on his forehead that usually popped out when he was really heated make an appearance.

I expected him to walk into the center and leave me there seething, but instead he took a deep breath, fixed his face and lifted the paper bag in his hand.

"I got you a burrito bowl." He didn't snap his words or tell me I was acting like I had no home training out here in the street. In front of his father's center where everyone on the block knew him.

None of that. Cool, calm and extremely fucking collected, he handed me the food. "Since you texted saying you were running behind, I walked over to Chipotle and got you something to eat."

I knew I had to look like I wanted the earth to open up and swallow me. He dropped his shoulder and stepped back, both hands in front of him. "Don't get mad, but I forgot to get you the Tabasco sauce you like." His mouth twitched and my face was so hot I wondered if it was making steam when the cold December air hit it.

I deflated as I looked inside the bag and saw that he'd gotten me a side of the corn salsa I loved.

"You're a fucking cheeseball. Thank you." I sounded tired and a little flustered—which dammit, I was.

He just shook his head and hiked a thumb over his shoulder. His head angled toward the center. "You can eat in my mom's office. She went home already." He looked at his watch, then gestured to my duffel bag. "Take a few and eat, so you don't get all hangry. I'll start setting up."

There was zero judgement in his eyes, and mine were almost filling up with tears, because I could not remember the last time someone did something like this for me. That someone saw I was close to my limit and just took some of the load from me.

I clutched the still-warm bag to my chest and nodded as I tried to get my shit together. I didn't need to burst into tears over a burrito bowl.

"You really came in clutch, J. I was going to be ravenous by the time we finished." I lifted my phone, which was still in my hand. "I just need a second. See you in there."

He didn't comment on my obvious disheveled state and smiled. "Okay, just let Jenny at the front desk know who you are and she'll show you where the office is." With that he walked in.

I really needed to think about the state of affairs of my job and life. This was not like me, I didn't fall apart. I didn't cry on sidewalks.

When I looked down at my phone Bri's message managed to at least get me out of my previous mutinous state.

Sanchez just texted. She's at her aunt's. We're going to have to figure out what happened, but that's more on us and CPS, not you, not right now anyway. Go teach those sixty-year-olds how to get freaky and we'll hold down the fort over here. And EAT something.

I had no words left, so I just sent him a long row of heart emojis. After one last deep breath I walked into the center, ready to do my workshop and determined to not let things I could not control take away from this night.

By the time I'd polished off the entire bowl and had something to drink, Juan Pablo had all my stuff set up in the room. There were chairs in a semi-circle facing the front, and a projector was ready to go with the first slide of my presentation already up. He had the packing cube I used to carry my demo toys on top of the desk sitting next to the handouts, and was looking very pleased with himself.

I had to admit that the food had gone a long way to bolster my mood and with just under ten minutes to go before our class was supposed to start, excitement started bubbling up inside me.

"Thank you," I said, as I admired the room. It was well lit and roomy. There was also a door, so we'd have a private space to discuss whatever came up.

He pushed his lips out and I knew he was trying not to smile. "I love the title of the presentation."

I turned my attention to the screen as if I didn't know what was there.

Keep Coming: Great Sex at Any Age

I chuckled and started unzipping my goodies bag to make sure I had everything I needed. "My friend Mirna came up with it. She and I usually co-facilitate this, but she's visiting her grandkids on the West Coast."

He made a noise that sounded like he approved, and was considering something. "You've got like a whole network of people holding it down for you when it comes to this stuff."

I nodded, considering his comment, when I heard voices coming from outside. My heart started racing when I realized those were probably my workshop attendees. I turned and tried very hard to keep a straight face as I lined up tubes of lube, dildos, cock rings and vibrators on a towel. To his credit J didn't even crack a smile.

I talked as I worked. "I've met a lot of people through the online store and trade shows. I've also been doing those toy parties." I leaned against the desk and kept an eye on the door in case anyone came in. "That's where I got the idea for the workshops. I kept going into these different spaces and got really mixed groups. I mean you know how it was in our communities, the sex talks were not happening. And when we did get them it was like three words."

He nodded knowingly and offered them up. "Don't do it."

I laughed without any humor. "Right. So just the lack of education was enough to get me thinking. But I also got a lot of non-binary folx and older people, and they all had questions, had things to say. Then Bri and I started talking about his experience and how things were for him during transition and after. How he dealt with intimacy, the changes, good, bad or unexpected, et cetera." I shrugged, not wanting to go on for too long. "I noticed there was a need there, in our communities, you know? There is so much to unpack for enby folx, and for black and brown bodies in general about pleasure, and our right to it."

I waved a hand at two women standing by the door. They were both Afro-Latinas, and could've totally been someone's abuelitas, but they had a pep in their step as they walked in.

"Come in, please." I looked up at J again, who was already moving away from the desk. "You light up when you talk about this stuff, Pris. It's a good look on you." He fidgeted a little bit. I wondered if he was going to say something extra or try to be funny like he did sometimes when he was out of sorts, but he didn't. "Can I stay? Listen in? I promise I won't interfere."

This boy. He was really trying to ruin me, again.

I dipped my head as I waved at a couple other people coming in. I looked at my watch and saw that we had another five minutes. "You can stay, J." I winked and tried to keep my stupid heart from lurching in my chest. "I'll even let you ask a question."

That smile he gave me—it was the one that in the last fifteen years had consistently fucked me up and made me like it every step of the way.

Juan Pablo

"So that thing is not what you use for pegging, then?"

I really didn't need to be sitting here listening to Doña Rosa, my barber's mom, asking about prostate massagers. But I sure as fuck was not getting out of my seat until Priscilla was done with this class.

We were about five minutes from the end and I'd managed to push through half a dozen boners and one particular tricky situation with a cock ring demo that for real had me holding my breath so long I lost time.

Pris was in her element though. I don't know how she did it, but she managed to make a sex talk for older folks fun, engaging—and God help me—sexy. I mean my mind was fucking blown.

Also, she looked happy.

It was such a far cry from how I'd found her outside of the center earlier. Face drawn, upset…exhausted. No, here, she was a different Pris, one that I hadn't seen in ages. And she had all these people enthralled and chatty, about sex toys. I'd been certain she would talk the whole time because the audience would be too embarrassed to ask questions. But Pris had put everyone at ease within

minutes and it had legit been one of the most interactive
workshops we'd had at the center.

I drifted back into the conversation as Pris was wrap-
ping it up. "Now who's going to carve out some time for
solo play?"

Everyone raised a hand and Pris clapped, delighted.
"Excellent. Okay, so who has some stuff written down
they're going to buy tonight?"

All hands up again, and I was *not* going to let any im-
ages of these aunties getting sexy at home in my head.

Instead I lifted my own hand way up. When Pris saw
me she busted up and winked. "Awesome. Thanks so
much for joining me tonight, and I hope you found some
of what we talked about useful and gave you a little fuel
to feel empowered about your body and your pleasure.
Remember to ask your partners for what you want, and
screw polite."

The room broke out in applause and fuck, the smile
on her face broke my heart. I wanted to see her like this
always.

I stood back as people came up to her to ask more
questions or say thanks. Some people pointed at a toy,
clearly wanting more info and she got to every single
one of them. I waited in the back, observing with too
many things swirling in my chest. I wanted to go up to
her and tell her that all that sexy shit she was telling the
abuelitas had me mad revved up and a little confused.
That I wished I could take her home right now and fuck
her senseless. Instead I took four deep breaths like my
therapist showed me and waited until it was just the two
of us left in the room.

I walked up slowly as she started putting her stuff
away. "I'm right behind you, Detective Gutierrez. I don't

want to get popped on the mouth." I didn't need to see her to know she was smiling. When she turned around she still looked happy as hell.

"You're not cute."

She did not sound mad at all, and she handed me a little black pouch. "Here. I wanted to give you something, to say thank you for dinner and for almost punching you in the throat before." Her mouth was twitching and I knew I was full on cheesing.

I took the bag and looked inside, trying really hard not to laugh.

"So you're giving me a used prostate massager to say you're sorry."

She balked at that and I swear I was going to choke from trying not to laugh.

"It's not used. Oh my God, J, that's gross. It's brand-new. I just got it the other day."

"Thanks." I bit my bottom lip at her contrite expression and felt sort of proud of myself that I didn't say something greasy, because I was *feeling* her right then. She was in gray slacks, a yellow sweater and black ankle boots. Her hair in the bun I knew meant she needed to wash her hair soon. The little diamond studs I'd gotten her for Christmas like ten years ago in her ears.

I knew this woman like I knew myself, but I had no fucking idea how to convince her to give us another shot. To come home with me, so I could take care of her in every way possible. I didn't want to bring up what had gone down after my parents' party, the night we'd had. Because even though it had been awesome, she'd still slipped out of the house before I woke up. A simple thank you in a text later that morning the only evidence it had happened at all.

I got myself together and tried to sound like I wasn't agonizing about everything. "This was great. I can safely say we'd love to have you back. Rafa's going to be calling you for sure."

She nodded as she finished zipping up her bag, her face open and relaxed. "I'd love to do it again."

And of course, I came out of my face without any fucking warning. "Do you want to come to my place and watch a movie or something?"

Netflix and chill? Really, Juan Pablo?

I belatedly remembered I was holding a vibrator in my fucking hand and waited for her to answer.

"Wow that's pretty tired." She didn't sound mad though. "You could just say you want a repeat of the other night." Something in her voice told me there was a lot more to it than that. She was looking for something and if I didn't get this right, I'd put us back where we'd been before the wedding.

I closed my eyes and struggled with what to say. I didn't want to play games with Priscilla. "I have a feeling that if I say something out of pocket, I'm going to get iced."

Her face got serious then, and my heart thumped hard against my chest. "Damn you really have changed, J." Her tone wasn't exactly friendly, but it was definitely not salty either. It was as if she was still trying to process what had happened with me.

"I just don't want to play around, and also don't want you to think I just want you to come over so we can jump into bed." I lifted a shoulder, feeling decidedly out of my depth. "I want to spend time with you." I raised both hands up in a gesture that was pretty close to supplication. "I'm up for whatever you're up to, Priscilla. No strings, no catch. I miss you." To my utter fucking humiliation I choked up on that last part. But I didn't look away. I wanted her to know I meant it.

She dipped her head in a hard nod, as she fiddled with her phone case. "Let's do it. It sounds like just what I need, actually." She almost flinched at whatever she remembered. "I'm too hyped to sleep." I thought she was done, but then she looked up again and her smile was real and big. "Thank you, J."

She leaned into me and gave me a chaste kiss on the lips, but she lingered there just a moment longer than I expected and my dumb heart was beating so fast I was sure she'd heard it.

When she pulled back, she still looked mad happy. I didn't punch the air, but shit, I wanted to. "Okay, let me lock up and I'll see you at mine."

I was going to let Priscilla set the tone and the pace, but I was not going to waste a chance to let her know her being back in my life was my foremost desire. Never again would I let her walk around not being certain that she was everything I wanted.

Chapter Fourteen

Priscilla

I was on the elevator going up to J's house and even though I would never *ever* say it out loud it hadn't taken very long for me to feel right at home in his building. He'd given me the entry code, so I'd made my way up without having to get buzzed up. I wasn't going to make a thing out of the fact that I was looking forward to hanging out with J. I didn't want to ruin it by telling myself we would only end up hurting each other, or worse—that this would be the time we wouldn't be able to come back from. No, I'd needed this ease and I was going to enjoy the fact that I'd been able to turn my evening around after a shitty end of the day at work. I was tired of handling everything on my own.

Juan Pablo and his new Zen thing had gone a long way to put me at ease tonight and I was not going to question it. I didn't want to go back to my place, which was comfortable and had what I needed, but didn't exactly feel homey, even after being there for almost a year. It wasn't like me to not make a space my own, but lately I didn't seem to feel settled anywhere. Tonight, doing the workshop, being in a space where I could help people feel more in tune with themselves and their sex lives had refilled my very empty well. I loved it, and it was getting harder to ignore that recently a few stolen moments working on my side hustle was what got me through most weeks.

As I pondered that very unpleasant reality my phone buzzed in my jacket pocket, right as I got to J's floor. I stepped onto the hallway as I read a message from my mother.

Call me, mija. Just wanted to know when you're going to be home for Christmas.

I sighed and immediately felt guilty. Lately speaking to my mother was something I dreaded, and I felt shitty about it. About all of it. I didn't have to wonder why. I knew. It was because half the time she wanted to hear about the job. How the promotion prospects were going. How I was putting away the bad guys. Honestly, I didn't have the energy. The other one, of course, was the fact that she'd ask where I was and I'd have to either lie to her or tell her I was at J's and that was *not* happening. Instead of answering I put my phone on vibrate and rang J's doorbell.

If anything came up from the job my work phone always had the ringer on.

As soon as J opened the door, my shoulders loosened. If I'd been a more reasonable person, or at least the me from a year ago—who seemed somewhat better equipped in not actively looking to fuck myself over—I'd have taken it as a warning and taken my brown ass home. But that Pris seemed to be out to lunch and the one in her place had her nose wide-open and was not shying from the almost certain mess in her future. At this point, the only thing keeping me from doing something incredibly dumb with Juan Pablo was the bloating and all-around PMS discomfort. Basically I was back to my teenage years' levels of self-control.

"Hey, come in." He'd had a bit of a head start. I'd gone by my place to drop off my stuff and change out of my work clothes, so he was leaning on the doorway wearing a tight long sleeve Henley and sweats that were riding *very* low. I could see the jut of his hipbones, which alerted me to the fact that my eyes had made it further south than was advisable.

"Hey," I said, as I walked past him, doing everything I could to avoid eye contact. Still without looking at him I handed over the bottle of wine I'd brought from home. "I picked up some of that Garnache we discovered on that trip to Ithaca." Reminiscing about trips to see my parents was the opposite of sensible, and yet here we were.

He gripped the bottle and as he pulled away his long fingers flickered over mine, and no that was not a fucking shiver.

"Thanks." His voice was low, like he could tell I was mad skittish and didn't want to scare me off. "Let me go open it. I don't know what you want to watch, but I'm up for pretty much anything. Other than horror, you know I don't fuck with scary movies."

I rolled my eyes as I sank down on the long end of his sectional and grabbed the remote. "Holy shit, Juan Pablo, how many buttons does this thing have?" I asked, baffled.

He laughed and got busy pulling glasses out of the cabinets and opening the wine. "You'll figure it out."

He actually wagged his finger at me like the big cornball he was.

I scooted up so I was sitting closer to the lamp and
tried to figure out how to turn the TV on. "Please tell
me you saw *Get Out*," I said, while I finally got the giant
flat screen on the wall to turn on.

"Hell, no. I couldn't sleep just from the trailer." I
turned to see him walking in with two glasses in hand.
He looked genuinely freaked out just from talking about
the movie, and it was so fucking adorable. I wanted to
forget the wine and the movie and kiss him silly. I teased
him instead.

"J, that's like mandatory. Milo didn't make you watch
it?"

He sucked his teeth and carefully handed me the glass
before sitting down next to me on the couch. I was not
going to get all in my feelings about how this was like
the old days, because that would not get us anywhere
productive.

He took a long sip of the wine and made a big show
of turning on the gas fireplace before he responded. He
had his index finger in the air.

"First of all, Camilo is not the boss of me. His ass is
blessedly too busy running Tom's life to be all up in my
business." His thumb popped up and I was having a hard
time keeping a straight face. "Second of all, he knows
those movies give me nightmares, and unlike some people—" this time he raised an eyebrow and pursed his
lips right in my direction "—*he* takes people's triggers
seriously."

Wow, this therapist was not messing around.

"Damn, okay, point taken, you didn't need to go that
hard. I got it. But that movie's required watching. Be-

sides," I said, pointing my glass in the direction of the TV. "We've watched horror movies before."

He pursed his mouth again and I could see that he was trying really hard not to say something out of pocket, and honestly that more than anything else completely disarmed me. I wondered if he'd say something bratty or if he's just push out whatever he had on the tip of his tongue to say. I wasn't sure how I'd feel either way.

When he finally looked at me he seemed so serious I almost felt bad that I'd started the conversation.

"Those times we watched horror movies…uh." He paused to take another sip of his drink. "I thought we both knew I was secretly reading a book on my phone and trying to tune out the nightmare inducing horror on the screen."

He looked a little mortified and straight up adorable and, I legit snorted. "For fuck's sake, Juan Pablo!" I was literally cackling. "You're too fucking much. Fine I'll find something not horrific."

His mouth twitched like he was super happy he'd made me laugh, and I wanted to kiss him. So bad.

I was playing a dangerous game. And yet, I could not for the life of me come up with a reason strong enough to make me leave. I fiddled with the remote after figuring out how to make it work until I found the *Great British Baking Show*. I raised an eyebrow in question before turning on the first episode of the latest season.

"Happy?"

J bit his bottom lip and it was really very hard to be this close and not kiss him. Because if that mouth was around I wanted a taste of it. That wasn't ever going to change. It hadn't after all this time. I didn't think it ever would.

His shoulders relaxed and he threw an arm over the back of the couch—noticeably not on the side I was sitting. "Perfect."

We both sank into the couch and watched a couple of episodes, furiously looking up recipes on our phone whenever we saw something that looked delicious. Every emotional part or stressful moment making us drift closer and closer to each other, so that by the time we were finishing Cake Week, I was practically on his lap.

I was starting to doze off when the smell of popcorn woke me up, and before I could even sit up Juan Pablo was walking back into the living room with a bowl of fluffy popcorn in one hand and balancing wineglasses in the other. "I knew the smell of popcorn would lure you back from sleep."

"You know I can't resist Orville's siren call." He laughed, handing me a refill and placing the bowl on the couch next to me.

He sat down next to me and in no time we both had our hands on the popcorn bowl. "You looked really happy today doing that class. Totally in your element." I knew him too well not to know he'd had that on the tip of his tongue all night. But I was not going to go down that road unless I had to. So I just hummed and kept myself busy shoving handfuls of popcorn in my mouth.

When he realized I wasn't going to respond, as he always did, he called my bluff. "Have you thought about doing it full time? I mean those ladies were into the class. Two of them asked me if we could make them a permanent thing."

I considered him for a second, really looking at him. I wondered if this was just another way for him to get back on my good side. Of extending another olive branch.

I could blow it off again, but I didn't feel like it. Somewhere deep inside, in a little drawer I rarely even let myself open, I did hold the dream of doing something like this for a living. Of being an activist, and educator. Of putting into my community in ways I knew it needed. Maybe even going back to school for it. But it just seemed so fucking reckless.

Without really looking at him, I made myself say it though. "I mean, sure, it could be great and I really love doing it. But that's not really an option, not as a job."

I could tell that he was really thinking about what he was going to say, because my job was always, always a source of tension between us. And we'd had more than our fair share of arguments when it came to it. He looked at me, and I could tell he was gaging how much telling me what he was really thinking would piss me off. In the end, he ran a hand over his mouth and went in.

"I just want you to know that in no way do I think what I'm about to suggest is easy or would happen any time soon." He paused for effect, because deep down Juan Pablo was the OG Drama Llama. "But you could slowly start doing something different. Like change careers."

It was exactly what I thought he'd say, but what surprised me was the emotion that flared in my chest as he said it. But I was more frustrated with myself and the fact that I was too scared to take a chance on something I really wanted, more than annoyed at him. Still, my first instinct was to get defensive. Lash out at him for saying things that he knew would upend my life. I tried very hard not to bite his head off since I knew he was trying to help.

"I've thought about it." Wow, I didn't even curse him out.

Growth.

"But I can't do that. I can't leave a union job, with security, benefits, *a pension*, to do something that's a glorified hobby, just because it makes me feel good. That's not my life, Juan Pablo."

"Pris, it's not like a glorified hobby. Mi reina— Fuck." He sucked his teeth at the slip up. We were certainly not back to endearments yet. "You had that room at attention. I was expecting at least a few eye rolls, but we were all hanging on your every word. And to have older Latinx men and women talking openly about sex? Yo, that shit was beautiful. For real."

Juan Pablo never said something he didn't mean. Never, even when it cost him a friendship or, in our case, when it meant there would be a fight. J spoke his truth, as he saw it, always. That's why, for the most part, he kept his opinions to himself.

But hearing him say it now, it was like he was handing me a gift I'd been too afraid to wish for. And holy shit did I want to take it, but I couldn't. This wasn't my reality. It wasn't even *his*.

I shook my head again, harder this time. "Nah, J, I can't. I just can't." My voice shook, because I wanted to ask him how to make it work. What he saw that I couldn't, but this road was not good for me. I could not just throw all fucking caution and responsibility to the wind because I wasn't feeling my job.

I held up a hand when I saw that he was going to argue. "Please." I closed my eyes, finally feeling the tiredness of the day. Of the long week I'd had. "Today has been nice. I don't want to get into a thing over this."

I was pleading, and he could see it and hear it clearly, and he kept whatever he was about to say to himself. "Okay."

With that he turned the show back on and settled the bowl of popcorn between us again. And we went back to the show in silence, the tension of all the things that we didn't say making the air so thick I could practically see it. I needed to go.

I was about to stand up and do it when a sharp pain in my belly made me sit back down. Of course.

My period would start fucking with me just in time to make this situation that much more shittastic. "Dammit." I groaned as a particularly eye-watering cramp came right on its heels. With any other person I would've just dealt with it in silence, but this was J, so I opened my mouth.

"Shit," I said, grabbing my belly.

"You okay?" He was already up, his entire body poised, as if he was ready to pick me up and whisk me to the nearest emergency room.

I grimaced as another spasm shot through my back. "Cramps."

"Oh shit." He started moving, gesturing toward the kitchen. "Do you still like ginger tea? I have some, and I'll put the warm pad in the microwave for you. Here." He handed me a throw that was hanging over the back of the couch. "I'll go put the kettle on."

I took the blanket with numb fingers and spread it over my legs. I sat there digesting the fact that he had the tea I usually drank when I had cramps and remembered I put a hot pad on my back when the pain got really bad. J had never been squeamish about periods or "woman stuff." He'd grown up with three older sisters and Irene

raised him not to be an asshole. But he had never been…
nurturing. Neither of us had been. That was one of the
things that always seemed to work for us. Neither of us
was sentimental. We were practical. Got our shit done,
and if we ever needed a hand, we asked for it.

This was different. Such a departure from our usual
playbook, and it shook me. To know that in these past
couple of years J had worked on himself, found ways to
be different, better. And I was drowning in self-doubt,
my entire life one big unsatisfying mess.

"You don't have to take care of me," I said, realiz-
ing shit was about to get real, and I was going to cry.
And I couldn't even blame it on PMS moodiness. "I'll
go home."

"But I have stuff here." He looked crestfallen. Like
I'd mortally wounded him by turning down his offer to
help. And if I was a stronger woman I'd have taken my
ass home. Instead I looked up at his handsome face, and
those brown eyes that were looking at me with so much
longing and said, "Do you have any Motrin?"

He beamed, like I'd made his entire year by letting
him coddle me. There were so many levels to how all of
this could potentially fuck with my head, but it felt so
nice here with him. I just wanted some more. More of
not having to grin and bear it on my own. More of being
taken care of, for once. I knew this was the kind of shit
that was going to make staying in friend zone hard, but
I could not bring myself to care just then.

God, I wanted to kiss him. Pull him down to where
I was, find a position that didn't make me feel like I
had ferrets gnawing at my lower back and then, I'd kiss
him. Hard.

"Why are you looking at me like you want to take a

bite out of me?" His mouth was all twitchy, like he was working real hard on not smiling. I looked down at his white crew socks and then back up to see him run his hand over his fade. Everything about Juan Pablo felt comforting and oh so tempting at that particular moment.

"For a guy that's had a front-row seat to how moody I get when I have cramps, you're taking a lot of risks."

He snorted, as I folded my arms around my belly and leaned my head against the couch.

"Let me go get your Motrin. Actually." His face changed then, like he was really taking his life into his own hands with the next part, but he asked anyway. "Why don't you stay over?"

He said it as he was walking away and I knew it was to avoid seeing whatever face I'd make. It was a good time to ask him what he thought was happening here. To make it clear to him that the only way this could work was if we didn't muddy the waters again. That the night after his dad's birthday has been good, too good. And I was scared that if we kept falling into bed together, we'd fuck things up royally. That having him back felt like a lifeline.

I was about to say all of it. But when he came back to the room a few minutes later with a steaming mug of tea and put out his hand to pull me off the couch, I took it.

"You can take my bed." His voice was husky and low, and even in my less than comfortable state, I was having a hard time staying on task.

"J." I really did mean to step back, but I pushed closer instead. He brought both hands so they were pressed to my lower back, right where I needed soothing. My eyes were half open, as if I was still trying to fool myself into thinking I wasn't really going to kiss him. I watched his Adam's apple bob up and down as he held himself back, not making a move until I did it first, and again I was blown away by all the ways in which Juan Pablo had changed.

I turned my head, so my mouth was right under his. His beard prickly on my lips. He smelled good. So good. So I opened my mouth, flicked my tongue over his lower lip. Just a caress, but like I knew he would, he ran with it.

He gasped as our mouths touched and without hesitation kissed me deeply. He was gentle too, careful not to press too hard on my belly. He managed to somehow watch the places I ached at the same time he touched and licked me just how I craved. When he lowered his mouth to kiss my neck he let out a groan that I felt in my own gut.

"You feel so good, Pris." The yearning in his voice, the deep longing there, made my knees weak. "You always feel so good."

I covered his mouth with mine, trying to stave off whatever words were primed to come out and break the spell. I wanted to stay like this, feel the rasp of his tongue on my neck. His teeth grazing my ear until I shivered. The way his touch filled places that no one else ever could.

"Juan." I didn't even know what I wanted, I just had to say his name.

"Nena." He slipped a hand down my back and gripped my ass hard as I panted, the cramps and pain forgotten for these few seconds. Just as I was starting to wonder what exactly I'd started my phone started buzzing against my thigh. I sighed, pushing back from J and pulled the phone out of the pocket in my leggings. When I looked at the screen I saw that it was my mother's number. It was almost 11:00 p.m. and she knew I was off.

"It's Mamí, you know she'll get worried if I don't answer," I muttered tiredly, as J tried his best to get himself back in control.

"Sure, tell her I said hi." His voice sounded resigned, he knew better than to expect I'd pick up where we left off after I talked to my mother. But I let it go to voicemail as I considered what I was doing. I'd had an emotional day—hell, an emotional week, month—and everything I hadn't let myself feel was sitting right under the surface. I kept feeling like all my priorities were out of whack. That the things I seemed to have valued above everything were smothering me, and if that wasn't enough of a mindfuck, it seemed like the only person I could talk about it with was the man I told myself I needed to stay away from.

I sent a text to my mother, without any indication that I was at J's house. He'd gone into his bedroom, so I just stood there waiting, I wasn't sure for what. No, that wasn't true, I was waiting for him to come out of the bedroom and try to convince me to stay, so I could tell myself I was just being nice. But he didn't come back. I waited for a minute, then two until I went looking for him. I found him sitting on the bed with the hot pad in his hands.

He turned to look at me and smiled sadly, his lips still a little bruised from my kisses. "We'll take this as far as you want, Pris." He shook his head, and heaved out a tired breath. "I want you in my life. I'm not going to lie and say I don't want a repeat of the other night." As soon as he said that he widened his eyes, as if seeing the hot pad for the first time. "I mean obviously not today, but like anytime. I am open to whatever you want."

My laugh at his attempt to work in the appeal for more sex was shaky, but the cramps were coming back, so I wasn't sure if it was because of J's words or my own body. I stood, letting what he said, the obvious want in his voice, wash over me. To be wanted like this, desired, just as I was, had always been a heady thing. And I'd always struggled with believing it. Believing him.

He looked down at the floor, shaking his head, and when he looked at me again, I could see in his eyes that he was desperate for me to see how much he meant every word. And when in the past I'd harden myself to his promises, this time I just didn't have the strength to walk away.

"I swear I will not fuck this up."

I shook my head and came to sit with him on the bed. "I was the one that kissed you, J." I took the pad from his hands, just to find something to do. "I don't want to mess this up either. It's been nice hanging out today. I've missed you too."

He dipped his head and looked at me again, looking more serious than I'd ever seen him. "We'll make it work. Figuring out a way to be around each other cannot be harder than staying away."

I laughed and ran a hand over his fade, running the pad of my finger along the sharp angles of his lineup. I was so mixed up about this man, and about myself. I wanted to let whatever was starting to brew between us happen and deal with the consequences later, but as if to remind me just how bad things had gone the last time, a sharp pain shot through my abdomen, making me double over.

"Shit."

With that Juanpa stood up and waved a hand at the bed. "Get in there. I'll go get the tea and heat this up." He rushed out of the room with the pad in his hand and I curled up under his covers, amazed to realize that even though this was the first time J had ever done any of this stuff for me, he still knew exactly what to do.

Chapter Fifteen

Juan Pablo

"Damn, J, you real pressed. What's up?"

I was so far in my own head while working on Yariel Cuevas, one of the Yankees players I gave PT to on the off-season that I practically jumped at his question. I didn't answer right away and kept massaging his shoulder as I considered what to say.

Yariel was a friend—hell, he'd been a steady hookup when I'd started dating about six months after Pris and I broke up. He was a real one. Unapologetic about his sexuality from the first day he stepped on the field. Even after things had fizzled out with us we'd stayed close. I'd been over to his place to hang out with him and his boyfriend on the regular and I knew he'd probably be a good person to talk this over with. Of course I could talk to one of the guys, but they all were too invested when it came to me and Priscilla and even when they understood my worries, they couldn't really be objective.

I slowly moved his pitching arm around as I worked out a way to say what I'd been stewing on for days. "Priscilla and I are kind of involved again." I was impressed with myself for summing up the increasingly complicated situation between Pris and me. It had been a week since the night of the workshop and Pris had been at my house almost every day. We'd kept it platonic the first couple of times, but as soon as she felt up for it, we were back in my bed.

We were now in this weird in-between where we were together, but not really, and it was driving me nuts.

Yariel looked up at me and blew out a slow breath. During those first months of our friendship he'd gotten more than one earful about Priscilla and all the ways in which I'd fucked up. "Isn't that good news? Why have you been scowling since I got here?"

I let go of his arm and pointed at one of the machines we usually worked with.

"Five reps on each side, then we switch." I was still thinking about what to say as I walked over to the machine and got him set up for his exercises. "It's just that we've been doing this thing where she comes over and we watch shows and I make dinner. I'll throw my arm around her, make out…a whole lot more sometimes." My heart rate sped up, thinking of the night before. She'd come to my place after work and we'd fucked right up against the door. I didn't even have time to properly say hello.

My face heated from the image in my head. "But she's got a very clear limit. We can talk about anything, but if she comes over obviously heated or fucked up from work, I'm not allowed to ask questions." Yariel clicked his tongue as he did his reps. His head was down but he was clearly listening as I talked.

"The fact that she's miserable at her job is not up for discussion, even though I can see how she basically tenses up anytime she gets a text from her captain or one of her colleagues. That's not my business, because I'm not her man." I ran my tongue over my bottom teeth as that fun fact sunk in again. I'd let my dick trap me into a situation where I couldn't really be there for Priscilla, not how I wanted to be.

Yariel stopped what he was doing and turned around on the machine's seat to look at me. We were in one of the PT rooms at the stadium which on a random afternoon in December meant we had the place to ourselves. Not that Yariel had any issue with talking about his personal life—the guy was an open book.

He gave me a look like I wasn't going to love what he had to say. "Wasn't the reason you broke up last time related to you being an asshole about how much she worked?"

I gritted my teeth as I positioned him on the machine again and worked on supporting his back as he pulled on the thing. "That's a pretty short version of the events, but yes," I said testily. "She almost got shot on the job and had been getting three hours of sleep for weeks, and when I told her I was worried about her she decided I had something against her being a cop."

Yariel took his time on his answer. I knew that he and his boyfriend had their struggles when it came his job and how all-consuming it was. Dating a professional athlete was no joke, at best you came a close second in the priorities list. He flashed those light hazel eyes at me before finally opening his mouth. "But you do have something against her job."

Damn, I didn't know why I thought this fucker would go any easier on me than the guys. "It's not that I have something against it, I just have feelings about it."

He gave me a dubious smile and turned back around

to grab the levers for the machine. "You have *baggage* around it. Your father got injured in the line of duty. You grew up seeing your mom constantly worried about him. You know that and she *certainly* knows that."

Yes, and when she told me she couldn't deal with me putting my stuff on her while she was trying to do a dangerous job and begged me to get some help I blew her off until she got tired of my bullshit.

"She does." I pressed my lips until they were a flat line, waiting for more of Yariel's hot takes.

"Did you tell her you're seeing someone?"

I nodded once, sat on the bench across from him and handed him a bottle of water, since we were clearly going to have a heart-to-heart. "I did tell her, and she was happy about it."

"Did you tell her you're seeing a therapist because after you two broke up you were a mess for months and you've been on a quest to be a better human for *her* since then?"

I pursed my mouth and looked up at the rafters in the ceiling, very much not wanting to keep talking about this.

"Nope. Because she'll think I'm just trying to earn points or something. And that's not why I'm going to Dr. Badia. At least not anymore."

Yariel cut his eyes at me like he'd been taking private lessons from Milo as he chugged water. After smacking his lips like an ass, he opened his mouth to ream me out again.

"So she's supposed to guess? She went *through it* with you, for years. Gave you a thousand chances and she's, what? Going to magically figure out you got your shit together this time? Also how do you expect her to trust you to hold it down for her with the job and be real with her when you've been hating on it forever?" He shrugged, but in his eyes I could see he was worried about me. "I mean, if I were her, I'd think that her struggles with her job were the best news ever for you."

I really needed to get some friends that lied to my ass on occasion.

I sighed and got up again, ready to get on with the session. "I'd never be happy about her being miserable at her job."

"Did you *tell her* that?"

"Damn, Yari, chill." I put my hands up, palms out. "I will. I mean true, in the past I would've just been happy to hear her wanting to do something else, but it's not even that. Those workshops and shit that she does are mad good. You should see the shit she writes on her blog and talks about on her podcast."

The last week, I'd pretty much scoured the internet for everything that Pris had ever written or recorded, and I was legit blown away. "I haven't ever heard any-one mix social justice with sex and pop culture like that. Her shit is lit. She could probably write a book, she's got so much to say."

I stopped talking and noticed Yariel was rubbing his chin like he was scheming something. "What's her web-site's name?"

"Come As You Are."

He laughed at that. "Dope. I'll take a look, if I'm into it I'll tell my agent about it. This is the kind of shit she loves."

I grinned at that and went in to give him dap. Yariel was working on a tell-all memoir about his experience as an openly gay Major League player and Dominican man, so he probably did know people who would be into Pris's stuff.

"Bet," I said clapping Yari's hand hard. "Maybe if Pris can finally see that she has a real career option on her hands she might feel differently about taking bolder steps to make it happen."

Yariel stood up and grabbed his phone from his pocket and the goofy smile that showed up on his face told me that his boyfriend had sent him a message.

"He's waiting for me at home." The way Yariel said that made me ache. That's how I felt whenever I knew that I'd get home to find Priscilla there or that she was on her way. It was how it had always been with her, and I was so close to getting that back. I could feel it. I just needed to grow a pair.

I clapped him on the shoulder and pointed at the massage table. "Let me work on your deltoids for a moment and then you can shower and go see your man. And thanks for the advice, brother. You gave me some homework."

After I'd cleaned up the machines and was heading back to the center where I had some afternoon clients, I took my phone out as I walked to my truck. I typed out a message without giving myself too much time to back out of it.

You coming by tonight?

I was thirsty and at this point it made no sense denying it. I had to tell Pris the truth. All of it. How I felt about her and all the ways I knew I'd let her down. I hadn't been the boyfriend she deserved, even at our best.

I'd relied on her to do all the emotional heavy lifting. It wasn't enough that now I knew better, I needed to tell her too. I had to stop assuming she would just "see" how I'd changed. Part of changing was being able to say shit.

When the message bubble came up, I could feel a cheesy grin just like Yariel's from earlier blooming on my own face.

Maybe. But FYI the offer of some wine and popcorn would sweeten the deal.

I tried to count to sixty before replying, but gave up after thirty.

Done.

Priscilla

"There's been a lot of phone action and smiling in your life lately." Bri's amused tone told me he meant that I'd been mostly grinning like an idiot.

I shook my head as I typed a message to Juan Pablo. Because we were on a multiple texts a day basis now.

I looked around to see if anyone was watching before I answered Bri. "It's not that deep. We're just hanging out."

Bri wasn't buying it and stretched his neck, hoping to get a look at my very NSFW text conversation. The messages between J and me had always been a bit on the filthy side, but he'd been keeping it PG, not wanting to cross boundaries. In the past few days though, things had gotten decidedly more heated.

I glanced at the message bubble, trying hard to keep from turning the phone away so Bri couldn't see what Juan Pablo would send. But I didn't want to make a big deal out of it either. So I kept my hand off the screen when the bubble popped up. As soon as I saw what he'd written I yelped and pressed the phone to my chest while Bri lost his shit next to me.

I put my finger over my lips, trying very hard to keep

a straight face. "Shhh stop, Bri." He just cackled harder. "Oh my God, why are you so loud right now?"

"Let me read it again." He was literally choking from laughing so hard, but I kind of wanted to re-read it too, and it wasn't like he didn't know what J and I were getting up to.

I looked both ways to make sure no one else was coming by then turned the phone so he could see it, and as soon as he read it, we were both howling again.

Imma make that kitty purrrrrr for me tonight.

"This is amazing, Priscilla. He and Reyes need to meet ASAP." Okay, double date suggestions were definitely dangerous territory. So I focused on responding to J's dirtbag text.

How could that bastard have me busting up and so turned on I had to literally fan myself all at the same time?

Are you using pet names for my body parts, Juan Pablo Campos?

Those three dots popped up almost immediately and when I read the message I actually giggled.

Don't matter what I call her... She always comes for me.

This light-skinned cornball was going to be my undoing. That didn't stop me from encouraging his ass.

We'll just see who's purring first.

I pocketed my phone as we were about to walk into our weekly team meeting, needing to focus on my job regardless of how entertaining I found Juan Pablo's constant bullshit. As always we were the first two to arrive. Bri had his tote bag with the usual array of goodies the Child Advocacy Center provided for the meeting. Soon we were arranging everything on the table and getting the coffeemaker started as Bri did his best to interrogate me before the rest of the people started arriving.

"So are you still doing the whole 'we're fucking and sharing our deepest darkest secrets, but not dating' thing?"

I didn't have to look at him to know he was probably barely keeping a straight face.

"When you say it like that, you make it sound really stupid." I wasn't even faking sounding hurt. I was all fucked up about it. So far, every time we hit a snag that in the past would have ended in a breakup J somehow managed to navigate it with a cool head. And that's what had me thinking about a future. About getting back together, again, which was so not where my head needed to be.

I lifted a shoulder as I fiddled with a cherry I'd grabbed from the bowl Bri had set on the table. "I just don't want to fuck with this. J's exactly like he used to be except now the sharp edges, the cluelessness, those are gone. Did I tell you about the ginger tea?"

Bri dipped his head, a lopsided smile on his lips. "Yes. He does seem like he's moved into a new phase. A man that doesn't shy away from being a nurturer, that's sexy as fuck. And not in the creepy 'let me feed you from my hands' way." Bri shuddered and I laughed. We'd had one too many conversations about shifter romances. "It sounds like he's actually paying attention to what you need."

"I know." I felt all warm inside just thinking about it. "It's been good, and honestly I just don't want to muddy the waters with anything that's going to start a disagreement or an argument."

That elicited a disapproving groan from Bri. I knew he would not be happy about me avoiding hard conversations to keep the peace, but it wasn't like that. Not really.

I raised a hand to suffuse whatever he was thinking. "Nothing's even come up. I mean stuff…about here," I said in a lower tone of voice, as I circled a finger in the air in front of me. "I've told him I'm not as happy as I used to be on the job, but that's it."

Bri gave me an assessing look and was about to say something when Joseph Sanchez, one of the child protective workers on our team, walked up, talking closely with Chase, another one of the other detectives in my precinct. I looked at Bri and raised an eyebrow in question. Chase worked in Vice, so he never came to these meetings.

As soon as Sanchez looked up, I knew something bad had happened. His eyes were bloodshot and he had huge circles under his eyes, like he'd had a very rough night. And long nights in child welfare work were usually the stuff of nightmares. Chase acknowledged me with a nod but pulled out his phone as Sanchez came over to the other side of the room to talk to Bri and me. My heart pounded as he got closer, all the warmth of the conversation from a few seconds ago replaced with dread.

"The stepdad ended up in the hospital last night. Admitted with a leg injury. Maybe a knife. We have a feeling it was her." He didn't need to explain. I knew he was talking about April.

"It was him; he was probably trying to come after her." Bri's face blanched as my voice boomed in the room. "She probably was sleeping with something to defend herself."

Sanchez looked back at Chase, whose face was unreadable, then turned to me again. "She didn't say, Priscilla. We asked her multiple times." He looked to Bri for some backup, but my friend was not going to help him out, not with this.

Usually I was more diplomatic about stuff like this. It was a team, after all, and I tried hard to not talk over people, but before Bri could even speak I was talking again. "Of course she didn't say anything. We never interviewed her alone. We never pressed the mother—or *him* for that matter."

Sanchez put both hands up, like he had no idea what I was so worked up about. When he responded it was in that "she's getting hysterical again" tone men used with me all the fucking time in the workplace. "I get you're angry, but we can't go on hunches. Not when it comes to taking kids from their homes. There was no imminent danger, and protocol is protocol."

I was about to get even louder when my lieutenant walked in. His face was grim and when I noticed Chase was trying to look everywhere but at us, my stomach sank.

As soon as the lieutenant was close enough I opened my mouth. "He needs to be arrested, lieutenant, right now. He's the one. He's *been* the one."

The lieutenant also looked like he'd been in the same clothes all night. That's when I knew they'd responded to this without notifying me at all. They'd shut me out, on purpose.

"Gutierrez, the only facts that we have right now are that the stepfather was admitted to the hospital with what seems to be a knife wound, and she's missing. The mother said she ran out of the house, and we still can't find her. He's in the hospital and not going anywhere for a couple of days." He'd shoved both his hands into his pant pockets, but he pulled them out to extend his hands in a "What are you gonna do?" gesture which had me seeing red. "He's also not talking. At this point we're not sure what happened."

I thought I'd black out from holding in everything I wanted to say, but I knew it wouldn't go well for me if I did. "Can I go talk to him?"

His expression told me what he'd say before he opened his mouth. "I put Chase on the case. He was on last night and I think he can handle it from here."

Bri spoke up as I was still trying to figure out how to protest without getting myself even deeper in the hole.

"There's the question of finding April too. It's best if Priscilla is involved. She knows her well. April likes her. Whatever is happening in that family we need to think about mitigating the trauma this child has already experienced. Adding new people is never a good approach." I loved Bri in that moment, but I knew ultimately law enforcement decided who went out and who didn't. Bri was an advocate, a social worker—he advised, but the lieutenant and the DA called the shots.

The lieutenant didn't seem too convinced, but to my surprise he conceded with a shake of his head. "Fine. But you are not to interfere with the case once the child's found."

I gritted my teeth, wanting to scream that the case was *mine*. That I'd been working it since day one. That I'd been saying this guy was suspect from day one. When I turned to look at Bri, his expression told me he was worried I'd do something to get me in trouble and fuck, I almost did. I wanted to unload on the licutenant about how shitty it was to be passed over all the time. How tired I was about all of it. But then I remembered Bri's words and that this wasn't about me, it was about April.

"I always do my job," I bit out, as Sanchez came over to talk to Bri and me. Lieutenant Dennis didn't even respond, he just turned around and walked to where Chase was standing.

I took a couple of deep breaths and once again asked myself how much longer I could do this.

When my phone buzzed, my stomach turned. I'd been messing around with J while April was hiding somewhere, probably scared for her life.

I ignored it, and turned to Bri and Sanchez. I had work to do.

Chapter Sixteen

Juan Pablo

As soon as Priscilla walked into my bedroom, I knew things were going to be intense. It was almost 1:00 a.m. and it was the first I'd heard from her since she'd cancelled on our plans to hang out a couple of nights before. She'd texted out of the blue asking if I was up, and now ten minutes later she was here.

I'd given her a key to the apartment on her last visit, so she let herself in, and found me reading in bed…waiting for her.

"Hey." She looked and sounded exhausted, and it was all I could do to keep the questions of what had been going on the last couple of days to myself.

"Hey, yourself. I'm glad you texted." I put my reader on the table on top of the stacks of books I always had there and moved to get up, but she lifted a hand, shaking her head.

"No, stay there. I'm going to shower first. Is that okay?"

I kept the eye roll to myself and gestured to the door of the en suite bathroom. "Of course. Towels are on the shelf."

I looked down and saw that she'd taken off her boots, but she was still wearing work clothes. She'd never done that before. She usually went home and changed into something more comfortable before coming over. Which meant that she'd been working until now, one in the morning on a Saturday.

Without saying anything she lifted her arms and pulled a hair tie from her wrist to put her hair in a messy bun on top of her head. Her mouth turned up as she walked into the room. "I don't suppose you have a shower cap."

I shook my head, smiling. "Nope, but I do have this," I said, smoothing a hand over the pillow she'd been using which was covered in the white satin pillowcase I'd bought after she started staying over.

She nodded again as she started taking off clothes. I sat back on the bed, with the covers off, my dick hardening with every move she made. She slid out of her navy blue slacks, revealing a triangle of black lace barely covering her. The silence in the room was charged and I wanted to get up and touch her so bad I was shaking.

I sucked in a breath as she went to pull off her turtleneck instead of her panties. Once that was off, I had a full view of all that brown skin. Her bra matched her panties, and my mouth went dry when she walked up to the bed, her hands by her side, so I could get a good look at her.

"Take them off," I demanded, practically sitting on my hands now.

She put both of hers on the edge of the bed and leaned in, without even acknowledging my request. "No. I'm giving orders tonight. I'm going to shower and when I come out, *I'm* going to fuck *you*."

My cock got so hard I was sure it would make a hole

in my briefs. I licked my dry lips, looking over at the bottom drawer of my dresser where I kept my toys and her eyes veered in the same direction. Again I made an attempt to get up from the bed, but she shook her head.

"I'll get it." She walked over to the dresser, went down on her knees so that I had a full view of her ass in that lacy thong, and pulled the drawer. She sucked in her breath at whatever she found. I did have a lot of stuff. Hell, she'd given me most of it.

She pulled out a long black velvet pouch and looked inside. "This one?" she asked as she pulled out the neon green vibrator I loved.

I couldn't talk, so I gave a sharp nod.

After a moment, she gently lifted out the harness we'd bought together years ago, and that she'd used on me dozens of times. My heart thumped in my chest with anticipation. Breaths coming in short pants. I saw her grab a cock ring and thick butt plug too before walking over.

She put the harness and the vibrator on the edge of the bed and walked on her knees to kiss me hard, tongue stealing into my mouth hot and sharp. There was an intensity to her tonight that was igniting a fire in my veins.

When she pulled back she held up the cock ring I assumed was about to go around my cock and balls.

"If I put this on you will you leave your dick alone until I'm done in the shower?"

I swallowed hard, loving and hating this game.

"Yes," I croaked, already tugging on the elastic band of my briefs.

Once my cock was out she made short work of getting the cock ring on, as I sat there with my chest heaving like I'd run for miles. She was close enough that her breasts were just inches from my mouth. But the game tonight was that she asked for what she wanted. So I waited.

"You want these?" she asked, voice full of mischief with smile to match, as she worked on taking off her bra.

"Always." She pressed in just enough that I could lap on her with my tongue, still I didn't move until she told me how she wanted me.

"Suck on my nipples, and use your teeth." Her words were sharp—an order, not a request, and fuck, I was so turned on I could barely think.

I leaned in and closed my lips around her and sucked hard. "Mm." She moaned and took my hand, placing it right over her pussy. "Do me with your fingers." Her hips were rocking back and forth, fucking my hand. And my dick was so hard I swore it would just snap off if I touched it.

"J." She hummed as I bit one nipple while pinching the other. My other hand was pressed to her heat, thumb right over her clit. Working it just like I knew she liked.

She sucked her teeth after a particularly sharp pinch and pulled back. "Enough." She was flushed, sweat beading her forehead and her eyes glassy. But I could see there was something slightly off. Something about the way she was looking at me. Like she wanted to get lost in what we were doing.

"Put that in," she said, handing me the butt plug, then pointing at the vibrator. "As soon as I come out of the shower, that cock's going in your ass."

With that she got off the bed and gave me a full view of her ass as she bent over to take her thong off. I was proud of myself for not leaning in to take a bite.

When she slammed the door of the bathroom closed

I slumped against the headboard, my dick bouncing against my belly.

Whatever was going on with Priscilla, she was going to fuck it right out of her head. If I was a better man, I'd ask her what happened, make her talk. But I was only human.

Priscilla

I let myself have another minute under the hot spray of J's shower, trying to get myself together. The last couple of days had been a blur. We'd worked around the clock on April's case without making much progress. I'd done what I could and when the lieutenant sent me home, I came here.

All I could think of on the drive in was how bad I wanted J. How I needed to feel connected to something, and he was the only thing that came to mind. And without having to tell him what I needed, he knew. J could get me out of my head and back into my body better than anything else could.

I stepped out of the shower and let myself think about him waiting for me on the other side of the door, hard and needy. He'd let me have him, play with him, give him pleasure, taste him and then he'd turn around and do the same to me. My core clenched, already wet from thinking of what was to come. I ran a towel over my hard nipples, between my legs without trying to relieve the need there. It would be so much better to wait.

Before stepping outside I tossed the towel in a basket

by the door and looked at myself in the mirror, my dark brown skin still a little damp, but clean. Soft from the warm water. I loved my body, my curves, every bump and stretch mark and I knew Juan Pablo did too. He knew this body as well as me, and I wanted to give all of it to him tonight. It felt so necessary it scared me. I'd long ago given up on thinking of him as a touchstone for my life, as something to rely on. But tonight when things had felt so heavy and so daunting I thought I might break, being here made it better. I redid the bun on my head, feeling some of the dampness from showering without a cap, and walked out.

J was standing by the bed totally naked. He could've been radiating heat. All those muscles somehow more impressive than usual tonight. J was beautiful, he'd always been beautiful. But now at thirty-five there was a strength in him that hadn't been there before.

"Are you all right?"

If Juan Pablo only knew this was when he was most dangerous to me. When he looked at me with equal parts hunger and softness.

I thought about hedging or giving him a half answer. But I knew if I didn't say something, he'd keep asking. "Later. I promise. Right now, I don't want to talk. Come here." I stepped up to where he was, wanting to be close to him, and felt the rush of blood in my temples, knowing I was about to lose myself in what Juan Pablo and I could do together.

As soon as I was within reach he wrapped his arms around me and pressed his nose to my ear. "You smell so good."

I had an arm around his neck and the other one on his ass, my fingers digging in, gripping him hard. He sucked in a breath when I tugged on the plug, almost as if remembering what I'd asked him for. What I'd said I wanted. "Are you going to let me?"

"You can have whatever you want..." he said, between nips on the skin on my shoulder and neck. My hands were busy stroking. His cock, his ass. All the places that I wanted, but when he spoke, he was demanding. "But I want to lick you first." All the air left my body. It was hard to think with his hands and mouth on me like that. Instead of answering, I stepped back and widened my legs.

"Is that an invitation?" He wasn't really asking and the way he was running his tongue over his bottom lip told me he was more than ready to take me up on it. But he didn't kneel between my thighs like I thought he would. That wasn't the game. Tonight was all about teasing, playing.

He ran his thumb over his chin and leaned back, looking at me. His eyes took me in, lingering on whatever part of my body he wanted. When he lifted his gaze to mine, his light brown eyes could've been embers.

"Where should I put my tongue first?"

My breath hitched at the question and without hesitation, I pulled his hand to my core, and used his thumb to graze right over my clit. The sensation was like an electric shock. I felt it in my whole body.

"Stop teasing, J. The more you make me wait the more I'm gonna take out on your ass later." I wasn't joking and still he laughed. Our eyes locked together as he used his fingers on me, making me tremble.

"You say it like that's supposed to dissuade me. You know I love it. Especially when right after I can bend you over and do you hard."

That fucker always got the last word. Before I could even think of a response, he was already on his knees, and lapped at me as though he had all the time in the world. I leaned on his shoulders panting, my hips thrusting into his mouth as he licked me.

"Ummm, J. Just a little more, I'm gonna come." That just made him double down, both hands tight on my ass as he pressed his face to my pussy, until he had me screaming.

"Oh my Gooooood." I threw my head back, nails clawing at J's shoulders as he tongued me through an orgasm that turned all my bones liquid. I circled my hips to get more of his mouth and fingers until I couldn't take it anymore. I stepped back and watched him run the back of his hand over his mouth looking extremely satisfied with his work.

I took one breath, and then another, to get myself together. And when my vision was fully back I pointed at the harness that he'd placed on a towel on top of the dresser.

"Put it on me."

Without taking his eyes off me, he grabbed the harness and walked over until he was right behind me. I could hear him breathing hard. He didn't waste any time reaching in front of me and getting the vibrator in place. His hard dick pressed to my back as he worked.

"You gonna do me with this cock, Priscilla?"

My gut was molten lava, and there were goose bumps all over my skin. He knew how hot this made me. How much I loved doing this with him.

Right after he finished securing the harness he reached in front of me. One hand on my breast and the other on the vibrator. He stroked that silicone cock hard, just like I usually did to him, as he tugged on the loop on my nipple. His breath hot in my ear.

"How do you want me?" He was circling his hips tight against my back and his cock was like a fire iron against my skin. It would be a miracle if one of us didn't black out after all this was done.

I pinched my other nipple and gave him more access to my neck, already so revved up I was practically incoherent. "Get on that fucking bed, Juan Pablo. Ass in the air. Now." I growled that last part and the motherfucker laughed. But within seconds he was on the bed, and fuck, the arch of his back.

I could write sonnets to the curve of Juan Pablo's ass. The way his spine dipped, and all that caramel skin. It made all the air escape out of my lungs.

I got on the bed after him and ran my hands over those wide shoulders and narrow waist.

"Stop teasing me, Priscilla." He was hissing, ready to get things going, but I was in the mood to stretch it out. So I teased him, tapping on the end of the plug, making him yelp. I pressed my chest to his back until my mouth was against his ear. But before I asked, I brought a hand to stroke his cock. "How bad do you want it?" He bucked so hard he almost threw me off, and I laughed.

"You know how bad, dammit, Pris. Give it to me." I could feel how hard he was gritting his teeth, his body taut with want. It was a heady thing the way J and I could be together. No inhibition, no shame, ever.

We just asked (or begged) for what we wanted, and almost always got it. I sucked hard on his earlobe then pushed back. Still not giving him what he'd asked for, knowing how much better it would be if we waited.

"That's nice," I crowed, running a finger over his cleft.

My skin felt on fire from the moment. He was giving me something big tonight. And I needed to give it back. I squeezed some lube on the silicone toy and then slowly pulled out the plug. J's ass pushed into my touch, looking to be filled. I positioned the vibrator at his entrance and slid in as J moaned.

"More, Pris." He was propped on his hands pushing his ass back until I was all the way in.

"Gonna go hard, J."

He grunted in response and soon, we were really fucking. The slap of skin and the sounds J was making were driving me crazy. I draped myself on top of him thrusting in hard until I felt him shaking under me. I could feel him fighting hard to keep the orgasm at bay.

"I want to be inside you when I come." I was surprised he could make words, but I wasn't going to fight him on that. I carefully pulled out and quickly undid the buckle of the strap-on, as J sat on the bed. I watched as he gripped his dick hard, and rolled a condom on. His chest was dripping with sweat and he was gritting his teeth so hard I could hear them.

When he was done, he gave me that fucking smirk that made my clothes practically disintegrate from my body then made a circle with his index finger. "On your knees, Priscilla."

I leaned in just long enough to kiss him hard, our tongues tangling roughly. When I pulled back I huffed, feigning annoyance. "You're lucky that pegging you puts me in a malleable mood."

His circled his finger around again, that smirk still fixed on his lips. "You love getting done like this."

He knew that for a fact, so I wasn't going to argue. As soon as I turned around I felt him shift, his damp skin touching mine. He ran a hand over my back, then smacked my ass hard. Dick right where I needed it. He teased my clit as I tried to get him inside.

"Come on, J. I know you wanna come." I was begging and didn't really care.

Without a word he slid in and soon we were rocking hard against each other. My tits bouncing under me as J gripped my hips and thrust into me. "Mueve ese culo, Priscilla." He grunted hard and slapped my ass.

"Fuck, J, I'm so close."

He was past words and all communication came in either grunts or growls as he fucked me into a frenzy. With one hand he started working my clit as he pounded me. "Oh God. Don't stop. Just…like that." My orgasm came out of nowhere and it knocked the air out of me. I dropped my arms as J thrust into me a couple more times. His face pressed to mine.

"This is so good." I felt him seize up behind me and the condom fill, as he flopped on top of me. After we'd finally caught our breaths, J carefully pulled out of me and got up on what looked like very wobbly legs to get a towel from the bathroom.

My mind felt empty and my body was throbbing in the best way possible. This had been exactly what I needed. The fact that everything else about today had been an utter disaster, just a dull nagging on the edge of my brain.

J handed me the warm wet cloth and got back in bed with me.

"So now that we've fucked that mood out of you, do you want to tell me what's going on?" The concern I'd seen in his eyes was clear when he spoke. He gave me a lopsided smile as he put an arm around me, his skin still a little clammy form the exertions of the past hour.

To my utter surprise, when I opened my mouth, I heard myself saying *yes*.

Chapter Seventeen

Juan Pablo

"I don't want you to tell me how to fix any of this. I just want to vent, okay?" I nodded, hearing the reluctance in Priscilla's voice. Whatever it was, it had her twisted in knots.

"I promise, I won't mansplain or interrupt with advice unless you explicitly request it," I assured her and shifted again, so that her head was on my chest.

My limbs still felt like jelly and my head was throbbing—fuck I was probably dehydrated. When Pris and I went hard like that, it took me a minute to recover. But I felt good. Not just about the obviously bomb sex we'd just had, but because Pris had come to me after what was clearly a hard day.

I grabbed a water bottle from the side of the bed and drank deeply then passed it to her. "Shit, Priscilla, you wore me out, ma." I wasn't even gonna apologize for calling her that. Thankfully, like me, she seemed to also think that we were past trying to pretend we weren't back to being fully in each other's lives. That's how it was with us, being together had always felt easier than being apart.

"I got taken off one of my cases." She sighed, but instead of pulling back, as she usually would whenever she was upset, she pressed closer. Her mouth against my neck while she talked. "You know I can't give you any details, but it's one of my kid cases and it's a fucking shit show. I've been making noise about how we've handled it from the beginning." Her voice was tight, but it wasn't just frustration. Whatever had happened was worrying her, which explained the intensity of the last hour.

"And you weren't getting a lot of support?" I tried to keep my voice as low as possible, because this, Priscilla telling me about her job issues, like in detail, was practically unheard of. Even a hint of judgement would shut her down on me.

She took her time to answer, her lips pressed to my neck. My heart fluttered in my chest, as I lay there with her. So fucking happy I could cry from having this again. "It's not even about support, they just weren't listening. I mean, some people were. Bri and I came to the same conclusions and were trying to talk sense into the rest of the team from day one, but people didn't want to push. The CPS worker is good, but again was not taking the time to look at the big picture. Bottom line, we fucked up and now this kid is going to pay for it." Her voice shook on that last part and I turned my head, nuzzling her neck. Kissed her cheek and then her mouth.

"I'm sorry." I didn't want to offer solutions, or minimize what clearly was a fucked-up situation. And what else was there to say? There wasn't a single pep talk that would make this shit any easier on her.

She kissed me back, her nails raking the back of my head, as she slid her tongue into my mouth. It was a long kiss, and I know she was using it as a distraction, but I'd never been strong enough to deny her. We separated reluctantly and she went back to talking.

"I'm pissed that they didn't listen to me. That this kid had to be in a horrible situation for weeks more than she should've been, when we could have removed her from that. But mostly, I feel like I'm just a cog in a machine." She exhaled, and when she spoke again she sounded small and really fucking tired. "It's sort of always been like this in some ways, so it's nothing new. It's the nature of the job. We can't fix everything. I don't know why it makes a difference now, but it does. It's just I can't shake this feeling that me being there doesn't even matter, and that scares me. I don't want something happening to someone on my watch because I was too burned out to do my job."

I scoffed at that, because no matter how I felt about Priscilla's job, she was a damn good cop. I sat up shaking my head and pulled her up so that we were sitting face-to-face. "You would never do that. You'd get out first." And I don't know if it was the endorphins still running through my veins or if it was how sad she looked, but before I could talk my dumb ass out of it, I was trying to talk her into staying in the job. "There's not a better detective in the NYPD than you. Your lieutenant is a fool if he doesn't know that."

The side of her mouth turned up a bit and she shook her head like I was talking crazy. "I know you're not trying to get in my pants again, because my lady parts are on recess until morning, *at least*." She whirled fingers in the general direction of my crotch, a doubtful expression on her face. "And I know you're going to need some rest."

"Hey," I balked. "I just sexed you up for like a full hour. I am not getting the credit I deserve."

She threw her hands up and then gestured toward her "lady parts."

"I just said you took me out of commission until morning. What do you want? To see me with a limp?"

I busted up at that and soon we were both giggling until we ended lying down on our sides. I ran a finger over her forehead where a frizzy curl had escaped the bun on her head. "I'm not trying to talk you into or out of anything. I just want to be here for you."

"I know. Thank you." She pressed her lips to mine in a gentle kiss, her eyes still sad when we separated.

I thought about my conversation with Yariel, about his text from yesterday saying his agent had read Pris's blog and loved it. That she wanted to meet her, and I dearly wished I could hand her this new possibility. But after tonight, and hearing how much she needed to feel in control of her life, I knew I'd overstepped. I'd been promising her that I'd changed. That I wouldn't make the same mistakes of the past, and yet I'd gone ahead and blabbed to Yari with the intention of fixing things for her. So, I could present her this neatly packaged new career, when she was still grieving the fact that the one she'd made for herself no longer fit her and ruin everything we'd manage to rebuild. Or I could keep my mouth shut. So I said nothing and laid there dying inside while I watched her struggle.

"We can't be fucking around at that cabin." Her words pulled me out of my troubled thoughts and it took me a moment to figure out what she was saying.

"The cabin" was Easton's family lake house. Some kind of mansion Upstate we were all invited to for a couple of days next week, after Christmas. The whole crew would be there and that meant we would be the only two who were not paired off. And because our friends were meddling assholes, I knew she'd want to keep whatever it was that we were doing under wraps. Hell, I was kind of glad that we wouldn't have to deal with the twenty questions from our friends. Still it stung to hear that she didn't want them to know.

I nodded, as I worked on unclenching my jaw, so I could say something. "The last thing I want is being stuck in a house with Camilo all up my ass about my sex life."

She twisted her mouth, trying not to laugh at my very poor choice of words. But when she spoke she sounded better. "I'm going up to Ithaca tomorrow and will drive to the cabin from there."

"P and Easton are coming down to Odette's for Christmas Eve, so I'm going up with them. Can I catch a ride home with you?" I was being fresh, but there was no way I was blowing a chance to drive down together. Especially not after two full days of having to keep my hands and my dick to myself.

She nodded and burrowed into me with a contented sigh. "Let's sleep, Juan Pablo."

I wished I could tell Pris how much more I wanted with her. But I didn't need to add my own shit to everything she was already dealing with. So instead I reached over and turned off the lamp by the bed and gathered her tightly to me. This wasn't perfect, not by a long shot. But it was what I could have right now, and I would take it.

Chapter Eighteen

Juan Pablo

We got to Easton's family mountain lodge in the Adirondacks after dark, and there were already some cars in the driveway. The plan was still for me to get a ride back with Priscilla, since Camilo and Tom, the other pair that lived in the city, were taking a private flight out of Rochester straight to DR for New Year's. Because that was how bougie that little fucker was these days.

I saw Nesto and Jude's truck and Tom and Milo's Range Rover. Pris's car was nowhere to be seen, but I didn't want to act all thirsty again. We'd said we'd keep things casual and I didn't want to assume anything and fuck with our vibe. Instead I decided to spend some time busting Patrice's balls for hooking up with the most eligible bachelor in Upstate New York.

"Damn, P, this place is nice, bruh." I could see Easton smiling in the driver's seat as he eased into an empty spot in the enormous circular driveway. The lodge was pretty awesome. Up by Lake George and nestled in a copse of huge pine trees. It looked like a legit log home, but I assumed it was mad fancy inside. "How big is this place, Easton?"

Easton turned around to look at me, but not before he stretched to give P a hard kiss on the mouth. Then he beamed that megawatt smile my way. Dude was always happy as hell.

"Oh it's pretty big, my whole family comes here at least once a year." He smiled then and leaned over again to kiss P a second time, because one of the many changes love had made in my friend was that he no longer cared about PDA. Nope. Patrice would show his man some love anytime, anywhere.

I wasn't jealous.

"I usually only stay for one night, but Patrice was my plus one this year when we came up for Thanksgiving." The smile he gave my friend when he said that was so full of love, I was not surprised to see him practically melt from it. Before they pulled apart yet again I heard him whisper, "Always, bébé."

Jesus, we'd be rolling deep with the love fest for the next couple of days. I'd probably have to choke out my dick just to make it through dinner with the way these fuckers were dolling out the PDA. But I wasn't going to harsh their buzz. Just because everyone was coupled off and living the #relationshipgoals dream didn't mean I had to be a Bitter Becky.

"So you were saying?" I asked pointedly, as they sat in the car literally rubbing noses. I wasn't trying to sit here for another hour watching these two make out.

Easton snapped to attention, an apologetic smile on his lips. "Sorry, right. There are four bedrooms. So you and Pris will have to share one."

That little grin didn't look remotely remorseful and I should've seen this bullshit coming. They all had a hard-on for Pris and I to get back together—just as bad, or worse, than our parents did.

I didn't twist my mouth, but only because I wasn't going to get rude with the host. "Uh huh."

Right as we were getting out the car I saw headlights coming up the driveway. When it passed us, I saw Pris's serious profile as she carefully navigated the snowy terrain and parked right behind us. We made quick work of getting out of the car, our bags from the back, and met Pris at the stairs going up to the house's front porch. We did the mandatory round of hugs and kisses and I tried really hard not to stare at her ass in the leggings she was wearing.

She looked around at the well-lit wooden porch and the comfortable looking rocking chairs smiling. "Damn it's been a minute since I've been up here. I think the last time was that New Year's Eve a couple of years ago."

Easton smiled wide and nodded. "That's right. It was after the hottest summer ever." That was said with a suggestive smile directed at Patrice. Meanwhile my friend cheesed at his boyfriend like he'd hung the moon.

Pris and I turned to each other and made gagging noises as we walked up the few stairs to the entrance. I tried no to pout at the fact that I didn't get to kiss her like that. That I wanted to let her know that I'd missed her in the two days since I'd seen her. That I couldn't stop thinking about her, worrying about her job. That she was back to being the center of everything for me. I couldn't do or say any of it. That was the agreement.

I sighed as we got to the door, and when I looked at her I was relieved to at least see that her eyes looked a little regretful too. But then she pointed at the big picture window and we both smiled at the scene. Inside we could Milo curled up on one of the couches in front of the gigantic fireplace. Jude was arranging a charcuterie platter on the equally gigantic coffee table, and the smells coming from inside meant that Nesto was doing his thing in the kitchen.

Pris opened the door and hollered inside, "Feliz Navidad, mi gente!" Patrice and Easton were right behind us and soon we were all bickering and laughing. It had been a while since we'd been together like this. These next couple of days would be nothing but relaxation, and I couldn't fucking wait.

"Patrice, why didn't you tell me there was a hot tub?" Milo of course had to get himself whipped up before we even had a chance to put our bags down. "We didn't bring our suits and I'm never going to convince Tom to go skinny dipping with the rest of you here."

Tom made his way to us with the ever-present smile he had whenever his man was around, and wrapped his arms tightly around Milo. "I thought you got enough of that on the honeymoon?"

Milo scoffed at that as if it was the most absurd thing he'd ever heard. "Enough of easy access to your dick? Right, like that's ever going to happen!" We all rolled our eyes as Milo wiggled in Tom's arms, but for me there was that ache again there too.

I needed to quit that shit and be grateful for what I did have. For the next few days I was going to enjoy my friends and be glad that Priscilla and I were at least back to being able to vacation together.

I should've known our nosy ass friends wouldn't let me have a moment of peace with my damn thoughts without meddling.

"Pris, why don't you show Juanpa to the room. It's

the one we usually stay in." Easton was getting real slick these days, but if Pris was put out she didn't say anything. She just grabbed her bag and with a small smile waved toward the stairs. I winked as the others shuffled around getting settled in.

"Lead the way."

I tried very hard not to ogle her ass while we ascended the stairs to our room, but it was not easy when it was only a few inches from my face. I had never *ever* wanted to take a bite out of something so bad. My throat was bone dry just looking at it. I tried to mask the groan that escaped my throat, but Pris was no fool.

"Are your eyes crossed yet, Juan Pablo?"

At any other time just the hint that she was flirting with me would've had me running with it. But for the first time in such a long time we were in a good place, and I was loathe to mess with that. So instead of making a lascivious comment or joking around, I cleared my throat, told my dick to calm down, and changed the topic.

"The view's pretty spectacular from up here," I said truthfully, as I stared out the giant window of the staircase. As we made it to the landing Pris waited for me, looking as if she was trying to figure out what I was doing. I mentally wished her luck. Because other than the fact that I didn't want to ruin the vibe she and I had going, I wasn't sure of much else.

That wasn't true either. I was sure about *her*. About the friendship we'd been building back up for the past few weeks. Because that's what was different this time. It felt like I'd rediscovered Priscilla. Not as the no-nonsense girl I feel in love with a million years ago, but as a woman who like me, was trying hard to figure out what was next. What fit her *now* instead of trying to cram herself into the mold she dreamed up before she really knew who she was.

"Let's put our stuff away. Camilo must have a mimosa with my name on it downstairs."

I let her guide me into the spacious room we were going to share in silence and placed my duffel by one of the beds. I sank into the comfortable mattress while Pris did the same on the other one. Like the staircase, the room had a large window overlooking the evergreen forest surrounding the house. Even though it was dark, we could still see the snow-covered trees around the house. I smiled as I listened to our friends moving around below us.

The drive up had been pleasant, but we'd taken off early enough that I was feeling like I could drift off into a nap, but then I remembered something important to ask her. "Any news on your case?"

When I turned my head, Pris's face didn't look like she was enjoying coming up with an answer to my question. "No news worth talking about."

She twisted her mouth to the side as she copied my position on the other bed. She looked tired and more than a little frustrated as she thought about whatever it was that was happening at work. "I'm off the case. So I'm not in the loop. As far as I know, the child is in a safe place. No disclosure yet." She shook her head and sighed.

"I'm so tired, J. You'd think that after twelve years into this job there would be some fucking headway, some progress around this shit. But at times like this it feels like it's the same old thing. We should've never let this situation go on in that home as long as it has."

I had some of the details for the case, but not all, so

I was trying to figure it out. "You think the parents had something to do with it?"

She shrugged and almost instinctively picked up her work phone, looked at the screen then settled it down again under her pillow. "It's hard to say. On one end they seem supportive, but we know enough about grooming to know a kid could lie to protect an abuser." She shut her eyes tight and blew out a harsh breath. "But at the end of the day, I don't care who it is. If an eleven-year-old gets pregnant, then fuck, someone needs to get arrested, because at the very least the negligence was criminal. Even if she lost the baby."

These were the moments when I usually was flooded with feelings of guilt, sympathy and admiration for Priscilla. She had paid more than her share of dues and seen more than anyone ever should, and she could still be affected by the cases. I wondered if I would've gone into the force if I'd have lasted half as long as she had. A few years ago a thought like that would've made me resentful. I'd focus on my own guilt over going back on my promise to join with her, and would've said something shitty or dismissive instead of seeing how fucked up she was about this.

"And talking to your captain won't help."

She shook her head. "I don't want to go over the lieutenant's head. He's already frustrated with me about this case. And at the end of the day, now that she's had a miscarriage, the whole thing has gone to a weird gray zone."

She looked so tired and it was taking all I had not to go over there and offer to give her a massage or just call up her captain and get this sorted out for her. But I knew if I wanted to stay in Priscilla's life, the first rule was: no fighting her battles for her. I'd fucked up when I got Yari involved, and I'd been dodging him for a week already. He'd been texting again asking me if I'd talked to Pris. While I sat there feeling guilty as fuck Camilo burst into the room like the five-foot-eight pain in the ass he was.

"Well, this is cozy," he said, as he sauntered in with two mimosas in his hands. He sat on the edge of Pris's bed and held out the glass.

"Sit up, ma. I'm so happy I finally got my bubbly buddy." He looked over to me and smiled, then hollered downstairs. "Papi, J's up here!" He handed the wineglass to Pris who took it from him like it was full of the elixir of life while Milo primly crossed his legs and tipped his head toward the door. "Tom brought a bottle of that rum you both like. He poured you a glass."

I smiled at that, rubbing my hands together. "My man, always holding it down. But it still creeps me out when you call him daddy."

He sipped from his glass and raised an eyebrow while Pris cackled next to him. "It's cute that you think I'd care." He raised a shoulder, and took a long sip of his drink, smiling as we listened to Tom coming up the stairs. "He likes it and it gets me laid often. So it's not going away anytime soon. Hey, babe."

Pris and I both turned to find Tom grinning in Milo's direction. He'd probably heard everything and like he did with everything regarding Camilo, found it utterly adorable.

"What's going on?" Tom asked us as he passed me my glass and sat on the armchair by the foot of the bed. To my surprise Priscilla sat up and with her eyes closed did something she rarely ever did—she opened up.

Priscilla

I don't know if it was the light snow on the window or the small fireplace crackling in our room, or the earlier conversation with J that made me feel like it was safe to share some of what was going on with me. I mean if I couldn't do it with these guys who could I do it with?

I took a sip from my mimosa and patted Camilo's shoulder. "I'm sort of struggling with my job." I sighed, hating to feel like I was whining, but grateful that I had a captive and sympathetic audience. "My lieutenant is being an asshole."

"Oh no, babe, that sucks. You were so hopeful this precinct would be better." Camilo's eyes were full of worry and he immediately went full social worker on me. "Is it just a temporary thing? Any chance you can be assigned to another lieutenant?"

I shook my head, wondering if spilling my guts about this was the best idea. "Not right now. I've only been there a year, and it wouldn't look good." I slumped against the headboard and took another large gulp from my now almost empty glass. "Jumping from precinct to precinct is not a good look. So, I need to ride this out and hope things change. And not by me getting demoted."

Milo's stank face, as always, was just on this side of over the top. "You do such good work and you know I live for cops who actually understand systemic oppression, but, hon, have you ever thought about doing the side hustle full time?"

I very discreetly directed my gaze to Juan Pablo and saw him perk up as if his antennas were getting pinged. I did give him credit for not interjecting. Because he looked like a chipmunk with this cheeks full of nuts right now, and still held his opinion all the way in. I almost laughed at how hard he was concentrating on what Camilo was saying. It was like he was almost trying to give him talking points by telepathy.

And usually I'd hedge about stuff like this, especially when Nesto and Jude walked into the room and settled on the little love seat by the fireplace. Not a second later Patrice and Easton came in and sat on the bed with J. It seemed like we were in for a kiki like the old days and I was on the hook for the first round of true confessions. The thing was, I wanted to say it—talk about this stuff with my friends.

I sat up straighter and bent my knees in front of me until I could cross my arms around them. They were all waiting to hear, not telling me what to do, or talking over me.

"It's not that I haven't thought about it. I love it, you know that, Milo. But the risk of leaving a job with security to try this out, it scares me. For what I envision I'd need a storefront with a studio space, and there is no way I can find that in the city for a price I can pay," I said, feeling discouraged. "I want to have a place open to the public for classes and workshops. And the blog and podcast seem to be doing well, but I don't know if people would actually be interested in my stuff for the long run." There were various huffs and puffs coming from every direction and Juanpa in particular looked like he was going to burst. But to my surprise, the one who spoke up first was Tom.

"If you're serious about a storefront let me know. My business partners and I bought a building on Lenox Avenue we're rehabbing with the intention of selecting some nonprofits or minority-owned businesses to operate there. We're planning to go through a committee for the selection process." He looked over at Milo and smiled with that besotted smile he always had for him. "But you would come pre-approved, of course. Camilo is a devoted follower of your podcast and what we want are businesses or agencies that are bringing something to the community that wasn't there before. People with missions that will enrich the lives of those who've been there for generations. Consider it a formal offer." The last part was delivered with a kind smile, and then a blush after Camilo gave him a loud kiss on the lips.

My heart skipped a beat at the possibility. At the idea that if I wanted it, I could have a space to give my business a serious try. To finally explore this dream I'd had burning in me for a while now. But just under that flame of hope was very real fear. That I'd let down my parents or worry or *embarrass them*. Still, it was undeniable that I wanted it. That the offer Tom was so casually making felt like it could alter my life forever. Fill a space that was growing emptier by the day.

I looked at Easton, whose intense gaze told me that like J he wanted to say more, to push me to grab this chance. But being a cop had been my dream, always, and I didn't know how to feel about the relief rocking just from the possibility of being able to do something else. I wondered if it was me, if I was not suited for it all along. If instead of stubbornly refusing to consider anything else if I would've been better off going in another direction like Juan Pablo did.

If I'd wasted all these years.

I was a mess of conflicting feelings, but for the first time in a really long time I felt almost brave enough to admit that I didn't know what I was doing. That I felt lost. I turned to look at J, whose brown eyes where trained on me like he was trying to decipher what was going through my head word by word. As if it meant everything for him to be able to do so. I let myself feel the love these men had for me. I took it in even though right now I couldn't reach for what they were offering.

"Thanks, Tom. I'll keep it in mind. I'm not ready to give up on the NYPD yet. I practically start shaking just at the thought of not being a cop anymore. It's who I am."

Multiple protests cropped up at once and Easton actually stood up. "Pris, you know that's not true." I had to laugh at my friend's obvious affront.

"Okay, East, chill," I said, handing him over my glass. "Let's get some more wine and take this party downstairs, because even if I love the attention of seven gorgeous men on me, I am not so into this 'True Confessions' moment. Thank you again, Tom, truly."

I pointed a finger at Camilo for the next part. "And that's not a greenlight for you to try and wear me down until I say yes either."

He clutched a hand to his chest like the little drama

queen he was. "What me? When have I ever told people what to do with their life?"

That finally got the tension to break as everyone proceeded to laugh their ass off at Camilo's shamelessness. Soon they were all getting up and walking out of the crowded bedroom and headed downstairs. When it was just J and I left in the room I felt his hand on my shoulder and the slightest brush of a beard on the nape of my neck. With my hair up in a pineapple the bare skin there tingled with Juan Pablo so close. There were a thousand reasons for me not to lean into him or to tighten the arms by my hip around my waist, but I couldn't come up with a single one.

"You all right?" The huskiness in his voice eased me, and I wanted to rest my head there forever.

"I am. I'm good," I said and meant it. I closed my eyes, expecting him to say something that would make things weird or would make me pull away. In the past he would've pushed against me tighter, pressed his lips to my ears, making me shiver. I almost hoped he would, but I also trusted he wouldn't cross the boundary, or any other, I asked of him.

He just swayed with me for a moment. Letting the conversation and the lifeline Tom had so casually handed over sink in. He knew there was no way I could talk about it. That there was no decision I could make right now. But knowing that my friends had my back meant something.

And seeing J hold back from trying to fix things was the most meaningful of all.

Chapter Nineteen

Juan Pablo

"Did Milo really just leave in the middle of Cards Against Humanity to go fuck Tom?" I didn't even know why I sounded surprised anymore. "Y'all are really doing the most. Damn. Nesto, leave Jude alone, he's trying to eat some popcorn." I was whining. But I was horny, tired and I'd been drinking, so my ashy ass friends were just gonna have to hear me complain.

"Juan Pablo, stop!" Pris was on the other side of the couch I was lounging in, with her feet on my thighs, and she sounded more amused than pissed at my litany of complaints, so maybe I'd just keep doing it. She'd been rubbing on my legs and generally getting me revved up all night. My poor dick was in agony. The past two days we'd been back to the times when we'd be at my parents' basement, trying not to get caught.

She winked at me as she gestured to Nesto for some more wine. "Jude's learned to live with the constant pawing." Jude smiled, his blond hair mussed from all the touching Nesto was doing.

"Oh I'm used to it, I also really enjoy it, so don't discourage him." I looked at Pris when he said that, searching for her reaction. When our eyes met I didn't find the regret in her eyes I'd been expecting, instead there was a spark there. Something good and hopeful, and I was sorry for not being able to act on it.

After another minute Patrice and Easton excused themselves, claiming exhaustion even though the fire in both their eyes indicated that sleep was not on the agenda anytime soon.

Pris and I were left sitting in front of the fireplace and from the tension in her shoulders I knew I was not the only one feeling more than a little flustered. Desperate for some kind of distraction I blurted out the one thing I knew would get both our minds off fucking in a hot second. "So what did you think about Tom's offer?"

She shrugged and ran a finger over the rim of her glass. "I mean what is there to think? It's a typical 'Tom is a Unicorn' type of thing."

I laughed at how deadpan she said that, but waited quietly because I knew she had something else in there. "I can't make those decisions right now. I have obligations. I have cases. I have bills to pay. Chasing some dream of teaching people how to love themselves more may never be a way to make a living and I don't know that I'm brave enough to take that risk, J." She looked crestfallen, ashamed to be admitting she was scared. I wanted to hold her, but I knew that doing that would only shut her down.

When she opened her mouth again her words were soft and just a little bit tentative, like she couldn't believe that she was saying them herself. "I'm discovering that there's so much in our parents' dreams that are tied to our own it's hard sometimes to untangle it all. And their dreams are always safe, doctor, lawyer, cop. The dreams of security, stability."

Her smile was bleak, almost resigned. It was an expression I'd never seen before. And that was when I really understood that Priscilla and I weren't those kids who fell in love anymore. We weren't even the people who broke up a few years later. No, we were a man and a woman who had lived and struggled, and paid a cost to dream our dreams.

When she opened her mouth again, it was like she was summoning the words from a place deep inside where they'd been hiding for a hundred years. "That dream of legitimacy, sometimes we have to be the ones who fulfill it for them. Papi wished more than anything to serve this country and for years he wasn't able to. Once he could, he was too old and I wanted to do it for him."

I took a small sip from the Zacapa I'd been nursing and laid my head against the armrest. "I know what you mean. My old man, all he wanted was to leave a legacy, to claim a little piece of the American story for him and his family. And I—"

I almost shied away from saying what was on my mind, because I feared it would put us back in a bad place. Bring memories of some of the worst moments we'd had into the room and I didn't want anything but her and I here. Still I said it. "I didn't give him the thing I knew would have made him feel like he had roots." I didn't need to tell her what that was. "I think that's why I was always so defensive whenever it came up between us. Why I could be such an asshole about your job. It took me a while, but I see now that my negativity was more tied to my own shit than anything else."

I didn't know why I'd said that, but once I did and

saw Priscilla's face relax I knew it had been the right thing to say.

She was thoughtful, but her mood had shifted; she wanted to say whatever was on her mind. "From the first day of the training academy I knew I'd have to work hard to stay in the force for the long haul. Not just because of the obvious misogynistic and racist bullshit that I've always had to deal with, but because there was something about the job and the work that didn't always fit with me." She closed her eyes and I knew she was searching for a gentle way to say whatever she was thinking. I knew despite the struggles she still believed in what she did. "Don't get me wrong, I think there are a lot more good cops than bad ones, and there are some fucking rock stars in the force, who believe in this work, in getting better. I just think I'm more of a community builder. I like a level playing field. Sitting with people and helping them figure things out."

I could see her doing that. Getting on her podcast and breaking shit down for folks, bringing in guests and getting down to the nitty gritty with them.

"You're good at that. You've been amazing at the workshops. We've got a waiting list."

She laughed at that, and I could tell how happy she was about how much people loved her classes. "I'm glad I can fulfill that need. Especially in our community. We've had our heads filled with way too much bullshit about what sex should look and feel like for black and brown bodies and if I can help get people at least thinking about things differently, or a little curious, then I will have done my job."

It was on the tip of my tongue to point out that with the demand at the center, how well her podcast was going and the fact that Tom had all but offered her a place where she could open her store, it seemed like trying this out for real was not as far-fetched as she'd thought even just a few weeks ago. But of course our fucking friends had to be obnoxious.

At first I couldn't tell what the thumping was, since I was so focused on figuring out how to push Pris a little on Tom's offer, but when she started busting up and looking at the ceiling I finally tuned into the noise.

"Sounds like the honeymoon is still going strong." She said it between gasps because she could barely speak from laughing. I sucked my teeth and jumped up from the couch. Turned around as moans started coming from the other side of the wall behind the couch.

"What the fuck?" By this point I was starting to fear that Pris was going to hurt herself from cackling. But the moaning together with the thumping from upstairs was giving me the giggles too. Our friends were horny freaks.

Pris had put down her wineglass so she could clutch her stomach and was shaking so hard the pineapple on her head was bobbing like crazy. "Oh shit, that's Patrice and Easton. They have the big downstairs suite." She pointed at the wall as another long moan came through the wall.

"What the hell is Patrice doing to him? He sounds like he's getting skinned!" I knew I sounded like a baby, but now that the shock had worn off I was getting a little bit turned on with all the porn sounds coming from every bedroom in the house.

Pris finally stood up, a silly grin still pasted on her face. "I don't know if *skinned* is the right verb, but whatever it is, sounds like Patrice is doing a great job." She tugged on my hand as I stood there, half horny as fuck and half mortified. "Let's go to our room. We can watch *Stranger Things* or some other scary show that will calm you down."

"I'm calm!" Wow my voice was super high and now she was looking at the tent in my pants. But I'd promised myself I was not going to be the one to break our no-hookup agreement. My heart sped up from embarrassment, but also because I caught the exact moment when she realized she wasn't as unaffected by the fact that we were basically engulfed in fucking noises. Her eyes ran up and down my front and stopped for a couple of heartbeats on what I knew was a raging erection. I had to fight the urge to smack my dick down. The only thing that kept me from doing it was the knowledge that I'd probably pass out from the pain.

I wasn't trying to be any kind of hero right now.

And damn the way Priscilla was licking her lips had me feeling some type of way.

Fuck. I wanted her.

She went from looking goofy to flushed and, oh shit, this wasn't good. I almost tripped trying to get to the stairs, and the moment I started moving she jumped back like I'd shocked her. I pointed in the direction of the stairs. "Uh, I need to shower." She nodded slowly and pointed to the kitchen.

"I'm gonna tidy up here." She took off for the kitchen like a rocket and I was on my way up the stairs in a hot second. I was going to strip my dick raw in that shower as soon as I locked that door behind me.

I got to the room in two seconds flat and was skinning out of my sweats as soon as I was on the other side of the door. Motherfuckers had me acting like a thirteen-year-old.

Priscilla

I was squirming. Like my pants were on fire. We went from deep conversation, to wanting to tear each other's clothes off in the freaking family room in seconds. And the fuck fest wasn't over either. As soon as Tom and Milo stopped, Nesto and Jude picked up the relay baton and there had been nothing but Si, Papi. And Just like that, Nesto, for the last fifteen minutes. I was starting to fear that Juan Pablo had either knocked himself out in the bathroom or was going to give himself pneumonia, because there was no fucking way there was any hot water left.

"Shit." I was so turned on, but I would not succumb. No, things were going well. J was supportive and awesome and I would lie if I didn't say that I was feeling things. Things I'd thought were long gone for me. But there was a difference. J had been a friend to me in the past few weeks like he'd never been when he was my boyfriend. And I was not going to bring in our very well-intentioned, but nosy and opinionated Peanut Gallery into the mix, until I was ready. If J and I got into it tonight, not only would they most likely hear us—since these walls were apparently made of rice paper—they'd want answers for things I was still figuring out.

Still I needed to take the edge off. If J walked out of that bathroom in nothing but a towel, like I knew he fucking would, I was going to jump him.

I went to the door of the bathroom and tapped on it gently. "Hey, are you okay in there?" There was a grunt and then what sounded a lot like panting, and I could see the shadows of his feet as he approached the door.

"Hey, yeah I'm good. Just need like another five minutes."

I could make myself come in two. Good *Lord* this was ridiculous, but fuck it.

I dove into my bed and quickly got under the covers, with the sounds of Nesto and Jude's sexcapade in my ears and the image of J on the other side of that door, gripping his cock hard, pinching his nipples, and making himself come. The way he spoke when I knocked on the door, there was just a hint of tension there that I recognized all too well. And yep, I was going to do this.

With one hand I reached over for the lamp on the table between the beds and switched it off, the other I slid into my yoga pants, my breath hitching at the wetness I found there. My stomach tightened with need as I ran the pads of two fingers over my engorged clit. I was wet and ready but this didn't feel like nearly enough when J was just a few feet away.

The thought of him naked and turned on was explosive, and soon I was circling my fingers hard over my clit, my limbs and gut going liquid with the orgasm I could already feel coming. I was almost there. I cupped my breast and tweaked the nipple, already panting. My mind flooded with Juanpa doing this instead of me. Like on the beach in the DR. How he grinned and looked up at me. His lips glistening from my heat. The way he licked them after, like tasting me was the greatest delicacy in the world. I arched my back as another shot of pleasure zinged every nerve in my spine and tried hard not to cry out. The muffled groan that came from the bathroom, just as my orgasm was edging out all rational thought was the last straw and soon I was clutching a hand to my chest as an orgasm washed over me.

Just as I was done getting myself together again the door of the bathroom cracked open and as suspected Juan Pablo strolled out in nothing but a towel. I almost laughed at just how accurate my prediction had been.

He was busy running a boar bristle brush on his fade and the way his bicep tightened made me want to jump him. He'd had his head down as he walked out, but after I turned on the small lamp by the bed, his eyes snapped up and locked with mine.

I was flushed, I knew that. And if anyone could recognize the signs of me in post-masturbatory bliss it was Juan Pablo. I didn't say anything, too distracted by the mouth-watering picture that J freshly showered made. I dropped my gaze down to the knot right over his groin, then up to that flat stomach and the tattoos that I'd seen him get over the years. There was the one on his chest that he had gotten with the guys so long ago. The little map of Puerto Rico with a heart over the spot where Aguadilla Pueblo, his father's hometown, was. He had one for his mother too, her last name in heavy black font under his collarbone. I knew that if he turned around, there would be one with the date of our first kiss. It had been a dumbass idea when we were eighteen and still the thought of him having part of our history etched on his skin made my chest flutter.

I wasn't sure what we were doing tonight or at all, but the ache between my legs was coming back with a vengeance with J flexing for me in every sense of the word. He did little circles on his scalp with the brush for a few seconds, and ran his tongue over his bottom lips. When he leaned against the doorway, eyes holding my gaze I knew we weren't playing anymore. No, this was a pre-fucking stare off and who ever broke first would be left holding the bag whenever we blew shit up.

I caved first.

"Are you all done in there?" I sounded winded, because I'd been holding in my breath to keep from jumping him.

His eyes were practically trying to pierce through my skull to figure out what was going on in there. He looked hard at me for a few seconds and then pushed himself off the door frame and stepped to the side.

"All yours." He waved his hand with a little flourish while I prayed to all the deities I knew that his towel stayed in place until I found refuge in the bathroom. I quickly got up from the bed and managed not to trip all over myself as I avoided all eye contact and was in the clear. But when I brushed past him in the doorway, the scruff of his beard made contact with my cheek as he whispered close to my ear, "I know that smell."

I gasped and clapped a hand over my mouth as I hurried to shut the door behind me. Once I was in the bathroom I leaned against the door and took three deep breaths, trying to clear my head. And the first thought I had was, *This is stupid.*

Why was I pushing J away, when it was obvious we wanted the same things?

I kept setting all these silly boundaries, not because of him, not anymore. But because of me. I felt like everything else was in a free fall, but I could control things between us. I could call the shots, set the pace, and he'd let me. He just wanted to be with me, and he was letting me define what that meant. And maybe I'd been scared to get all of him, because I knew how it hurt whenever I lost it. But wasn't I cheating myself worse with this?

Juan Pablo the boy I'd always loved, was a man I could build a life with. More confident, more open, more communicative. All the things that I'd always said I wanted from him. All the things I'd told myself a million times would make him the man of my dreams.

And I had to wonder if now I wasn't enough for him. With my hang-ups and my indecision maybe I wasn't the person *he* needed. Maybe J was better off with someone who could dock into the life he'd made. I certainly couldn't see myself trampling into that beautiful, pristine apartment with all my baggage.

But maybe those were just excuses. He wanted me, I wanted him. That was enough to start.

I pulled open the door with the intention of letting Juan Pablo know exactly what I was thinking. But as soon as I stepped into the room I him found standing there like he was still waiting for me. I took one step toward him as the towel around his waist fell to the floor in a fluffy heap.

"Did you forget something?" Everything about him in that moment was fucking devilish and exactly what I wanted.

"We have to keep quiet," I said, feigning annoyance

as I went in for a kiss. By the time I came up for breath I was half naked and tumbling to the bed with him.

We could talk later.

Chapter Twenty

Juan Pablo

We'd managed to get through the next day without any more covert masturbation episodes or our friends fucking so loudly the bears could hear them. We also managed to have extremely hot and noiseless sex, so I was counting this vacay as a win. It had been a good break but now it was time to head back to reality.

Jude and Nesto had taken off at the crack of dawn so Nes could get back to the restaurant, accompanied by Tom and Milo, who were off to the DR. Patrice and Easton were going to hole up at the cabin on their own until after New Year's, so it meant that Priscilla and I were the only two headed back to the city.

Since there was a storm warning for the afternoon, we got going after breakfast. After more hugs, we had our bags packed and were standing on the snow-dusted porch saying goodbye to Patrice and Easton who looked ready for us to go so they could get back to bed.

"Brother." I got pounded hard on the back by P. "Text us when you get off the mountain and if it starts snowing get a hotel room. Don't fuck with snowy roads, Juan Pablo." I rolled my eyes as I pulled out of Patrice's tight embrace then looked at Pris, who was mean mugging me for not taking P's advice seriously.

"Will do. If snow gets heavy we'll get a room." P still fretted about anyone getting on the road and he was especially fearful of the snow, but my reassurance seemed to relax him.

Pris gave Easton a big kiss and he squeezed her tight. "Okay, friend. I'm going to be down there in a couple of weeks. Dinner?" It sounded more like a warning than a question and the way Priscilla snapped her head made me think they were going to have a heart-to-heart she might not be fully up for.

"Yes. We'll talk." The pointed look Easton was giving her was making me very curious, but when I looked at Patrice he just shrugged, like he had no idea. It was hopeless, he wasn't ever going to tell me anything Easton didn't need me to know.

I opened the passenger door to Priscilla's Crosstrek. I didn't even pretend like she was going to let me drive.

As I slid into the seat she stared at me slack jawed. "You're not going to fight me about driving?"

I shook my head as I took my time doing my seatbelt. "Nope. Your car, you drive. But, I'm glad to take over if you get tired." I adjusted my knit cap and looked straight ahead, ignoring what I knew were stares of disbelief.

My heart thumped a little faster in my chest wondering what was going through her head. My inability to let anyone drive on the interstate if I was in a car was notorious, but giving up control was one of the things I'd been working on with my therapist.

"Wow." She sounded genuinely surprised, if only just a tiny bit suspicious. "P, it's like we're witnessing a personality transformation right before our very eyes."

Patrice, that traitorous motherfucker, just laughed, but when he spoke the affection there made it hard for me to get mad. "Nah he's still a pain in the ass."

"Priscilla, stop clowning, we're going to get stuck in the snow."

"There he is," she said, voice brimming with amusement. "I knew this had to be a momentary lapse."

I rolled my eyes without responding as she got into the car. She had her usual vacay attire for winter. Leggings, UGGs and a hoodie. She also had her short North Face on. She looked good enough to eat, and I meant that literally. It was really a miracle and a testament to her stubbornness and my therapist's skill that I hadn't blown our cover in the past two days.

Once we were out of the mountains the drive was easy. Pris had always been a careful driver, even if she had a bit of lead foot. We'd talked about our friends, how happy they all were, and even though she and I were still on shaky ground, I felt good. Hopeful. When we were getting closer to my place, I finally got the courage up to say what needed to be said.

"Pris, what are we doing?"

She didn't take her eyes of the road, but her back stiffened at my question. Like she knew it was coming and she's been bracing for it. We passed a long stretch of bare birch trees while she thought and I had to bite my tongue not to fill in the silence or worse, take it back.

Just when I thought she was going to ignore me, she finally turned her face toward me for just a second, and to my relief she was smiling.

She shook her head, her lips still turned up. "A week ago, I wasn't sure I could've told you. I would've been too in my head with all the stuff going on at work to try

and figure it out. But you know something?" I waited
for her to answer, knowing it was a rhetorical question.
"I figured something out in the last couple of days…"

Her brows furrowed like she was thinking hard on
how to say it, and my pulse raced. I could feel the blood
rushing to my head. I wasn't sure what she was thinking,
but it felt like our entire futures were riding on this moment. Like it was our final chance to make things work.

"It's fucking hard for me to be soft." She scoffed at
that, as if she was stating the obvious. "I always feel
like if I'm not showing every person in my life I have
everything handled, that I'll let them down. That I won't
be me anymore." My instinct was to tell her that wasn't
true. That no one expected her to be perfect, but I held
my tongue, because I knew in a lot of ways, it was true.

No one needed to tell Pris those things when she could
see them for herself. When growing up the only women
that looked like her on TV were tired stereotypes. She'd
been in the force for almost fifteen years and I knew how
rare it was to see women like her in leadership positions.

No matter what I said to her now, we both knew she
was right. So instead of dismissing the truth of her words,
I put my hand on her knee and tightened it. Wanting her
to know that I heard what she was saying, the burden
of carrying that. She sighed, fidgeting in the driver seat
still sparring with her thoughts. "With us, it became even
more complicated once I joined and you didn't."

"I'm sorry," I croaked.

She shook her head hard, gripping the steering wheel.
"Don't, J. Please. You don't have to do that. I know why
you didn't do it, and even if you didn't have perfectly
good reasons, you had every right to go the way that was
best for you." She waved a hand in the air, as if to redi-

rect herself back to what she'd been saying. "The reason why it was hard was because I kept telling myself I had to prove to the world I'd made the right decision. The more my own doubts crept in, the more I tried. Eventually, I was holding myself so tightly, I couldn't let anyone in."

I swallowed hard, and looked at her. "Pris, this isn't all on you. I was doing my own version of that too, and I didn't make things easier for either of us by being an ass about your job, and flying off the handle all the time." I bit my lip, and just fucking said it before I lost my nerve. "We're good together, Priscilla. Fuck, I think we're perfect. If the mind-melting sex we've been having wasn't enough."

She chuckled at that. "We are pretty good at the sex part."

I groaned and gripped my dumb dick, which got hard from just her saying the word *sex*. "We're amazing at it. I'm hard just from thinking of that shower sex from last night."

Now she was the one groaning. "Dammit, J. Don't derail us, this is a serious talk."

I threw my hands up, exasperated at myself. "Sorry! Pris, like I said before. Right now I'm willing to take whatever you're ready for. But I just need you to know that what I want is *everything*. My life is where I want it, but it's not complete, it's not really real without you. I'm not gonna say you're my soulmate because I know you have feelings about that, but I just need you to hear me say this… I love you. I have loved you since I was fourteen years old and kissed you in my Nonno's yard. And unlike before, I'm willing to put in the work to be the man you deserve. Baby, whatever you need, my body, my life. Yo soy tuyo, Priscilla."

She gasped at that last part like she'd been punched in the chest, and when she looked over at me her eyes were full of tears. I leaned over and wiped then with my thumb.

"You asshole. Why are you doing this now, when I can't do anything?"

I laughed at her rage, but the way her hand reached over to my thigh, and gently stroked, let me know we were fine.

"I got a lot going on, J. I can't seem to make any decisions lately, but you're right. We've been so good in these last few weeks. I love you." I sucked in a breath, when I heard her say it. It was weird, because we'd said it hundreds, thousands of times even. But it felt different now, after I'd lost hope I'd ever get those words from her again. She rolled her eyes at whatever face I was making, but she looked happy. "I do. I don't seem to know very much else right now, but I know that."

I wanted to say things, ask questions. I wanted to make promises and ask her to do the same, but I could wait, give her time now that we were both open to really trying.

"I'm here for whatever you need, Pris." I needed to say this. "I want us to be a partnership, a team. We've never done that, we always tried to keep our lives separate and I know part of it was us trying to avoid clashes about our careers. I didn't want you to think that I thought you needed me handling your business." I fidgeted, just a little bit freaked out about how she might react, but it was important to say this, if we didn't have that clear, we'd be doomed again. "Whatever you decide with your job, I'll support you. I just want you to be happy."

She gripped my hand hard and in a voice that was

soft, but very clear told me what I'd been needing to hear. "Okay. I want to try."

I believed her. I felt it too. We rode in comfortable silence until we saw the exit for Yonkers. Just as we were getting to the turn the light snowfall we'd had for the last few dozen miles thickened, and I turned to her. "You need to be at work tonight?" Being a detective, she was supposed to have more normal hours, but there was no such thing as nine to five for cops.

She shook her head as she took a careful turn into the Cross County Expressway. "Not until after New Year's." She perked up as though she remembered something. "Actually, do you want to come with me to Bri and Reyes's place tomorrow? They're throwing a party. You'll like them." And just like that, the doors to each other's lives were open again. I knew it wouldn't take much for us.

I grunted in approval as she slowly drove us down the snow-covered streets of Yonkers. "You gonna let me be your date?"

The smile on her lips was pure sin as she maneuvered the car. "I may let you kiss me at midnight."

"I'm in, then." She laughed at my very suggestive tone, as I looked down at my phone which had been buzzing with incoming texts. When I looked at the screen I froze. I was a message from Yariel that was either coming in at the best or worst time possible.

Yariel: Hey, Pa! Listen. Did you talk to Priscilla? My agent's hot about working with her. She's already talked to an editor at my publisher and they want to see a book proposal ASAP. If she wants to make a move, I wouldn't sleep on this. Call me anytime, Hatuey and I are around.

Come thru tomorrow if you want, we're having some people over for New Year's.

Fuck I should've never talked to Yariel. Priscilla was going to be so pissed. All the shit that I'd told her—and tried to show her for the past month—would mean nothing. But I also couldn't keep this opportunity which could literally change everything from her. Not after the offer from Tom.

I was reading the message for the third time when Priscilla's hand on my shoulder made me look up from my phone. "Hey, sorry."

"Is everything okay?" I quickly put my phone in my pocket. I needed a minute to figure out what to say.

"Yeah, everything's fine." I realized that the car had stopped and when I looked ahead, saw we were in front of my building in the guest parking. The snow was really coming down now, and I was glad we were at least off the road. "You want to come up?" She was going to kill me with those smiles.

"Yeah, I just need to—"

She never got to tell me what, because her phone rang and then everything went to hell.

Priscilla

As soon as I saw the number, I knew my night, my New Year's plans and everything else was going to be screwed. A call while I was on vacation from Sanchez, our child protective services liaison, was never ever good news.

I help up a finger at Juan Pablo who was now looking out of the car window with increasing concern. "Gutierrez."

His voice was strained, and two octaves lower than usual. "I'm calling you as a courtesy, because we have worked well together." Sanchez was never one to beat around the bush, but he sounded royally pissed. That was concerning—the guy had been at CPS for over fifteen years; he'd seen it all and was usually not one to get emotional.

"Okay," I said, and my tone must have been sharper than I was going for because J frowned at me. Sanchez and I didn't see eye to eye sometimes, but he was a good worker and if he was bringing something to me, surely there was some fuckery going on.

"The stepfather was brought in for questioning.

They're still talking to him, but it looks like they're going to let him go."

"What?" I asked, incredulously.

"She hasn't disclosed and he's not saying anything. We have nothing. At least that's what Chase is saying." His frustration was only ratcheting up my own anger. "They keep tiptoeing around it. But I think you and Bri are onto something. The home situation…something's not right there."

I breathed through my nose and reminded myself that getting agitated with J in the car was just going to mean more shit I didn't want to deal with later. "He hasn't confessed because no one thinks he did anything. That child is being abused, all the signs are there, Joseph. She had a fucking miscarriage for God's sake. She's twelve." So much for not screaming.

"I know things are definitely not right, which is why we have her with her aunt for now. But arresting someone without a confession or even a disclosure is not going to stick."

My head was pounding hard, and again I tried not to vent my frustration on Sanchez, who really was doing me a favor by looping me in. "They're not asking him the right questions. Chase doesn't work these kinds of cases. He doesn't know what he's fucking doing. They keep treating this like some kind of innocent mix-up. That man is preying on that child. Who knows for how long it's been going on?"

"We will keep our eye on him and on April. Nothing's going to happen to her. She's safe."

I was so fucking tired of all this. "We really need to re-think our definition of safety when it comes to children." Even as I said it, the frustration from earlier seemed to boil over into something dark and ugly. "I'm going over there."

As soon as I said it, J shifted in his seat, his eyes like saucers as he looked at the heavy snowfall.

"I wouldn't do that, Priscilla. You're not on this case anymore, and I won't appreciate it if you let the lieutenant know I called you about this."

That wasn't a suggestion, but I was feeling reckless and fed up. "Thanks for calling, I appreciate it."

I ended the call and turned to find Juan Pablo looking at me like I was a ticking time bomb. "Looks like I'm going to have to go in after all."

"Was that about that case you got taken off of?" I bit the inside of my cheek and stared at him as he waited for the answer he already knew.

"They have the perp there for questioning and I'm going to try to talk to him." He was not backing down from the stare down, but I wasn't either.

"But they took you off the case, it's not safe to drive and we were in the middle of something important, Priscilla."

Something about his tone hit me the wrong way and I almost snapped at him. "Juan Pablo, I have to do my job."

He didn't answer, but it was obvious he was thinking, *What job? You're off the fucking case.*

"Pris, please. I was about to tell you something. Please let them handle this, you're not even on duty."

With every word out of his mouth I got more defensive. I wanted to tell him that it was fine for him to take the day off if he needed to, but he wasn't the one with a job where you literally had lives on the line. That I couldn't just switch off my responsibilities. But I didn't,

I didn't want to be cruel or petty. And in the end he was right. This wasn't even my case anymore.

"Okay, why don't you tell me whatever you were going to say."

He looked around the car as if he was suddenly confused with what was happening. "You're not coming up?"

I sighed, pushing my head to the headrest, tired as fuck and resentful that once again what had seemed to be a perfect fucking day was now ruined with a single phone call. Because I knew this conversation would only end in a fight.

"J, please. Just tell me." I kept my eyes closed, but my lids could've been a movie screen. I could clearly see his face. Tense, his lips pursed, frustrated with me.

But there was more to his silence, whatever he was going to say worried him. "You know my friend Yariel?"

My eyes snapped open at the question, because he really thought he was slick. "You mean the shortstop you were fucking for like a whole year?"

He cleared his throat and his neck turned red, but his face stayed serious. "Yes. He's a friend. He, uh." His eyes kept looking away, and before he opened his mouth I knew things were about to get worse. J could keep it together, but when he felt against the wall, when he was desperate, his heart always was faster than his head.

"I told him about your blog and your podcast and he mentioned it to his agent." He was talking so fast I was having a hard time following, but as soon as the word *agent* left his mouth, I felt a surge of anger in the pit of my belly.

"His what?"

More fidgeting and eyes everywhere but on me. "He's writing a memoir, about coming out in the majors and his boyfriend now, their life together. He has a book deal and an agent. He said she loved your blog and your content and she wants to talk to you about a book deal, Pris."

"You did *what*?" I wasn't even pissed, I was freaked out. This felt like too much. I was okay with options, taking my time with things. But I didn't want to know this. I didn't want to have to make this decision right now.

"Pris, I didn't show anyone anything. I just mentioned to Yariel that *my friend*—" he really emphasized the word, as if to remind me who he was. What we were "—is an awesome columnist and that you're kicking ass on your podcast, and that I thought you could write a really hot book about sex, wellness from a really bomb point of view."

"I didn't need you to push me on this, J."

He pursed his lips, jaw clenched and I could see he was working hard on what to say next. He knew I fought dirty and I was in a mood where anything he said would be enough to set me off. A twisted, fucked-up part of me almost wished he'd sent something to the guy without telling me, or that he'd say something to piss me off, because that way I'd have an excuse to pop off. To tell him to get out of my car, say something ugly and end this right here.

"Morena, I'm not pushing you." That bastard knew I melted whenever he called me that. "It's just an opportunity. You don't need to do anything with it. You don't even have to call the agent. It's your call. She read your blog, listened to your podcast and loved it. I just want you to shine, and do what you love."

That should've made me happy, glad that Juan Pablo was so into this part of me. That I had his support, but it didn't. I felt stifled, my heart racing at the idea that there was a chance I could make a go of this. Because if I tried and I failed, I didn't know what I'd do.

I felt the desperation crawling up my throat. I should've told him I was scared. That this felt like too much pressure, but instead I shut down.

I gripped the steering wheel hard, my eyes focused on the snow that was somehow thicker now. "I need to go to work."

"Work?" He sounded baffled. Like he was sure he'd heard me wrong.

"I need to go to the precinct. I have responsibilities. I don't have a grandfather with property all over the Bronx, Juan Pablo." He flinched at that and I just kept going.

"I have myself and my work. If I leave the NYPD now to chase some fucking hobby because I'm unhappy at work, what will happen a year from now when it all goes south? Tell me, what?"

"It's not going to go south."

I scoffed at that, now fully invested in blowing up everything we'd managed to salvage in the last month.

"And if it takes longer to get off the ground, I am here. I am your partner, I'm on your team, Priscilla. We all are. So what if you have to lean on me for a little bit?" He tapped his shoulder and I could see that his eyes were watering. "You can lean on me. You can, I promise you."

I shook my head hard, but I wouldn't look at him. "I can't, J, I have to go."

"You're running, Priscilla. This won't work if you keep running." He sounded so defeated, and let down.

"I need to go." I was barely able to get that out. We sat there for a few breaths, then J had the last word.

"I will never stop loving you, *never*. But, Pris, I can't be with you while you hold me at arm's length. You love me, I know you do, but you won't let anyone see your wounds, mi vida. I can't stand watching you suffer and not do anything. I don't want to take care of you. I want to love you. To live with you. To be your man, Pris, and to do that, you have to let me in."

After that he opened the door, the wind howling as he jumped out. "Please be careful, and text me just to let me know you made it home okay. I hope it works out at the precinct." With that he stepped out and I heard him get his bag out of the back before heading into his building.

I watched him until he went inside, and after rubbing the tears out of my eyes, I pulled the car out of the parking lot and into the snowy street.

I felt as desolate, as cold and gray as the streets I drove through. Juan Pablo had offered me everything I'd said I wanted. He'd shown me that he could be the man I'd always said I needed. And in the end, I'd been the one to trample on it all.

Chapter Twenty-One

Priscilla

"You can't be here." I'd barely walked in when Chase intercepted me outside of the interrogation room.

"What do you mean I can't be here?" I was not in the mood for bullshit and Chase was really barking up the wrong fucking tree. "I just want to ask Mr. Baker a couple of questions," I said, shouldering myself into the observation room. He was still in there, looking slick as always. Three-piece suit on point, wing tip shoes and dead eyes. His expensive lawyer sitting next to him, ready to pounce.

"Chase, are you going to tell me you think this guy is innocent? Look at him!" I said, waving my hand at his smug face.

Chase let out a sharp breath and rubbed his eyes hard. "I know how to do my job, Priscilla. Antagonizing him isn't going to get us anything."

"I just need five minutes, just five, and I'll fucking have him."

"Gutierrez." My back went up at the way the lieutenant called my name. He was never friendly, but he'd never been hostile. But right now he sounded like the

sight of me was making his blood boil. "You're no longer assigned to this case. You're not even on duty right
now. Why are you here?"

That question hit me like a ton of fucking bricks.
Why *was I* here?

Chase was doing his job. Even if it wasn't what I'd
do, it wasn't my call. That's how things worked. I'd be
furious if someone tried to come and overstep on one
of my cases. I was acting recklessly because I was running. I was here so I didn't have to sit with Juan Pablo
and tell him about my fears. Or even more terrifying,
my hopes. I could barely cope with the idea that in the
last two days I'd been basically handed two opportunities that could change everything for me. I didn't know
how to process the prospect of doing this differently. Of
having to count on others.

Of having to rely on Juan Pablo.

"Priscilla."

Oh my God, was I crying in front of the lieutenant?
"Go home. You need the time. I don't want to see you
here until the second." His eyes had lost the annoyance
from earlier and now all I saw was concern. "We are all
here for the same reason you are, we don't want anything else to happen to that child. That's why she's out
of the home, that's why there's an order of protection.
If anything happens, I'll call you myself. But you need
to let this go."

I nodded numbly and walked out of the precinct without saying a word. By the time I got into my car I was
sobbing. I didn't know what to do with myself. No that
was a lie, I wanted to go back to two hours ago and have
a redo with Juan Pablo. I wanted to be in his warm living

room, sitting in front of the fireplace. Instead I'd pushed him away and hurt him.

And as if she could sense I was struggling, my mother's number flashed on the Bluetooth screen.

"Mami." My voice was all clogged up from crying, but I was fucking done trying to keep it together. I was sad, and scared I'd ruined things with J and with my job.

Before I could even speak she knew. "Que pasa, mija?"

I took a deep breath and felt the tears streaming down my face. My nose was running. I felt so scared, but the desperation to finally say it won out. "I think I want to quit my job." My heart was thumping so fast in my chest I thought it was almost certainly going to beat right out of it. My voice sounded exactly like I felt—small and terrified waiting for my mother's judgement.

"Mi amor, is that why you've been like this? So distant? Ay, mija." The heaviness of those last words cut me to my core. "Have you been putting yourself through hell on your own?"

I thought about that before I answered. I had, in the beginning. For months I'd been going through the motions every day feeling more and more like the life I'd been single-mindedly working for didn't fit me at all. I'd sat with that truth like a lead balloon in my stomach, but then J had teased the truth out of me. He'd held space for me to finally speak the words out loud, my friends had been there too. And that had helped. But I'd still not let myself own it, because it all came down to this.

My mother and my father.

Their disappointment. I'd always thought I'd put up with almost anything if it meant that my parents could still be proud of me, but every day the weight of that felt like it would eventually bury me.

"I've been talking about it to J." Just saying his name made my breath hitch, because I'd hurt him tonight. When he'd tried to be there for me, I'd hurt him. "We had a big fight about it today."

There was some tongue clicking and teeth sucking. "Ay, Priscilla." My mother was trying her hardest to be there for me, but the news that I was sabotaging her plans for J and me was a low blow. "Is this about your shop? Is that what you want to do?"

I couldn't tell if her tone was reprimanding or just curious. "Yes, kind of." She just made a noise of approval, but didn't ask anything more, waiting for me to explain. "I've been doing this blog, and I started a podcast."

My mother let out a soft laugh at that. "Mamita, you think I didn't know about that?"

I was sure flames were going to start sprouting from my face. Because the thought of my mother hearing the episode about ass play was literally too much for me to handle right now.

"Oh my God, Mami, please tell me you haven't been telling your friends." I wasn't exaggerating the panic in my voice even a little bit.

"Some of my friends. I only listened to a few, the ones that I uh…thought I'd like. But, mija, how could you think that I wouldn't be interested in something you're doing? Your father and I love you and are so proud of you no matter what you do. Even if I don't necessarily understand all of it." She sounded more than a little flustered and I was starting to really think she actually listened to me go on for forty-five minutes about rimming, pegging and prostate massagers.

Kill me now.

But somewhere under the incredible cringe-worthiness in this conversation, I felt oxygen coming back into my body. My mother and I were talking about my podcast and there was no yelling or shaming. I'd told her I didn't want to be a cop anymore and there had been no condemnation. We were *talking*.

And the thing was, I knew my parents loved me. I had never doubted that ever. But they came here with nothing, and they sacrificed so much. I didn't want them to feel like I'd tainted their legacy. That I'd broken my part of the deal. How could they talk to their friends about me now? To the family back home?

"I just want you and Papi to be proud of me. You were both lawyers, for fuck's sake."

"Priscilla, language." I laughed at that, because my mother never let a curse word slide, not even in a crisis.

"Perdon, Mami. I'm serious though, you left so much behind, and dealt with so much sh… I mean, crap for me to have everything I needed." My mom and my dad had come in the seventies after finishing law school in the DR, hoping that an educated couple could make headway here. But there hadn't been many options other than manual labor. My mom had worked in restaurants and my dad in a bodega Uptown. They'd managed to turn that into good jobs, but it had been a struggle for a long time. "I feel so selfish, like I'm being wasteful. I don't know." I started crying again, as my mother tried her best to soothe me from hundreds of miles away.

"Mija, let's do the Facetime, so I can see you." I laughed at the way she said Facetime. I called her from my phone, still sitting in my car. But when I finally saw my mother the last of my control snapped and a deep sob escaped my throat. I felt so alone at that moment, and what hurt most was that I knew it didn't have to be that way. That I could be with J now or Bri, or even my parents. But I'd been pushing them away at every opportunity.

"Oh, Priscilla, mi amor, I need to be looking at you when I tell you this." My mother's skin was lighter than mine, but we had the same face. She had a few wrinkles now at sixty-seven and the little moles around her eyes were multiplying almost by the day, but it was still the face that had always shown me love, unconditionally.

"We will always be proud of you, mija. No matter what you decide to do, we will always support you. I don't care what it is." She paused and wagged a finger in front of her face as I smiled. "As long as you're happy. That is all we care about. You've always had a good head on your shoulders, mi amor. We trust your judgement, we trust *you*. You're a helper and a doer, always, since you were little. We know that no matter what it is you end up doing, it'll be something that will help people."

"I just don't want to end up in a situation where I worry you, Mami. I don't want you thinking I can't take care of myself."

My mother looked at me like she couldn't believe what I was saying, her head shaking in apparent disbelief. "You have never given me a reason to worry, and that's not because you have a good job, but because you're a good woman and I know what you're made of. I want you to feel free to live your life, in whatever way you want."

She closed her eyes and I saw her reach out, almost as if she wished she could touch my face through the screen, and I wished she was here too. "I was lucky. Your abuela Miguelina was a strong woman and your abuelo was a fair man and he listened." I smiled thinking of the strong, tall woman that we'd gone to visit every summer. "Girls got married off all the time to older men, richer men, but your grandmother wouldn't hear of it. She wanted me to go to college. And when I came home with your dad, and people talked." My father was very dark skinned and it had been the source of many unpleasant conversations among my mother's very light-skinned family.

"I'm sorry that happened to you, Mami." She waved a hand as if to say, it's all in the past.

"When I brought him home my mother only wanted to know two things: If I loved him and if he was good to me. The rest we could figure out together. She didn't want me trapped by her choices."

I let out a long breath and looked at my mother's tired eyes, but there was so much love there, love that could catch me if I needed it and maybe it was time for me to try and let go. "I've never felt trapped, Mami."

She dipped her head and smiled again. "Maybe not consciously, but we have so much to prove, mi amor. Even if we didn't tell you, we asked for a lot. But it's different now and I got nothing left to prove. Do your thing, mija. If I don't understand something, I'll ask."

I was completely wrung out. But now that things with my parents didn't seem so terrible the pit in my stomach about Juan Pablo was getting wider by the second. "I think, I messed things up with J, Mami."

I expected her to dismiss my words, or tell me J was crazy about me, but her eyes got really serious, more serious than they'd been so far. "That you have to fix yourself, Priscilla. Let him be there for you, learn to lean on those of us who yearn to catch you, mi hija querida."

I was crying again, but this time it was different. *I* felt different.

We ended the call after I promised her that I would call her after I got home, so she knew I was okay. Then I remembered J had asked me to do the same.

I took a detour, but I'm headed home. Will let you know when I get there. I'm sorry about earlier.

His response came almost immediately, like he'd been waiting for my message.

Thanks for texting. There's nothing to apologize for.

I waited for another minute, my eyes fixed on the screen waiting for the three dots to pop up promising another message, but nothing came.

Everything had been said. I knew where I stood with J, now I needed to meet him halfway.

I picked up my phone and sent another message.

Is your man's offer still on the table?

I waited with my heart in my throat for a response and within seconds it came.

Of course. Tom was serious. You just have to say the word. And why are you texting me? I thought you'd be riding Italian/Puerto Rican dick all the way into the New Year. Don't act coy. We all know you two are fucking again.

I didn't even have the energy to act affronted.

The Italian/Puerto Rican in question is not very happy with me at the moment.

The message had barely sent when my phone was blowing up with a call from Camilo.

I picked up ready to be reamed out, but when he spoke all I could hear was the love and concern I'd been getting from all my people today.

"What happened?"

I didn't deserve them. Actually that wasn't true, I did deserve all of it. I just needed to start acting like I knew it.

I took a deep breath, closed my eyes and told him.

Chapter Twenty-Two

Juan Pablo

"I'm coming!" Who the hell popped in at noon on New Year's Eve anyway?

I'd fallen asleep after finally getting Priscilla's text that she'd made it home. I was still hurt and for the first time ever wondering if I just wasn't what she wanted. If when she saw me she just didn't see her future. Because I didn't know what else to do. I didn't know how else to prove to her that I was in this for the long haul.

I got to the intercom by the front door and hit the speaker with my head still buzzing with a hundred different conflicting thoughts. It only occurred to me when I heard the doorman's voice that no one ever showed up to my place without texting first.

"Hey, Mr. Campos. I have Bri and Reyes here. They said they're here to see you."

I was stunned and wondered if I'd heard him right, but before I could ask anything he spoke again. "Bri says he's Priscilla's coworker."

I nodded as if he could see me and finally got my shit together and answered. "Yes, of course."

As soon as I put the receiver back, I looked around

the apartment and realized I'd never put away my bag. It was in the middle of the living room where I'd left it last night. There was a half-eaten bowl of popcorn and a fair amount of fun-sized bags of Sour Patch Kids all over the couch that I'd taken from my stash of leftover Halloween candy. My house, which was usually pristine or, as Camilo liked to say, an homage to "Reformed Fuckboi Chic," was a hot mess and I didn't even care. I avoided the mirror in the hallway as I walked back to my room to put on a shirt and wondered if Priscilla had sent her friends to get all her shit back from my apartment.

I went to answer and as soon as I opened the door I figured this wasn't going to be a social call. I guessed who Bri was from the many times Pris had talked about him. He was lean, medium height and had very bright blue eyes and fiery red hair. His boyfriend, Reyes, was tall, hairy and had kind brown eyes. I stepped to the side so they could come in. Just because I felt like shit and probably looked worse, I didn't need to act like I had no home training. "Please, come in."

I waved them over to the couch and we all tried to act like this wasn't awkward as fuck until I finally broke. "Did she send you to get her stuff?"

I surprised myself when my voice didn't crack. But I wasn't okay, not by a lot. I ran a hand over my face, feeling exhausted just from the effort it took to say that. Bri was looking at me like I was the sorriest asshole on earth. "We were deputized by Camilo to check on you."

Of course.

I didn't have it in me to even be pissed at him for interfering, he'd tried to call me last night and I'd just texted back that I'd call him today. So him deploying people to my house wasn't even a surprise. "I'm fine."

Reyes, who so far hadn't said a word, scoffed at my obvious lie.

"Okay, I'm not fine. But I'm also not sure what I can do. I don't want to be pushy or make Priscilla feel like I'm not giving her space. I didn't handle things in the best way last night and I think instead of her feeling like I was being supportive, she probably ended up feeling like I was pressuring her or pushing my own agenda."

Bri was looking at me as if he was trying to read what I wasn't saying. But after a moment he smiled, and leaned forward. "You should come to our house tonight. We're having a New Year's party and Pris is going to be there."

I shook my head forcefully and stood, not sure where I was going to go. I couldn't leave them sitting in my living room and go hide in my room like I wanted, but I had to move. "No, I'm not going to go there and make her feel uncomfortable. That's not cool."

Bri smiled even wider at my answer, like I'd gotten a test question right and now I was really fucking confused. "That's fair, and I told her I would re-invite you. You know Priscilla, she needs time to come around, but I know she loves you. Since you guys reconnected she's been slowly coming out of the funk she's been in."

Reyes squeezed Bri's shoulders as he talked, as though he needed to feel that physical connection, and once again I ached in the presence of that kind of partnership. Love that was so strong you had your own language.

I stopped pacing and looked at Bri, hoping that he was right, and she'd be open to talking to me. "Are you sure? Maybe I should call her first." I'd shut off my phone last night after she'd sent a very short text telling me she'd made it home, but maybe now in the light of day, she'd see things differently.

Bri stood up and Reyes followed, still quietly letting his man handle the business they'd come here for. "Call her. I think she'd like that. She's doing a lot of thinking today. She has a lot of decisions to make." He smiled at what I was sure was a startled look on my face. "You guys can work this out. I know it."

I wasn't nearly as confident as he was about that but went in to give them both dap anyway. "Thanks for coming to check in on me, and I'm sorry that little shit, Camilo, got you out of bed for this."

Reyes laughed at that and finally said something. "He's friends with Bri. They know each other from work stuff, and he's always been great to him. If somebody's good to my man, they can call me anytime for anything."

Bri blushed, his cheeks flaming red, as Reyes leaned in to give him a kiss. When he looked up again Reyes clapped my shoulder, as he took Bri's hand with the other. "Come through tonight."

"I'll think about it, thank you." I walked them both to the door and then went back to my bedroom to get my phone. I paused to slide a hand over Priscilla's satin pillowcase and looked around, noticing her things everywhere. Her tub of Palmer's on the night table, the copy of *Pleasure Activism* she'd been reading for the third time, bookmarked with an old Metro Card. A pair of Nikes she'd left here so we could go for runs together when she stayed over. If I went to the bathroom I'd find even more of her there. That old shower gel I'd stopped using because it reminded me too much of her was back in the shower. Her toothbrush and her bonnet were in there too. We'd finally gotten a chance to be together in this place. In the apartment that I'd always wanted to see her in. I wanted to have that forever, for this to be her home. For *me* to be her home. If she needed time, I would give her time, but I would also make it very clear, that if she was willing to fight for us, I would be there with her. Shoulder to shoulder.

The messages and missed calls flowed into my phone, but Pris's number wasn't in any of them. Camilo had sent a few asking how I was and then saying he'd asked Bri to check on me. My mother asking about plans for tonight. Nesto worried about me, after most likely getting the tea from Milo. Patrice saying Easton had talked to Priscilla and that she was okay, but they wanted to know how I was doing. All our people, holding it down for us while we figured things out.

I took a deep breath and tapped out a message to her, hoping that she would respond.

Good morning. I hope your night wasn't as shitty as mine. Camilo already had Bri stop by here to do a welfare check, I'm almost 100% sure you're next.

The three dots made an appearance a couple of times then disappeared, but after a few moments a message came.

Milo does the most. JFC. Good morning... Night was pretty shitty.

I made myself send the next text because I wasn't going to ambush her in front of strangers.

I got re-invited to Bri's party...

A minute went by, then another and I was starting to

wonder if she was going to leave me on read, which in my book would be a big fucking NO to the question of me attending the party.

Maybe I'll see you there.

That was definitely not a no.

Priscilla

I wasn't sure what I was even doing. I hadn't been this fucked up about anything in a while, and that was saying something considering the half-dozen breakups with J along the years and the ongoing drama with my job.

But I'd been on my own thinking about what I wanted all day, making plans, doing pros and cons lists until my hands hurt from writing. Thinking, dreaming, wondering if I could really take so many chances at once. Because my job was a big one, but so was letting myself believe J and I could really do this again. That this time it would work when we'd messed things up so many times before.

I'd gone over every possible scenario in my head until I'd gotten sick of it and gotten in my car to go to Bri and Reyes's party, but instead, my car somehow drove its damn self to Juan Pablo's building. Almost as if I was in some kind of fever dream, I found myself in my New Year's Eve attire, knocking on his door at 5:00 p.m. He'd texted he'd be at the party and I'd been vague and weird, because that seemed to be the only thing I could manage today.

The party wasn't for another couple of hours though.

I'd told Bri I'd come early and help. Instead I was showing up at J's house unannounced, and I hoped I was doing
the right thing. I rang the bell once, not wanting to use
the key he'd given me, and waited with my heart pounding so hard I felt the pulsing in my ears.

I heard noises on the other side of the door and had
to press a hand to my diaphragm to regulate my breathing. The lock clicked open and before I had time to think
about what I would say he opened the door. I wanted to
kiss him, tell him I wanted a do-over for last night. Thank
him for giving me space, for believing in me, for offering
a shoulder. For a lifetime of being the only person in the
world who could truly see all of me, and never hesitating
to tell me I was perfect just the way I was.

But the only thing that came out of my stupid mouth
was, "Hi."

He looked surprised and unsure, which was something
that happened with this new Juan Pablo. In the past he
would always front like he had it all under control. He
never hesitated to let you know he had it handled. This
Juan Pablo asked for help, he said what he was thinking, he could be vulnerable, and that made him so much
stronger.

We stood there in awkward silence until he stepped
aside and lifted a hand to wave me in. "You want to come
in? I was just making myself a snack." I nodded and came
inside. Noticed the little Christmas tree we'd gotten together was lit, and that he had the fireplace on. I wanted
to change into sweats, take off my makeup and wait for
the next year of my life—which I was sure would be full
of changes—here with Juan Pablo.

He stood by the couch, his arms crossed over a Yankees hoodie, his expression unreadable. I could tell he

was thinking hard about what to ask, wondering what I'd come here to do. After all, he'd been very clear about what he wanted, I was the one who hadn't made up my mind.

"I'm going to leave the force."

He stumbled back like I'd slapped him, and I almost laughed. I lifted a shoulder and sank down in the armchair that I'd begun to think of as mine, and leaned down to unzip my boots. I needed somewhere to put my eyes when I said this.

"It's time. I haven't been happy in the job for a while. There are a lot of good people there and they can do the work better than I can right now. I want to try making a go of this project, of getting the space open." I lifted my eyes first, and found him still standing by the couch. "I texted Camilo and Tom. I told them I'll take them up on the space. And if the offer's still there, I'd love to talk to Yariel's agent. But that's not the only reason I'm here."

My temples throbbed as I stood up, needing to go to him. It felt right for me to be the one to make my way to him now, since in the past month he had come to me so many times. I needed to be the one to take this last leap of faith for us. To tell him that I could see how much he'd changed and that now I could also clearly see a future for us.

"I needed to tell you I'm sorry for last night." He opened his mouth to protest and I shook my head gently, and took both his hands in mine needing the connection when I said it. "No, J. I do need to say it. If this is going to work we both have to have more faith in each other. You've shown me in these past few weeks that you're willing to do that. That you're ready for whatever if it means we're working for the future we both want. And

I want so many things, so many," I said with a laugh. "But all of them, all of them, involve you. I love you. I do, so much and it seems like that's never going to stop." I shook my head, as our eyes locked together, his already a little watery with tears. "I love you, J."

He brought his face closer and his arms tightened around my waist. "You're everything I've ever wanted. And my dream, mi reina, my prayer, is that you will let me be there for you as you go for yours." I gasped, choking on my tears, as he pressed his lips to mine and that kiss was perfect. Strong and soft at once. I could taste my future in that kiss, feel the strength of what we had in Juan Pablo's arms.

"I love you, Priscilla. I'm so happy you're here." His voice was soft, and he spoke as he pressed tiny kisses on my neck and my jaw. I didn't want to move from here. Or leave this place again, until we'd had time with each other, until I felt grounded in this new chance I'd gotten with this man.

I pulled back and smiled at him helplessly. "Would it be rude to cancel on Bri? I'm supposed to help set up."

The smile I got in response was just on this side of filthy and how did he still make my stomach flip? "I'll make it worth your while if you do."

I laughed and kissed him again. "I have no doubt you will. So, what? Netflix and Chill for New Year's?"

He bit his bottom lip in that way that made every nerve in my body tingle with anticipation and went in for another kiss, but just as our lips met, he said, "As long as I get to give you your midnight kiss."

I whispered back, smiling against his mouth, "All my

New Year's Eve kisses from now until forever belong to you."

That was a promise I would work hard to keep.

Epilogue

Not quite a year later
Priscilla

"Are you crying?" It was hard keeping the amusement out of my voice, even though Juan Pablo had tears streaming down his face as he looked around my brand-new working space.

"Yeah, I'm fucking crying. Look at what you did, mi reina. This is amazing." He turned his head back and forth, like he hadn't been in here practically day and night for the last week helping get everything ready for the grand opening. He knew this place almost as well as I did. But even I had to admit seeing it bustling with people made it all look real.

I came closer and rubbed my thumbs on his cheeks and smiled at him. "You're a sap."

"And you're a badass." I preened and pushed up for a kiss.

I felt like a badass.

After a year of transitions—leaving the force, moving in with J and writing a fucking book—I'd reached the last one of my humungous milestones. I finally opened the doors to Come As You Are: Community Store and Growth Space.

Camilo's man had come through. I'd been able to open this place in the heart of Harlem and I couldn't wait to get to work. I couldn't believe this was my life. That I was doing something I felt passionate about and got to go home to a man that, even after twenty years, still gave me butterflies. I felt J's arms wrap around my waist and I leaned into him, my head right against his.

His beard brushed my face when he leaned in to ask me something. "What are you thinking?" I could almost taste the smile in his voice. The same giddiness that was cursing through my veins.

"I'm thinking, my cup is full, Juan Pablo."

He grunted and pressed his arms tighter around mine, that hot as fuck rumbling in his chest that still made me weak in the knees. "You sure we bought enough wine, you know how Camilo gets." I laughed with my lips pressed to his neck.

"They're here with Libe, he's always on his best behavior when she's around."

"That's true," he conceded. "She's the only one that can whip him into shape."

"I can tell from the jealousy in your eyes that you're talking about me, Juan Pablo," Camilo called as he made his way to us from across the room with the rest of the guys right behind him. I could feel J's grin from the way his cheeks popped against my face.

Nesto came in for a hug first. "Prima, this place is bomb. I love it. That Maldonado hustle always comes through, baby." Nesto's reference to his and my mother's maiden name made me practically burst with pride.

There were so many people whose shoulders I'd stood on so that I could be here tonight.

"I know that's right!" My dad responded as Nesto gave me another hug.

Soon Patrice and Easton were doling out hugs and handing out cold Presidentes, and Juan Pablo was getting everyone to the table for some food. We'd finished our opening day, let the neighborhood into this new space that I was going to steward for them, and now we were going to drink, dance and eat like my people did.

I had done it. I'd taken a leap and trusted that my man, my friends and my family would catch me if I fell.

I turned around to wrap my arms tight around Juan Pablo and looked up at his smiling face. "Did you think this is where we'd end up? With me teaching people how to have better sex?"

He lifted a shoulder and bent his head so that our lips were touching. "You're doing a hell of a lot more than that, mi amor." That pride in his voice when he talked about all this would never get old. "I love that you're doing this and that you're killing it in every way." He pushed his lips into mine as our nearest and dearest yelled around us to "get a room."

"But I always dreamed whatever I was doing, when I was done with it, I could come home to you," he confessed, making my heart leap.

"So you're saying I made your dreams come true?" I asked, breathless from the moment.

That smile was going to be the end of me. "Baby, you know I've always dreamed big."

* * * * *

Reviews are an invaluable tool when it comes to spreading the word about great reads.
Please consider leaving an honest review for this or any of Carina Press's other titles that you've read on your favorite retailer or review site.

Acknowledgments

It's been an absolute privilege to write these books. I started this journey with the hope of being able to add the stories of my people, as I knew them, to this genre I love so much. I am filled with gratitude that I was able to do so, and for the people who have helped me along the way.

I am endlessly thankful for every single person who in this year has tweeted, reviewed or emailed me to say what these stories have meant to them. Nesto, Camilo, Patrice, Juan Pablo and the rest of the Dreamers world are fictional characters, but they were inspired by so many people who have made my world better. That these glimpses of their stories have meant so much, to so many, is more than I could've ever hoped for.

As always there is no way I could do this without the support and love from so many wonderful people:

Kerri Buckley, my editor. We made it! Four books in one year, and we're both still standing. I could not have asked for a better steward in this journey.

The Carina PR and Marketing team, for all you do to get my stories out there and your constant support.

Linda Camacho, my agent, for everything.

My writing community. My RWA-NYC friends, you continue to inspire and amaze me.

Always to my partner and my girl who have buoyed me through this year in a million different ways.

Finally, to every Dreamer out there. Those who came from our islands so many years ago and built communities out of nothing, and for those still coming today, armed with nothing but a suitcase, a body ready to work, and a head full of dreams. I hope we can continue to make space for you to thrive.

About the Author

Adriana was born and raised in the Caribbean, but for the last fifteen years has let her job (and her spouse) take her all over the world. She loves writing stories about people who look and sound like her people getting unapologetic happy endings.

When she's not dreaming up love stories, planning logistically complex vacations with her family or hunting for discount Broadway tickets, she's a social worker in New York City, working with survivors of domestic and sexual violence.

You can find her on:

Twitter: www.Twitter.com/ladrianaherrera
Instagram: www.Instagram.com/ladriana_herrera
Facebook: www.Facebook.com/laura.adriana.94801
Website: adrianaherreraromance.com

And don't miss the book that started it all.
American Dreamer *is available now!*

No one ever said big dreams come easy...

For Nesto Vasquez, moving his Afro-Caribbean food truck from New York City to the wilds of Upstate New York is a huge gamble. If it works? He'll be a big fish in a little pond. If it doesn't? He'll have to give up the hustle and return to the day job he hates. He's got six months to make it happen—the last thing he needs is a distraction.

Keep reading for an excerpt from American Dreamer *by Adriana Herrera.*

"The future belongs to those who believe in the beauty of their dreams."

—Eleanor Roosevelt

Chapter One

Nesto

"So, this is it? You're really taking off to that wilderness upstate."

I looked up from where I was trying to shove another gigantic container into the back of my food truck, and saw Camilo, one of my three best friends, walking down the sidewalk wearing oversize sunglasses and holding an enormous cup of coffee.

Late as always.

He was supposed to be here an hour ago, but could he manage to make it on time to help me literally pack up my entire life? No.

"What the fuck, Milo? You're an hour late, pendejo! I've been waiting on you since seven a.m. You know I'm on a schedule, man. I can't have this truck sitting here all morning!" I cringed thinking of everything I needed to get done in the next twenty-four hours.

"We need to be on the road by nine if I'm going to be ready for the gig tomorrow. I shouldn't have let Mamí talk me into opening this thing the day after getting up there."

Milo looked at me shaking his head, then put down his coffee and crossed his arms over his chest like he had all the time in the world.

"Chill out, you'll be fine. Your mother already has your food order waiting at the commercial kitchen she found you. As soon as we get in, she'll be deploying people to make sure you're ready to go. Besides Juanpa, Patrice and I will be there tonight to help too. Don't worry so much, pa. It's only like a five-hour drive. We'll be there by two, tops."

I took a deep breath, because I knew arguing with Milo would probably mean I'd either get going even later or that he'd get himself so worked up he'd crash my damn car on the interstate.

"Dude, can you be at least a little sympathetic? This is a big fucking deal for me. I'm moving out of New York City, my home since I was six years old, to try and get a food truck business going upstate."

I reached over for another container and huffed in exasperation. "If I had a beard and a man bun I'd be a cancelled show on Food Network."

Milo's face softened, and he started chuckling while he finally got his ass in gear and walked a box to the truck. "You're so over the top sometimes. But okay," he said, raising his hands. Palms out. "It's only a six-month trial, you can always come back. Your truck is doing fine here. It's not like you're going out of business or anything. People love those burritos."

He grabbed his coffee and drank deeply before continuing with his pissy pep talk.

"I mean, true, it's hard to make a living out here with all the competition, but your food sells well. You've been killing it at Smorgasburg when you're down in Brooklyn. Those hipsters go crazy over your shit."

I shook my head forcefully at his words as I slammed the back doors of the truck closed.

I stepped away from the vehicle, taking a long look at it. Emblazoned on the back was the logo for my business, *OuNYe, Afro-Caribbean Food* in huge bold black font on a red background. The black and red contrasted with the flags of the Dominican Republic, Puerto Rico, Cuba, Haiti and Jamaica painted over the entire truck.

To name my business, I used a word from the Yoruba language. Which had been spoken all over the Caribbean by our ancestors, the West Africans who were brought there as slaves. *Ounje* is the Yoruba word for *nourishment*, and I'd decided to play a bit with things and put the NY right at the center.

The two worlds that made me merged into one word.

OuNYe was my baby. I put my blood, sweat and tears into getting this idea off the ground. Street food filled with the flavors of the Caribbean. My roots and those of Juan Pablo, Camilo and Patrice, my three best friends. The food we had grown up with and had been our connection to where we came from, while our families tried to make a life here in the Big Apple.

Now I was taking one last shot at making my living from it.

I looked over at Milo, who was still gulping down coffee. "I've been doing this for two years, and I need to be able to make a decent living. I'm not going to be sweating it out for the rest of my life, to barely break even. If I can't get it off the ground like I want to in Ithaca, I'm done. *Se acabo.*"

Milo clicked his tongue like it was taking every ounce of patience he had not to hit me upside the head.

"Oh my god, you gotta stop. You've agonized over this move for a year. You'll be doing business like gangbusters up there. You're gonna kill it. You know white people love 'ethnic' food wrapped in a tortilla."

He held up his hands with his index fingers hooked together, ready to start pulling out the receipts to shut down my bullshit.

"First of all, the concept is awesome, and your food is delicious. Second, there isn't any Caribbean food anywhere up there. Now, stop whining before I lose my temper with you! I've had like three sips of this coffee and you know better than to aggravate me when I'm not properly caffeinated."

I could only laugh. "You're an idiot."

This is why I knew Milo and the guys coming along for the drive up was a good idea. Because despite the fact that he was salty as fuck sometimes, the guy could give a hell of a pep talk. I walked to my Prius, which Milo would be driving up to Ithaca, met him by the driver's side door and handed him the keys.

"Here, don't drive like a fucking maniac. I texted you the address where we'll stop for lunch. There's a truck stop so we can park. Patrice and Juanpa already left in J's truck. They'll meet us there. Again, do not drive while reading something on your phone or text the guys while the car is moving."

"Pshh, you're being mad extra today." Milo blew me off. "Stress is not a good look on you, pa." He scrunched his face, pressing the point as he got in the car. "See you in a couple of hours." I stepped back and watched him set up the Google maps on his phone and drive off with a little wave.

I went back to stand by the truck and looked around one last time. It was a beautiful Sunday morning in New York City. The sun was shining and it was going to be a perfect spring day.

People in this corner of Manhattan, right up against the Hudson River, were already buzzing past me, heading to jobs and lives. Going after their little piece of the American dream. I choked up because this felt final, like it would never be *my* New York City again. This place was not just where I lived, it was part of my DNA, and I was convinced I would never feel at home anywhere else.

After twenty-seven years of calling this place mine, I was leaving.

I took one last look at my surroundings and inhaled the smell of fresh coffee and hot oil from the empanada cart down the street. I stood right off Broadway, on 155th Street, Boricua College on my right, Trinity Church Cemetery on my left, and the Hudson straight ahead. This had been my neighborhood for almost eight years, and I was going to miss it. I was going to miss all of it.

I sighed as I made my way back to the truck and climbed in. I got the map up on my phone, pushed down my sunglasses and started the truck.

I was ready.

I was going after my dream, to pursue my passion. As I headed out of the city, I looked out and said a silent "See you soon."

If it didn't work out in Ithaca, I'd be back soon enough.

I was a son of New York City, and she would always have me back with open arms.

The day ended up being perfect for a long drive. Just a bit before two p.m. I took the exit for Ithaca and began to feel the nervous anticipation of what was to come. I was adventurous when it came to travel or trying new things, but not with my livelihood.

Immigrants didn't fuck around with a steady stream of income. If you were making a decent living, you worked your ass off to keep it on lockdown.

Pursuing your passion? Risking everything on a dream?

That was for people with trust funds, not a Dominican kid from the Bronx.

While I coasted down the rural two-lane road that led to my destination, I thought about what this move meant. It'd been terrifying to leave a good and secure job to try my luck in something so unpredictable, and where the chances for utter failure were sky-high. Sure, I was confident in my skills, in my food, but I knew there would be a long way down if I failed.

This was not just a side-hustle anymore. I was going all-in with my business. It felt big, like it could change everything.

Before I got to my mom's, I decided to stop at the gas station where I was going to park the truck for lunch services, and check out the location. I was low on gas too, so I could kill two birds with one stone.

Navigating one of the many hills of Ithaca entering downtown, it was like I was seeing it for the first time. I drove by houses painted in bright colors and narrow streets full of trees laden with flowers. It was so green and quaint here. I wasn't sure how I'd fit in, being so used to the fast pace of the city.

I turned the steering wheel of the truck and wedged into an empty spot next to a pump. I jumped out and glanced around, taking in the location. I couldn't help the grin that broke out on my face. Of course my mom would somehow manage to find me the best possible spot in town. It was right by the public library and all around were commercial buildings. There would be a lot of foot traffic during the week.

I kept looking around as I filled the tank and didn't notice the car that drove up on the other side of me. It was a small, green Subaru hatchback with a Human Rights Campaign sticker on the back window. The guy who jumped out was gorgeous. He had the blondest hair I'd ever seen, and was wearing tight jeans and a black NPR t-shirt.

For some reason his shirt struck me as hilarious, and as he was pushing up his Ray-Bans to look at the screen on the pump, a laugh burst out of me. He turned around with a startled expression, probably looking for the jackass laughing at him for no reason. The intensity of his blue eyes, and the way his mouth pursed and then turned up into a smirk like he wasn't sure if he should get pissed or laugh too, made the laugh die in my throat. He was so pretty, and currently looking at me like there was something seriously wrong with me.

I put my hand up in an attempt to apologize for my bizarre behavior. "Sorry, man. Ignore me. I'm just a bit punchy from a long drive."

He didn't respond, just kept staring me, looking confused. I quickly finished up, and almost left without saying anything. But at the last second decided not to be an asshole and called out, "Have a nice day," before jumping in the truck.

I sent a quick text to my mom to let her know I'd be at her place soon and pulled out of the station. As I drove, I mused that if the blond was a sample of the men running around town, I'd need to look into some socializing opportunities. Then I remembered I was here to run a business, not to get laid.

I needed to get my head in the game and remember if this plan didn't work out my only prospect at the moment was going back to TPS reports and coming up with ways to make fro-yo sound "a little more urban."

After a few minutes navigating my truck through the tight residential streets of Ithaca I turned onto my mom's block and saw her waiting outside.

She was wearing a flowing white linen shirt, her long salt-and-pepper curls falling down her back. As a boy I thought she was the most beautiful woman in the world, and that was still the case. These days she was embracing the natural look; had given up wearing makeup and relaxing her hair.

I parked the truck in the empty space in front of her house, which I knew she must have been guarding furiously all day.

"M'ijo! You made it," she yelled out as I walked over to her. "Look at you, so handsome. Your hair is getting long, papí," she griped as she gave me a bear hug and kissed both my cheeks.

"Mamí, you look gorgeous. I like this blouse. Very Stevie Nicks."

Complimenting her on her clothes and how great she looked was first and foremost.

She smacked my arm but the big smile on her face gave her away.

"Muchacho, Stevie Nicks is a lot older than me!"

She pulled on the hem of the shirt as we walked, as if only now noticing what she was wearing. "Besides, this old thing? Your tía Maritza got it for me at some hippie clothes sale she goes to. You know how she is, goes overboard, buys too many things, and then I end up with half of them!"

I raised an eyebrow, because she was just as bad as Tía Maritza with the shopping.

"You two are hilarious."

She put her hand around my waist as we walked up the sidewalk. "Tell me about the drive. Did you have any trouble?"

I was thinking how much I'd missed having my mom and sister close by, when a pinch on my arm got my attention. "Sorry, Mamí. Drive was good," I said as we got to the door of my mom's little house.

One thing was certain, even if things flopped with the truck it would be nice to have family close again. My mom moved up to Ithaca eight years before. She wanted a more sedate environment for my little sister, Minerva, to go to school, and decided to join Tía Maritza and Tío Tonin who'd been here for years. I'd been out of college and working then, so I stayed behind. I looked down at her smiling face as she ushered me into the house.

"Good. Come in, your sister should be home soon, and your tíos are on their way over. We're all so happy you're here, papí." I got another squeeze.

. "The guys are inside," she said, trying her best to look grumpy, and failing completely. "They've only been here for fifteen minutes and Juanpa's already eaten all my food."

I just grinned down at her. "Don't even front like you're mad, Mamí. I know you love having a house full of people."

She looked up at me with a blank look on her face, as if she wasn't sure what my point was. "Nesto's home!" she called while she went for another hug.

I loved seeing my mom in her home. She'd busted her ass as a single mom for so long to give us a good life. She'd kept us out of trouble and was an amazing role model, but it all came at a cost.

She never stopped. She worked hard, and always knew what was up with school, with friends and on the block. All while going to night school, and sending money home to help the family back in the DR. If anyone deserved to slow down and smell the roses, it was Nurys Maldonado.

We stood by the door arm in arm and then my mom waved toward the kitchen. "Let me go start some coffee." She gave me one last peck on the cheek before she hurried off.

I spotted Milo sprawled on the couch messing with his phone. "Did Milo do anything to my car?" I asked my mom, who was already in the kitchen.

Mamí smiled in Camilo's direction while she bustled around. "Car looks fine to me, but you know Milo. As soon as he got here he started moaning about getting lost three times and cursing out Juanpa and Patrice for not picking up when he called them."

I looked over and saw my friends filling my mom's living room. My brothers. I wouldn't have them just a few subway stops away anymore. I tried to shake off the feeling of unease the thought brought me and focused on all the stuff we needed to get done before they went back to the city.

But before I could get to them, my uncle and aunt were barreling into the house making a fuss over me, and talking over each other asking about the truck.

"Nesto! M'ijo. Look at you. You look more like your abuelo every day. Doesn't he, Nurys?" my aunt asked my mom as she engulfed me in a tight hug.

Tía Maritza was a slightly thinner and older version of my mom. The same bronzed skin, the curly hair, tall and curvy. She didn't look a day over forty-five, even though sixty-two was just a few months away. She and Tío Tonin had been married for almost forty years and still looked at each other like they were high school sweethearts.

"What's good, Tío? You letting Tía Maritza feed you too much of that platano?" I asked, patting the little bulge around his waistband.

He laughed heartily as he went in for a bear hug.

Tonin as always had a big smile on his face, and at sixty-five his dark brown skin was still free of any wrinkles. My uncle had always been like a father to me. He taught me by example how a man should act toward those he loved. I hoped when the time came, like him, I could be the type of man who put his people first.

"It's good to have you home, mi muchacho. Your mother's been putting the pressure on us all week getting everything ready for you. We've been talking up the truck in town too, people are excited for the Caribbean burritos."

"That's good, man, I need to sell a lot of them if I'm going to make rent!" I said, clapping his back as he moved to put his arm around Tía Maritza's shoulders.

"Tía, you're looking younger every year." She preened and gave me another kiss.

"We're so happy you're here, papí."

"It's good to be here. How's Pri doing? I haven't seen her in a minute." At the mention of my cousin, my aunt's face shone with pride.

"She's great. She may be here tomorrow. Hopefully you can see her."

"Definitely." I nodded and looked over at the guys who were lounging on my mom's furniture. Juanpa's stank face told me he'd probably heard us talking about Priscilla.

He was ridiculous.

Those two had a love/hate thing going on since we were kids, and apparently they were back to hating each other.

"Yo, are you bums just going to lounge over here all afternoon? We got shit to do!"

Juanpa squinted up at me while he sipped some kind of Frappuccino looking thing.

"I'm taking a break, son. I just drove five hours hauling all your shit out here. Let me enjoy my independent coffee shop beverage, pa." He lifted his cup. "They got a drive-thru barista situation in town. This shit is fire. They need to open one of these places in the city."

He looked so happy sucking down on that straw.

"Okay, man, drink your sugar bomb first, but we need

to unload your truck before you leave tonight." Juanpa went back to focusing on his drink and doing something on his phone and just nodded, already distracted. I looked over at Milo who was hunched over, looking at something on Patrice's laptop.

"What did I tell you about calling people while driving my car, man?"

Patrice shook his head and grinned as he typed, but knew better than to try and make a joke about Camilo's driving. Milo flipped me off, looking like he was about to curse me out, when I saw my sister, Minerva, coming up the path to the house.

She was so tall, and was looking more like Mamí every day. She was just a few inches shorter than my six feet two by now. We didn't have the same dad, but everyone said we were identical as babies, same light brown skin with a tint of red. Whenever we ran or laughed too hard our whole faces flushed. Her hair was straighter than mine, and my eyes were a lighter brown, but we both had our mom's face. Full mouth, broad nose and thick eyelashes. Minerva's were so long they looked fake.

She was gorgeous, just like Mamí.

I went to meet her by the door and as soon as she walked in, I picked her up and twirled her around a couple of times.

"You're getting too pretty, baby sister. It's a good thing I'm here, Mamí!" I yelled over my shoulder. "We can start working on the protective fence around the house this weekend. Got to keep the boys away!"

"Stop it! You're so extra, Nesto." She hit me on the

shoulder, laughing. "What's wrong with you? Put me down."

"What, you're too big for your manín to pick you up?" I asked, squeezing her tight. "So, are you dating? What's his name?"

I crossed my eyes, making her laugh again.

"Stop it. *Loco.*"

"She had this gringito following her around like a puppy all winter," my mom said, walking out of the kitchen.

"He was here all the time, hanging around with a mopey face, and Justin Bieber hair, trying to read poems in Spanish."

She clicked her tongue and gave my sister her patented "pobrecita" face, which was half "I feel bad for you" and half "but really I should be mocking you."

"I didn't have the heart to tell him to stop coming over," she teased Minerva, who was giving her a death glare with the intensity only a sixteen-year-old could produce. My mom kept going though. "He sabotaged himself enough with that haircut and bad Spanish."

We all cracked up while my baby sister silently gave me and the guys the finger as she sat on the couch. Before my mom and Minerva got into something I decided to get people back on track, because the clock was ticking.

"Okay, mi gente," I said, clapping my hands together. "What's the plan? We have a lot to get ready if I have the truck scheduled for a lunch service in town tomorrow." I flashed a smile at my mom who was standing at attention.

"Mamí, I stopped by the gas station and that spot is

going to be lit." She beamed with pride at my comment. "You said you had all the food at the kitchen, right?"

"That's right. Everything's there ready to go."

The "I told you so" face Camilo was flashing my way did not go unnoticed.

I looked at my watch and saw it was only 2:30 p.m. "Excellent. We have plenty of time to get all the night before food preparation done. Milo and Juanpa, since you guys are driving back tonight we should go to the kitchen and get all the stuff in J's truck unloaded now."

Everyone nodded and people started getting up and ready to get going as I talked.

"I can get my clothes and stuff moved into the studio with Patrice tonight since he's here until tomorrow. The woman I'm subletting from texted today and said I can go into the apartment anytime. She left the keys with you, right, Mamí?"

She patted her bag, which was already slung on her shoulder.

"Yes, I have them here, I can't believe you aren't staying here even one night."

I had to nip the guilt tripping in the bud.

"Mamí, you know it'll be easier for me. The studio is in Trumansburg, right by where I'll be parking the truck overnight. It's closer to the commercial kitchen space we're renting. It just makes sense for me to be up there."

She sighed and came over to pinch my cheek.

"Yo se, yo se. I just wanted to spoil you a little bit. Anyways, I took the week off so I can help you with the truck, m'ijo. Tía Maritza will also help until you hire some people."

Mamí was already headed for the door but called over

to my sister who'd gone back to her room for something. "Minerva, vamonos, are you playing with that thing on your phone that gives you rabbit ears again?" She turned around to look at me. "She spends all day making faces at that thing!" She rolled her eyes, while the rest of us lost it, then went back to yelling in the direction of Minerva's room. "Vamos, muchachita! We need to help out your brother, and you have school tomorrow."

Minerva hustled out, looking flustered. "Ay, Mamí, why are you yelling? I'm ready." My sister hiked her thumb at me, as she walked to the door. "Vamonos, Ernesto."

That was it, my people were ready and so was I. The Ithaca chapter of OuNYe was finally off and running.

Don't miss American Dreamer
by Adriana Herrera.

*Available now wherever Carina Press
ebooks are sold.*

www.CarinaPress.com